CYBERWARFARE

THE TED HIGUERA SERIES BOOK 6

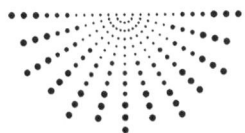

PENDELTON C. WALLACE

VICTORY PUBLISHING

ISBN **978-0-9991432-3-0**

Visit Pendelton Wallace's Web site at www.pennwallace.com

Contact the author at http://www.pennwallace.com/contact-penn.html.

Cover Design by Brandi McCann

🏵 Created with Vellum

CONTENTS

AUTHOR'S FOREWORD

I hope that you are reading both of my series, The Ted Higuera Thrillers and the Catrina Flaherty Mysteries. Characters cross back and forth between the two series. While I try to make each book a standalone read, they take place sequentially. *Cyberwarfare* takes place directly after *The Chinatown Murders.* The next Catrina Flaherty Mystery will take place during and after *Cyberwarfare.*

As always, *Cyberwarfare* is based on a true story. People don't believe that these cyber-attacks are really possible. Believe me, they are. Most of the attacks have already happened and the few that I made up are technically possible. People: Beware. This stuff is happening around us every day and our government is doing little to stop it.

Enjoy the story.

"I know not with what weapons World War III will be fought. But World War IV will be fought with sticks and rocks."—Albert Einstein

"Frankly, the United States is under attack. Under attack by entities that are using cyber to penetrate virtually every major action that takes place in the United States."—Dan Coats, the director of National Intelligence

"WASHINGTON — A newly drafted United States nuclear strategy that has been sent to President Trump for approval would permit the use of nuclear weapons to respond to … the most crippling kind of cyberattacks." – New York Times, By David E. Sanger and William J. Broad, Jan. 16, 2018

"I think we should expect to see an increase in Iranian cyberactivity against us,"—Michael Daniel, former White House cyber coordinator

"[Abolishing the office of Cyber Coordinator is] a strange signal to send … If anything, the threats we face are going to continue to get more intense and worse in cyberspace before they get better."—Michael Daniel

"… the U.S. Treasury named North Korean programmer Park Jin Jyok for working on behalf of Pyongyang in carrying out several cyberattacks against U.S. and global targets." – TechCrunch.com, by Zach Whittaker, September 6, 2018

CHAPTER ONE

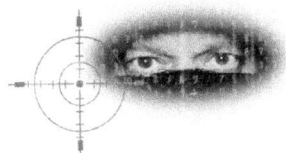

Ted Higuera sat in the dark at his large oak desk pushed up against the window with a million-dollar view. A half empty bottle of Herradura Añejo tequila on the desk sat with a plate of salt and lime wedges. Next to the tequila stood a bottle of Corona. He chugged the glass in front of him, then sucked on a lime slice.

From his Capitol Hill apartment, he saw the lights of Seattle's Denny Regrade gradually give way to Elliot Bay. The bay opened to Puget Sound. He watched the ferry boats and private yachts as little specks of light on the dark water. Across the Sound, he saw the lights of Kingston on Bainbridge Island.

He'd been trying to reach her for almost an hour. She didn't answer. Her cell phone number was not in service. She didn't answer his emails or return his texts.

Jesus Cristo! Was she never going to let him talk to her?

He dialed the ranch phone again. Somewhere, a couple of thousand miles to the south, the phone rang. And rang. *"Lo siento, perro no estamos en casa ..."* the answering machine said.

God-damn.

He hit the stop button and dialed again. This time, after five rings, he heard a pickup. His heart went into sprint mode.

"Ted, I've told you not to call here."

"Don't hang up, Mishis Gonzales." Ted slurred. Could he keep her on the line? "I need to talk to you. I need to talk to Maria."

He heard a deep sigh.

"I've told you, Ted. She's not going to talk to you. I'm not going to let you. You've got to stop calling here. Just let it die."

"Teresha ..." He didn't know what else he could say. "I have to know. I do know. Itsh my baby. I need to be part of my son's life."

"Teddy." Her voice sounded almost sympathetic. "I don't know how many times we have to tell you, it's not your child. Please stop bothering us."

His heart stopped. He heard a baby cry in the background.

Dios mio. He's here!

"Teresha, the baby, is he okay?"

The connection broke.

The bitch. Flaming mega-bitch from hell.

Ted gazed out the window but didn't comprehend what he was seeing. The entire view was dark. Despite his fuzzy vision, he still saw the lights of the ferry boats in the bay, but all the shore-side lights were gone. Seattle had slipped into total darkness.

He poured another glass of tequila.

LIEUTENANT COLONEL JOHN STEVENSON floated through the corridor, occasionally giving himself momentum by grabbing a handle or protruding object. At the intersection of four passageways, he changed direction and went "up." In his weightless world, there really was no "up," but the opening was above his head, so he considered it "up."

He pondered the irony of going up to the cupola to look down on Earth. The cupola was on the bottom of the space station in its orientation to the planet below. Stevenson mused on why they called this area a cupola. On Earth, a cupola was a small dome on the top of a building, usually to admit light and air. On the space station, it was just a dome module bolted onto the growing structure's belly with seven windows.

"Hail Mary, full of grace," he mumbled and crossed himself as he passed through the threshold. He always said a little prayer as he entered. From this perch, high above his home planet, he could see the hand of God.

He loved watching the changing face of Earth, two-hundred-fifty miles below him. He saw major features like oceans, big rivers, and mountain ranges, but small things like skyscrapers or aircraft carriers were lost in the distance.

Through the windows he made out the Atlantic Ocean. Off the coast of Africa, a thick swirl of heavy white clouds circulated around a dark hole. *Shit, someone's gonna have hell to pay.* Every time he looked at the growing hurricane, it seemed larger and more ominous.

As Earth turned on its axis, the land mass of North America gradually came into view.

"Is beautiful, dah?" Sonia Petkovic floated into the cupola besides him. She was in her forties but could pass for twenty-something. Her long black hair floated like Medusa's venomous snakes.

"Is beautiful, yes." Stevenson agreed. He looked her over; she was dressed in white shorts and a navy-blue polo shirt. "We're coming up on my hometown."

She pulled herself next him to look out the window.

"Where is home town?" she asked.

"Long Island, New York." He pointed out the window. "See there, the long, curving island close to the coastline. That's it."

"Is beautiful from here, but then again, everything is."

They floated at the window, watching North America slip into darkness as night approached that side of the planet Lights appeared, extending from New England to Florida in an almost unbroken network. In the middle of the continent, vast patches of darkness were broken up by small light clusters. The big cities stood out like beacons amid the surrounding blackness.

Finally, the West Coast came into sight. "Here comes Disneyland," Stevenson said, turning to the woman beside him.

"Where? The whole West Coast is lit up."

"At the south end of the coast." He turned back to the window. He saw the sprawling lights of the Seattle metropolitan area to the north, then Portland and San Francisco stood out among a host of smaller cities. Finally, he gazed at the Los Angeles area. From the north of L.A. to Tijuana, Mexico, it looked like one solid city. "The happiest place on Earth."

"Shit. What's going on down there?" Stevenson put both hands to the window and gasped.

"What the ...?" Sonia put her face against the glass to get a better look. "What happen?"

Disneyland, and all the surrounding metropolis, went dark. The lights went out close to the border. From Mexico to the Canadian border, one-by-one the lights went dead. A sea of black covered the continent, from the Pacific Ocean to the Rocky Mountains.

DR. WILLIAM EVERLY was God in his world. He commanded the minions serving his bidding and held the power of life and death in his hands.

An elderly woman whose heart had stopped on her way home from church, lay draped with green cloth on the table below him. Dr. Everly sat in a chair that looked as if it belonged on the bridge of the Starship Enterprise.

A rapid beep-beep-beep emitted from the heart monitor.

"BP one-sixty-five over one-ten," a nurse said.

Everly nodded and kept his eyes focused on the binocular device before him.

"Okay, we're going in." He put his hands in two cuffs and rotated them.

A Rube Goldberg looking machine sat poised over the old woman. It rested on a four-wheeled cart and had four arms Everly always thought of as "Doctor Octopus Arms." As he moved his hands, two arms of the machine moved in unison.

"Everything looks good here."

"All clear," the anesthesiologist replied.

The nurse held her breath as the robotic arms inched closer and closer to the woman's chest.

With deft movements, the doctor's commands were transferred to the surgical robot. One of the robot's arms ended in a scalpel-like device, the other in a pincher-like implement. The two unused arms lay back along the cart.

The blade moved closer to the woman's chest in tiny increments, touched her skin, and began a smooth cut. A line of red traced its way down her chest.

"Retract," Dr. Everly said.

Dr. Pauline West pulled the flaps of skin open, revealing the rib cage beneath. "Retract," she echoed.

The Michelangelo Machine, dubbed "Mickey" by the operating room staff, continued to cut.

"Retractor," Dr. Everly said.

Dr. West inserted a shiny stainless-steel implement into the woman's chest and pulled the ribs apart.

Dr. Everly slid back from the machine and took a deep breath. "Okay, good so far, people."

He put his eyes back to the binocular device and studied the ancient heart.

Then the lights went out.

The view in his binocular device went black. The beep-beep-beep went silent.

"Power outage," one of the nurses announced.

"Stay calm," Dr. Everly ordered.

The operating room staff froze.

"Emergency power should come on in a second," he said, as much to reassure himself as his crew.

Battery-powered emergency lights dimly illuminated the room. Dr. Everly waited for Mickey to come back on line. And he waited.

"What the hell's going on?" he asked. "Where's the emergency power?"

"It should be up by now," Dr. West said.

"Tanya, call the security desk. Find out what's going on."

A heavy-set woman peeled off her gloves and grabbed the red phone on the wall. She turned back to the doctor. "The phone's not working."

"Then get the hell out there and find out," Dr. Everly snapped in a raised voice, then stopped and took a breath. He took pride in always being in control. How close had he come to losing it?

The nurse flew through the swinging doors.

"Pulse, BP," the doctor said.

A nurse placed fingers on the patient's wrist. "One-twenty and thready," she said.

She put a manual blood-pressure collar around the woman's saggy bicep. After a moment, she looked up at the doctor. "BP remains the same, one-sixty-five over one-ten."

"Where's the fucking power?" The surgeon pushed himself up from his Captain Kirk chair.

"The backup generators didn't come up," the heavy-set nurse said as she burst through the doors. "The systems guys are working on it, but they don't know how long it'll take. The batteries for the emergency lights only have about an hour in them."

"Jesus Christ on a crutch," Dr. Everly said. "Okay, folks, we're going to have to do this the old-fashioned way."

He shoved Mickey aside and moved next to Dr. West.

THE EL NUEVO Chaparral was packed. With a full parking lot an attendant showed drivers where to find an empty space.

The pink stucco building sat on a hill over-looking Seattle's Lake Union. Hope Higuera always thought of the heart-shaped lake as the center of the city.

The L-shaped building with a domed cupola was perfect for a Mexican restaurant. The packed dining room was to the left when entering the brightly-tiled entryway, the bar to the right.

Cheerful Mexican music and the sounds of laughter filled the air. Hope, the proprietress, walked among the tables wearing a silk blouse and a skirt that showed off her tiny waist and hid her full hips.

"Donald, Marion, how're you doing?" Papa always told her that nothing was more important than remembering a guest's name.

"Hi, Hope," the chunky business man said as he half rose. "This is my cousin Marty, from Minneapolis, and his wife, Gloria."

"Hi." Hope held out her hand. "So nice to meet you."

"Señora, they need you in the bar," a young busboy said as he approached Hope.

"Thanks, Miguel." Hope excused herself and whispered to the busboy.

"Send a complementary order of Nachos to Donald's table, will you," before making her way into the bar

"What's up?" Hope asked the light-skinned, brown-haired woman tending bar.

"We can't get the spigot on the keg to work." Toni Walker wore a low-cut blouse and her store-bought double Ds strained to break free when she bent over the keg.

"Let me have a look." Hope moved beside the keg. She didn't see anything wrong. She pushed down on the tap with all her strength and turned it to the right. It slid right in.

I swear, she couldn't get her wings on by herself if the angels came down from Heaven to take her home. But she was a good bartender and a great draw. Every night on her shift, the bar was packed with single males.

The dining room personnel moved with choreographed precision. She made her way through the kitchen back to her office. She closed the door behind her and absorbed the quietness. Before the incident in Mexico, action was fuel for her system, but something had changed. Since being shot, she craved the peace of her closed off space.

She logged in to her computer. A whole string of black boxes appeared on the lower-right-hand-side of the screen. There were bunches of messages and Facebook posts. She ignored them and brought up the scheduling program.

She found the schedule filled out and ready to post. Automation was great; her scheduling program produced a product that was ninety percent accurate, but the schedule was her single best tool for making her staff happy. She wanted one last look before posting it.

Her screen flickered, then went black. The lights in her office went out. Her world was plunged into darkness.

What the hell?

She got up and felt for the door knob. The entire restaurant was dark. She felt her way along the wall to the back door and searched for the alarm. She turned her key and opened the door.

She stepped through the exit and looked out over Lake Union and the city. It was all dark. A city-wide blackout.

When she came back inside she was stunned by the silence. Her little brother, Carlito, dressed in chef's whites, was easy to pick out of the mulling crowd of employees.

"Hey, sis. What do we do now?" he asked.

"It looks like the entire city is dark." She rubbed her head. "Jenny, make sure the guests are comfortable. Get extra candles lit wherever you can put them in the dining room."

Jenny nodded and hustled away.

"Carlito, grab the flashlights from the office and get back into the kitchen." Fortunately, most of the cooking equipment was gas. "Keep putting those orders out as best you can. If you have something you can't make, let the server know so that the guest can re-order."

When she went through the door to the dining room, she saw that Inez had already gotten the emergency box out from under the cash register and was issuing paper guest checks to the servers. Servers and bus boys lit dozens of votive candles on every flat surface.

"Ladies and gentlemen," she yelled over the swell of conversation. "Please remain in your seats and stay calm. The entire city seems to be in a black-out. We don't know how long the power will be out. We can still cook and will continue to serve your meals. If you would like to cancel your order and go home, please tell your server so she may remove it from the queue."

A soft murmur spread through the dining room.

"Of course, there will be no charge for your food tonight. Let's all be good neighbors and take care of each other. It's a great night for a fiesta."

The crowd applauded.

"WE INTERRUPT your broadcast for the following special report."

"Good evening." A heavily made-up, fortyish blonde smiled to the camera. "I'm Janet Petersen. Welcome to a special report from *News Front*, coming to you from Washington D.C." The theme song crescendoed and the camera panned out to show Janet Petersen sitting behind an ebony anchor desk. "Our story tonight: The West Coast Black-Out."

"And, out," a voice carried over the set.

Janet took a sip of water and smoothed her hair as the show's credits ran.

She knew the hairdressers hated it when she touched her hair, but an old habit was hard to break.

"Back to you, Janet. In five, four ... " the stage manager mimed the last three numbers with his fingers.

"Five minutes ago, all electrical power to the West Coast was lost." Janet read from her teleprompter. To viewers, it appeared she were looking straight at them. "Here on the East Coast, we are still getting sporadic information from local stations out west. Our West Coast affiliates all have emergency generators and our news vans make their own electricity. I'll update you as more reports come in. As of this time, no one knows the reason for the blackout or even how it could happen."

She paused and put a hand to her right ear. "We're receiving a report now. Hold on a minute."

She nodded her head. "I've just been informed that the blackout extends from the Mexican border to Canada and from the Pacific Ocean to the western slopes of the Rocky Mountains. We're going now to a live report from David Garcia, at KCBS in Los Angeles."

A dark man with black hair appeared on the screen over Janet's shoulder. He stared into the camera a couple of seconds before speaking.

"Thank you, Janet. I'm at the Los Angeles County Administration building, trying to get a handle on what's going on here."

Automobile horns screamed in the background.

"All cell phones and land-lines are down. We're communicating with our field teams via satellite broadcasts. As you can probably hear, the traffic control system has gone down. We have reports of accidents throughout the city. News Chopper 7 has footage."

The screen went black, with tiny lights from cars illuminating the ghostly landscape.

"Thanks, David. This is Kelly O'Donnell in News Chopper 7." The lines of white and red lights on the freeways below her were frozen. "As you can see, the traffic below us is a mess. When the power went out, the traffic system failed. Cars hurled into each other in intersections all over the city. Traffic is at a standstill and people are abandoning their vehicles in the streets. LAPD asks all motorists to remain with their cars. As tow trucks clear the streets, drivers need to move their cars to allow traffic to flow."

Garcia held a finger to his ear and said, "Kelly, I hate to cut you off, but we're going to Brad Demming at the San Jose Creek Water Reclamation Plant. Brad what do you have?"

The screen behind Janet split, with a picture of David on the left and a short man with matinee-idol looks on the right.

"Hi, David. I'm here at the San Jose facility just outside of Whittier, California. I just spoke to Daniel Barnwell, the plant manager. He says that the plant has completely malfunctioned, and raw sewage is flooding into the streets. The Los Angeles sewage treatment system handles over five-hundred million gallons of sewage a day. At this time, there is no way to prevent that sewage from flowing through the system, untreated."

"Brad, doesn't the county have backup power for those plants?"

"Yes, it does, David." The camera backed out and Brad stood in front of a modern-looking building with a Los Angeles County Sewage Treatment Plant sign. The lights in the building were blazing. "Mr. Barnwell told me that their computer systems have gone haywire and the computers are causing the problems. Flow gates have locked shut all over the city and the sewage has no place to go other than the storm drains."

"Any word on when the plants will be back online?"

Brad shook his head. "No, David. They've called in all staff, but with traffic tied up the way it is, it could be hours before they're here. Once they have their people on-site, they have to crawl through their computer systems, line by line, looking for the bad code. It could take hours, days or weeks to locate the problem. In the meantime, the County Sheriff's Office has put out a notice to all beach-goers to stay out of the water."

"Thanks, Brad." David looked back into the camera. "Janet, as of now, no one knows what happened or why. We'll keep you updated as more information becomes available. For now, back to you."

"Thank you, David." The screen returned to Janet Petersen, in Washington, D.C.

"No one can tell us what's going on. I have reports that the President is calling the Joint Chiefs-of-Staff to an emergency meeting at the White House. Our White House correspondent, Julie Chin, is standing by with that story."

The screen behind Janet showed an Asian-American woman standing on the White House lawn. "Thanks, Janet." Julie looked down at her tablet. "We can't get confirmation of these stories but have been told that the President believes this is a cyber-attack on the United States. He has called his military and technical advisors to the White House in the middle of the night for an emergency conference. You'll recall that the President recently announced that any cyberattack against the United States would be retaliated against with nuclear weapons."

Julie held her hand to her right ear. "I'm getting another report in now. This story is just breaking. An ISIS website has claimed responsibility for the power outage."

CHAPTER TWO

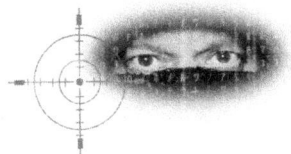

FOUR MONTHS EARLIER

Chris Hardwick pulled his Porsche Boxster into the parking lot of an old warehouse in Seattle's SODO district. East of the ball parks, fancy restaurants, and expensive condos, this was the industrial underbelly of the city.

He sat for a moment in the silver sports car. Although twelve-years old, it looked brand new and ran like a Swiss watch. Harry, his late dad, gave him the car as a high school graduation present and a bribe to keep him in Seattle and attend the University of Washington.

A lump filled his throat and his eyes dampened. Harry had suffered a heart attack during the Swiftsure sailboat race forty miles off-shore. By the time the Coast Guard reached him, it was too late.

Get with it, bud. He shook his head. This should be the most joyous time in his life. He just won the biggest murder case of his career. He had more clients than he could handle, he had the love of a good woman, life was good. So why did he have this feeling of sorrow, loneliness?

Chris slipped out of the expensive sports car and headed for the building, kicking at the weeds which protruded through breaks in the parking lot concrete and the McDonald's wrappers that flitted at the mercy of the wind coming off the Sound.

"Mr. Chris," a large African woman said in a British accent as Chris entered the door. "So nice to see you." She jumped up and wrapped him in a big hug.

"Abiba, it's been too long."

Although Chris was a tall man, he felt engulfed by the woman's embrace. She was every bit as tall as he and outweighed him by a hundred pounds.

She set him free. "You here to see Mr. Ted today?"

Chris gasped for breath. "Yeah, is he in?"

"He's in his office." Abiba wiped a tear from her eye. "Mr. Chris, you must help him. Ever since he got back from Mexico, he mopes around. I swear he spends more time with Señor Herradura than he does with his clients." The corners of her lips turned down. "With Mrs. Flaherty gone, we need him. You have to make him snap out of it."

"I'll see what I can do. I still have a miracle or two up my sleeve." Chris headed through the maze of cubicles toward the back of the office. As usual, a couple of dozen women sat in groups of twos or fours inside the workspaces carrying on the work of Flaherty & Associates.

Chris knew that Catrina Flaherty founded the private investigation firm to help women in trouble. When Ted came on board, he moved the company into the 21st century and brought in several high-profile security clients. The *hermano* was a smart guy; he shouldn't have any trouble running the agency without her.

Chris stopped at the office door to study his best friend. Ted Higuera was a short, stocky man. He could still bench press two-fifty and had the moves that won him the all-time high school rushing yardage record in the Los Angeles School District and got him the scholarship to the University of Washington.

Ted looked like hell. He had dark circles under his eyes, his curly black hair was uncombed, and his Seahawks T-shirt looked as if it died several months ago.

"Hey, amigo, what's up?" Chris asked as he entered Ted's office.

"Chris." Ted rose to embrace his buddy in a big *abrazo*.

Chris smelled the distinct odor of tequila and sweat about him. "I haven't

14

heard from you in a week. I thought I better come over and see if you're still alive." Chris took a seat in the padded cherry-wood chair opposite Ted's desk.

"Just barely, man." Ted returned to his chair. "Sometimes I wonder if it's worth it."

"That's bullshit, and you know it." Chris picked up the bottle of tequila and examined the label. "You've got more going for you than any hundred other guys I know." The bottle was two-thirds empty. "Is this from today?"

"Don't go gettin' all goodie-two-shoes on me." Ted's eyes widened, and his stare intensified. "I can take care of myself."

Chris put the bottle back on Ted's desk. "It doesn't look like it."

Ted's lips curled into a sneer.

Chris took in Ted's office. The bright cherry-wood furniture accented the soft gray walls. A picture of Papa and Mama, before Papa was murdered in Mexico, sat on his credenza, next to pictures of his two brothers and two sisters. His attention was drawn to Ted's little sister, Hope, in her *quinciñera* dress. *God, even at fifteen, you could tell she was going to be something special.*

In the picture, Hope wore a light-pink ballgown that emphasized her tiny waist and large bust line while minimizing her full hips. His heart skipped a beat. *This is really it.*

"I was just thinking..." Chris cleared his throat. "Ah... that we've sure come a long way."

A sign of life flashed in Ted's eyes. "Yeah. I never expected this..."

"Me neither. I guess we're all grown up now. You, the president of your own company, me with my own law firm. Who'd-a thunk it?"

Ted closed his eyes and was silent for a moment. "I remember how we never wanted to have adult jobs; I mean, I never thought about it, now here we are... I guess you're right. It's just that ... I mean ... first, I lose Maria. The baby should be due soon. I won't even be able to see my own son. Then Cat walks out on me."

"Hey, amigo." Chris pounded his fist on the desk. "She didn't walk out on YOU. She left because her life was in ruins. After she discovered that Harvey was a serial killer; well, you know what I mean. She needed to get a fresh start. You need to get a fresh start. I'm going to take you out and find you a girl tonight."

"Bullshit. I don't want another girl. I want Maria." Ted slumped in his chair.

"Get real. That's just not going to happen." Chris shook his head slowly. "C'mon, Ted. I came to break you out of this jail. Let's head down to the gym. I've got the afternoon off."

"Nah, I got stuff to do."

Chris spun the LED screen on Ted's desk to face him. The calendar application was up. "Yeah, it sure looks like you're busy." Chris rose from his chair. "C'mon, get your butt in gear, Higuera. We're going to the gym, then we're headed over to The Green Front for a beer."

"The Green Front? What's wrong with Hope's place?"

That was the last place Chris wanted to go. "I need to talk with you... someplace private."

SAM LIKED his life predictable and uncomplicated. Each day he rose early, spread his prayer rug, faced Mecca, and professed his faith. Then, he made a pot of strong tea and sat at the kitchen table with his Surface tablet and scanned the Internet for world news.

By the time he finished his second cup, sounds of life seeped into the kitchen. His twelve-year-old son, Amed, burst into the kitchen, grabbed a Pop-Tart and gulped a swig of orange juice from the container.

"Amed, how many times do I have to tell you not to drink from the bottle?" he asked.

"I dunno." His son smirked at him. "How many times have you told me so far?"

Before he had time to reply, his fifteen-year-old daughter, Amira, swept into the room, twirled, and dropped daintily into a chair.

"You are not wearing that outside," Sam roared. Once more she was wearing a short skirt and a low-cut T-shirt.

How could his wife allow his daughter to dress like an American whore? He considered himself fully integrated into American society, but he still had standards. He married Jennifer while in college, and she converted to the faith, but somehow, she couldn't adhere to the Islamic sharia law's dress requirements.

"Mom!" Amira shouted. "Dad's doing it again."

His kids were out of the house before he had time to say, "Good morning." Jennifer, who worked a night shift at the Kaiser Permanente Hospital in Bellevue, rarely rose before he left for work.

Jennifer never got the knack of Syrian cooking. He grabbed a bowl of yogurt, some fruit, and a bagel. A poor substitute for a real breakfast. At home, his mother would have breakfast covering the table by the time he made his way to the kitchen. *Modern American life.*

Sam loved his walk to work, especially on a late summer day. His three-bedroom apartment at the Trails of Redmond was less than a mile from the Microsoft campus. Nestled amongst tall evergreens, the air smelt of cedar needles and ferns, and salal crowded the path. It almost made him feel as if he was in a primeval forest.

"Sam, good morning to you," a small Indian man said as he joined Sam along the trail.

"Marhaban, Guppy." Sam smiled and fell in step with his friend.

As they walked past the rarely used recreation centers, half a dozen other H1B visa engineers on their way to work joined them.

The Microsoft campus spread throughout the valley. Modern three-story buildings were surrounded by acres of parking lots filled with BMWs, Porsches, and luxury SUVs. Green lawn filled the gaps between the buildings. Fountains graced courtyards filled with workers holding coffee cups in one hand and Surface tablets in the other.

What a pleasant place to work. Far from his birthplace of Halab in war-torn Syria.

Sam said goodbye to his comrades, made his way to his office and docked his tablet into his workstation. The large flat-screen monitor sprang to life. He started with emails. It was always important to keep up on the latest communications.

Next was his work-group wiki. Any new security threats discovered overnight would be posted there. His subordinates in India also posted the results of their day's work.

It worked well that way. He and his American team scoured the Web for security flaws in the Windows operating system during the day. They left instructions for the India team when they went home. When they came back the next day, the India team made their fixes and the American team tested them.

It was a big job. As head of the Windows security team, Sam had the whole world at his fingertips. Hundreds of millions of computers world-wide depended on his team to keep them safe from the cesspool of viruses, worms, Trojan Horses, ransomware, and other malware infesting the Internet.

Sam considered his team white-hat hackers, the good guys. The black-hat hackers were always trying to find new ways to break into systems and cause havoc. Stopping them was a never-ending task. As soon as one operating system breech was found and plugged, another was discovered. His team worked twenty-four hours a day to try to keep ahead of the hackers. Most of the time, the security flaws were discovered by the black hats, not by his team. Then his team had to hustle to solve the problem before it became an epidemic. It was a game they never won.

TED KEPT up with Chris step for step on the treadmills. Even though Ted had been a college athlete, Chris was the gifted one. Chris's dad, Harry, had been a Heisman Trophy candidate at the UW until an injury ended his football career. Chris inherited Harry's genes.

Ted wiped the sweat from his brow and looked over at this friend. He was tall, with long blond hair pulled back into a pony tail. His sky-blue eyes melted many a female heart. Ted chuckled to himself. *They shoulda cast Mr. Perfect there in the Thor movies.*

His mama didn't raise any fools. He knew what Chris was up to. Anything to take his mind off Maria.

"So, are things settling down for you at the office?" Chris asked between breaths.

"Not much. I'm keepin' Cat's business alive for her. It was her passion, and I expect she'll come back for it someday. Ya know we were spared from that run-in with the terrorist up in Canada for a reason. I feel like I need to defend people that can't defend themselves."

Chris smiled.

The tread mills slowed down.

"We've made a lot of progress in the cyber-security department," Ted said. "I got more clients than I can handle. I'm thinkin' about hiring an assistant."

"That sounds like a nice problem to have." Chris stepped off his treadmill and toweled his face.

"I'm so swamped with the business side of the business." Ted wrapped a towel around his neck. "I can't service our clients. I'm thinkin' that the company has grown too big to handle."

Chris headed for the showers. "I know you took some business classes at the U. Remember what professor Chin used to tell us?" He paused a moment. "Do what you're good at, then hire experts to do the things you aren't good at."

"I haven't thought about Chin in years. Yeah, I guess you're right." Ted felt the endorphins coursing through his system. He couldn't wait to get back to work and start straightening things out. "I've got two big security contracts coming up. I don't know how I'll find time to do them."

Chris spun the combination on his lock. "Here's an idea for you. You need to restructure the firm. When you and Cat were running it, you just kind of did your own thing and it worked. Now that you're alone, you need to build some processes. You should hire a replacement for yourself to run the cyber-security department, then hire someone to run the investigations business. That will leave you to run the over-all company."

Ted stripped off his workout clothes and dropped them into the bottom of his locker. "Papa used to tell me that the secret to success was to surround yourself with successful people."

The memory of Papa cast a dark shadow across his soul. The Cartel killed Papa in Mexico when he was searching for Ted's little brother. *If only you waited for me.* But there was no stopping Papa once he'd made up his mind.

He shook it off and headed for the showers. Chris made everything sound so easy. Where was he going to find someone who could run those departments?

CHAPTER THREE

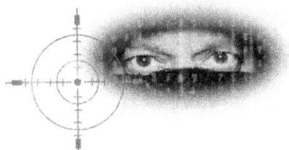

A true safe house did not exist. In this accursed country, the FBI, CIA, NSA, Homeland Security, and a dozen other covert agencies he never heard of had eyes and ears everywhere. That day, he felt relatively safe in the outskirts of Kirkland, but Uncle Sam could invade their space at any time.

Assad al Allah, a nickname meaning Lion of God, wasn't concerned for his own life. They could burst in, guns blazing, and send him to paradise where seventy virgins awaited his pleasure. It was the mission that concerned him. If the Feds charged in, could he save the mission?

Assad, a short, slight, dark man, checked the security monitors. A dozen hidden cameras guarded the house. Motion detectors were a pain when some stray dog wandered into their yard, but they would be a gift from Allah when the black-clad SWAT teams arrived.

Before they installed the first computer, the first router, they secured the premises. They took great care to dig an escape tunnel. It often amazed Assad how much effort his brothers in Syria took to plan and fund these missions.

To secure their network, buried deep in the dark net, Assad and his friends built a system that spoofed other networks and bounced around the globe to keep their IP addresses safe.

All of this to make one safe house. He had a dozen of them. When the FBI broke down the doors of this house, he and his followers would escape and be up and running in the house in Seattle or Bremerton or Tacoma before the Bureau swept this one. Praise be to Allah; they were unstoppable.

The bombings at the Boston Marathon, in Paris, Berlin, and Madrid moved the cause forward. Raids at crowded theaters and synagogues raised his spirits. How many of his brothers had already sacrificed themselves for the glory of Allah?

But those actions were child's play. In a way, they were proof of concept missions building up to the greatest attack ever planned. When they were done, the Great Satan would be cowering on its knees. He and his little crew here in Microsoft Land, with thousands supporting their efforts in other countries, would do the impossible.

The Great Satan built its empire on technology. They were the masters of the world at high-tech. It was that same technology that would doom them.

There was a steady hum of voices behind him as he labored at his workstation. A dozen other Muslim men, all trained in the United States, some even born here, worked as one to institute Allah's will.

"I'm ready, my brother," a heavy young man said to Assad. "We can do the test anytime you are ready." They spoke English because not all of them spoke Arabic.

"What's your target?"

The rotund young man smiled. "I thought we'd start out inconspicuously. I picked out a Subaru Outback. It's here in the Seattle area so we'll hear the news when it goes wild. When you give the word, my program will take over control of the car and crash it."

Assad al Allah smiled. "And you're sure this is repeatable?"

"Of course." The programmer opened a can of Coke. "If this works, and by the grace of Allah it will, we will be able to take control of virtually any car built after 2012, anywhere. We can take over thousands of them at a time, millions."

Assad placed his hand on his friend's shoulder. "And you're sure that we can increase the speed enough to assure a fatality in the crash?"

"It won't be a problem."

What originally was the living room housed four more workstations. At each station, a keffiyeh-wearing man labored diligently at Allah's work.

"Daaim, how are you progressing?" Assad moved to a tall, thin man with dark hair and hatchet features.

"Just watch." He pressed a few buttons on his keyboard and the microwave oven sitting on a butcher block came to life. He got up, grabbed a fire extinguisher and headed to the kitchen. "It takes several minutes to reach the flash point."

The microwave hummed and vibrated. "I turn up the power to max before I start the machine."

The two men hunkered down behind a thick plastic shield.

Assad smiled to himself as he watched the accursed machine run. *How many of these devices do the infidels have in their homes? Almost every house has a microwave, but most of them are not yet connected to the Internet. Only the modern ones will be able to start fires.*

As the thoughts passed through his mind, the microwave exploded, sending hot metal and plastic all over the room. A roll of paper towels a couple of feet away on the butcher block caught fire. What remained of the microwave burst into flames.

"See, it can start a fire." Daaim quickly extinguished the paper towels. "But, there's no guarantee that American housewives store combustible objects near. Out of a thousand devices we detonate, only a handful will start a fire."

"That's all right." Assad headed back to the living room. "They will cause enough fires to instigate chaos. With all the infidel fire departments called out, there will be more fires than they can handle. Allah willing, we may start a huge urban fire."

Assad sat at his workstation and brought up the Cayman bank account. He had set up the accounts with extreme caution. If the infidels ever caught on to them, it would take them months to follow all the false trails and blind leads to their money. They preferred to deal in cash, but Assad's sense of irony made this too delicious.

They bought lists of credit card numbers from their Chechen neighbors. Their brothers hacked large retail chains, banks, even government databases, to mine the credit card data. The Chechnyans were Muslims, but more interested in making a few bucks than saving the world.

Assad's program ran small charges against the stolen accounts. A few dollars here and there so the owners wouldn't notice. The charges went to false companies Assad set up to be the initial receptacles for the money. The money was aggregated and sent around the world to make the true recipients all but untraceable.

They were only small charges, but there were millions of them a month. From the USA to Britain to Europe, Australia, and Asia, Assad stole little bits until he amassed a fortune.

And it cost a fortune to keep this operation going. He must not only pay for the expenses of the operation inside his great enemy, but also for work, materials, and supplies in his homeland and Europe. This was truly a global enterprise. With Allah's help, they would bring the decadent Western World to its knees and open the way for the Great Caliphate the Prophet foretold.

IT STARTED at 6:02 a.m. The first computer showed an animated gif of a cartoon baby laying in its basket, crying. By 6:05, every computer on the network had the crying baby... And a pop-up box saying that the owner's data had been encrypted. To get the data released, the user was to send three hundred dollars in Bitcoin.

The employees at YTS were in an uproar. People dashed from desk to desk. Voices were raised. Excited people dumped papers on the floor.

Gosh darn it! This was impossible. Bear sat at his workstation and stared at the screen. *Impossible!* YTS Digital Security was the best in the world. No one, NO ONE, could hack into their systems.

Yet there it was. The CryBaby virus, taunting him from his own workstation. To make matters worse, the crying wouldn't stop. He couldn't even turn off the sound on his computer.

Bear had a love/hate relationship with the black hat hackers. David Brigham Jones, known to his friends and co-workers as Bear, loved the hunt. He considered himself the world's top cyber security analyst. Unfortunately, Justin McCormick, his life-long friend and boss, didn't.

Bear built YTS with Justin. He went to school with Justin. He stood by Justin while he served his seven years in purgatory for hacking into the New York Stock Exchange and manipulating stock prices when he was sixteen, forbidden by Homeland Security from touching a computer. Bear was employee number two at YTS Security. He knew every bit as much as Justin, but Justin got all the accolades.

It popped Bear's cork when *Time* magazine ran a cover story on Justin titled "The Most Dangerous Man in America."

Bull pucky. Without Bear there was no Justin McCormack. Yet Justin was publicly degrading his supposed best friend.

Justin humiliated Bear at the morning standup. Every morning, the team members met for a standup meeting, taking a couple of minutes each to say what they did the day before, what they were working on that day, and any obstacles in their path. It was routine.

But Justin turned it into a public drubbing.

"I guess we don't need to ask what Bear's working on." Fire flashed in Justin's eyes. "What're you going to do about it?"

"I'm not going to pay any fucking ransom." Bear saw the astonishment on his co-workers' faces. He hadn't sworn since grade school. "Oops! I'm sorry. Did I say that out loud?" His face turned red. "We'll wipe all the servers and rebuild them. We have good backups."

Bear's system of redundant Storage Area Networks (SANs) saved every file to mirrored servers every few minutes. In case one went down, the other took the load seamlessly. He had daily backups, so they could never lose more than one day's work. For high priority files, he did hourly backups.

All for nothing. The CryBaby virus locked up all the files on all the servers and workstations, mirrored or not. He needed to get his off-site backups and rebuild to the previous day's data. A whole day lost. Plus, all the work that wasn't going to happen that day as they repaired the damage. *Crud.*

"I want to know how this happened." Justin said.

The other employees kept quiet and took a step away from Bear.

"We won't know until we're back up and running. Most ransomware like this comes in attached to an email or as a link to a website. Until I can look at everything that came in yesterday, I won't know."

Bear glared at his frenemy. Justin was everything he wasn't. Tall, built like a linebacker, steely-blue eyes. He fit in any environment.

Bear looked at his socks and sandals. He knew he was no prize. Short and stubby, wild red hair, and a bushy beard. His superpower was his brain. Only Justin's was better, and he knew it.

"Tina, Jay, and I will rebuild the servers in a quarantined environment," Bear said. "When we're sure they're clean, we'll move them back to production."

Justin pursed his lips. "This is just a Band-Aid. Until we find out how they got in, we're vulnerable." Justin turned his back and walked to the large window overlooking downtown Seattle. "We're supposed to be the best in the world. If you let this happen, it could cripple our business."

The accusation stunned Bear.

"Our clients come to us because we keep them safe," Justin said. "If we can't keep ourselves safe, how can we keep our clients safe?"

The heavy red hair on Bear's arms bristled. "No hacker is as good as we are."

"You think? I'm wondering if you're still up to the task." Justin turned and walked out of the room.

CHAPTER FOUR

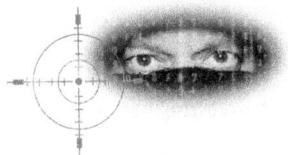

Mary Beth Henderson loved the changes to their offices. After a would-be murderer bombed their building, Cat and Ted rebuilt in 21st century style. Gone were the garage-sale desks and wobbly chairs. Mary Beth had never worked in cubicles before, but it seemed homey to sit in a group with the three other women on her team in a little cloth-covered bullpen.

Best of all, Ted insisted they build a picnic area, complete with a gas barbeque, in the parking lot for employees to take their breaks. Flaherty & Associates occupied the mezzanine of an old warehouse in the industrial area of Seattle with no good restaurants within walking distance. She had never worked anyplace that cared for their employees like Flaherty & Associates.

Mary Beth passed through the heavy glass door into the patio. Green lawns, a couple of potted trees for shade, a gurgling fountain, and cement benches produced a little oasis in the concrete jungle.

She sat on one of the picnic tables and opened her canvas lunch bag. She retrieved the Chinese chicken salad and a can of Diet Coke. After a deep drink of the Coke, she stopped and thought.

Life seems different now. Cat's gone. She just walked off and left the business to Ted. That isn't a big deal, really. Ted's a good guy. But he's a guy. The business was built by women for women. How will we fare with a man leading us?

And can I do my job without Cat? Would Ted understand the things Cat knew? Could he even understand a woman's life?

Her cell phone rang.

"Hi, Abiba," she said.

"Mrs. Mary Beth, I just got a call." The British accent seemed so normal to Mary Beth now. "Normally, this is something I would pass on to Mrs. Flaherty, but she's gone now. I think you should take it."

"Ah... Okay. Who is it? What's it about?"

"The woman wouldn't give me her name. She wanted to talk to Mrs. Flaherty. Said she was referred by a friend. When I told her Mrs. Flaherty wasn't available, she almost hung up. I had to practically beg her to stay on the line."

Mary Beth munched a bit of salad. "What did she want?"

"Her husband abuses her. She wants to talk to Mrs. Flaherty about her options."

"You can patch me through to her." Mary Beth put down her fork.

"She already hung up. I convinced her to come in for a meeting though. She's on her way."

"Crap. Is Cat's office available?'

"It's ready if you need it," the cultured voice on the phone said.

Mary Beth put her lunch back in the sack. *This is big time. Could be dangerous. The kind of thing Cat handled so easily. What'm I going to do?*

MARY BETH WATCHED from Catrina's window as a red Toyota Highlander pulled into the parking lot. A woman with long brown hair, wearing athletic shoes and scrubs, stepped out. She stood by her car for a moment, then shook herself and headed towards the front door.

Mary Beth read her body language. *She doesn't seem too sure of herself* she thought as she headed to her own desk. She could see the front door and Abiba's desk from her workstation.

The etched-glass door opened, and the woman stepped in. She was very good looking. Chiseled features, straight nose. *Must be a nurse or something.* She constantly touched a tissue to her nose.

"I ... I ... called a little while ago." The woman's voice was shaky.

"Hello." Abiba rose from her desk. With her size, she should have been scary, but somehow, she projected a loving grandmother feeling. "Let me get Mrs. Henderson for you."

"No. I mean ... I'm not sure. A friend of mine recommended Catrina Flaherty, but I don't know about anyone else."

"Just speak with her . . ." Abiba said.

"No." The woman turned towards the door. "This was a mistake."

Mary Beth leapt to her feet and met the woman at the door. "Hi, I'm Mary Beth Henderson." She held out her hand. "I didn't get your name."

The woman stared at her a moment. "I didn't give it."

"Would you like a cup of tea? Coffee? Water?"

"No. I think I should leave."

Mary Beth looked into her eyes and gestured toward the office. "Won't you just come with me?" She saw the pain in the woman's eyes. "I know where you are. I was there once. Catrina rescued me and my kids. She found us a safe place to stay. She gave me a job. She encouraged me to make something of myself. I wouldn't be who I am without her. I really do understand."

The woman's face softened. "Well, maybe." She took a deep breath. "Tea could be nice. Do you have Earl Grey?"

Mary Beth nodded towards Abiba.

"I'll bring it to Mrs. Flaherty's office." Abiba headed towards the break room.

"C'mon. Let me show you the way." Mary Beth led the woman through the maze of cubicles to the back of the building. "This is Cat's office. No one uses it now, so it's a good place for us to talk. No one will interrupt us."

"Thank you." The woman sank into a loveseat behind a glass-topped coffee table. "Where is Cat? She was recommended to me. Why can't I see her?

The detective sat on the other loveseat at a ninety-degree angle from the woman. "Cat is on an extended leave. She didn't tell us where she was going." She took a deep breath. "Let's start again." Mary Beth extended her hand and flashed a warm smile. "I'm Mary Beth Henderson. I'm a private investigator here."

The woman took her hand in a weak grip. "I'm ..." She paused to think. "I'm Jane. Jane, uh ... Williams."

Mary Beth smiled. "Good to meet you, Jane Williams."

Abiba entered the office carrying a silver tray with three cups and tea service. They looked miniscule in Abiba's giant hands. The women were silent while she poured the tea. Then Abiba sat next to Mary Beth.

Jane stared at her for a moment.

"Oh, it's okay." Mary Beth waved a hand at Jane. "Abiba sits in on all client meetings. She's more than just a receptionist, she has a ... ah ... unique way of looking at our cases."

"Mmmm – "Jane moaned.

"She was rescued by Catrina Flaherty, too. Her husband and mother-in-law were going to circumcise her daughter."

Jane gasped. "How do you circumcise a girl?" She was sorry she asked the question.

"The shaman cuts out the girl's clitoris with a sharp stick, while the mother and grandmother hold her, Mum." Abiba turned, blinked her eyes, looked out the window, and signed.

"We're here to help you." Mary Beth put a packet of Splenda in her tea. "Tell me about your kids, your husband."

Jane bowed her head and closed her eyes, as if in silent prayer. "He's a good man. A good provider. But he's so old fashioned. He wants my daughter covered up from head to toe. He's very strict. When we upset him, he belittles us. He tells me I'm an affront to God in front of my children. He calls my daughter a whore."

Mary Beth took notes in a spiral-bound pad.

"He was furious last week. He came home from a meeting so happy. Then he got a phone call. After that, he was a monster."

"He beat you?"

"No." Tears formed in Jane's eyes. "He told us how worthless we are. He never picks on my son, but he tears into my daughter, saying things I'd never imagine. He says that if I complain to anyone, he'll kill me. And my daughter. He says it would be an honor killing."

Mary Beth took a deep swallow. "My husband beat me. I can imagine what it must be like, having him belittle you like that."

Jane's head sank lower. "Sometimes I wish he would… Just to get it over with. It's like the sword always hanging over my head."

Mary Beth took a breath. "How can we help you?"

"I don't know. I mean, I can't." Jane fidgeted with the piece of tissue in her hands. "We can't leave. The children. They're in school. They have friends, activities." She shook her head. "No, he's a good man. I mean, he provides for the family, takes care of us. He doesn't drink or use drugs. He's a leader in the mosque. If I left him, I'd be banished from the church. The kids would be in limbo."

"I see. He hasn't struck you? The children? Ever?"

"No. But I'm afraid he might." Jane rubbed her hands together in her lap.

"He hasn't tried to choke you?"

Jane shook her head. "I said no."

"He has threatened to kill you though?"

"Yes." Jane's voice was so low that Mary Beth could hardly hear it. "And my daughter."

"Does he have a gun? Any weapons?" Mary Beth's pulse pounded in her ears.

"Heavens, no. He's a peaceful man.'

Mary Beth moved over to the other love seat and took Jane's hands.

"But …" Jane said. "He told me that if I ever try to leave him, he'll kill us all."

THAT WAS one of the longest hours of my life, Mary Beth thought as Abiba led "Jane Williams" to the door. Mary Beth flopped into Cat's swivel chair and thought back on her life.

Rudy was like that. The nicest man in the world. Until he drank. She couldn't count the number of times he beat her. She feared not just for her life, but for the kids' lives as well.

She met Catrina Flaherty at a self-defense class. Catrina somehow knew she was in trouble and took her aside. After several sessions of meeting for coffee or going to a movie together, Mary Beth finally opened up.

Catrina rescued her – what they called an "extraction" in this office. She was so strong.

Can I do it? What if the husband comes home? I'm not as big as Cat. I don't have the self-defense skills she has.

Mary Beth had a good sense of herself. She was a petite woman, not particularly physically gifted. With short brown hair and a trim figure, she felt like a soccer mom.

How am I going to get Jane out of this? Can I do it? What would Cat do?

CHAPTER FIVE

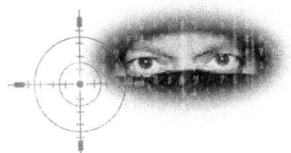

"Ohhhh ..." Abiba yelped. "Mr. Ted ..."

In his tequila haze, it took Ted a moment to realize what was happening. He leapt from his chair, dropped his glass on the desk, and ran to see what the problem was.

"Mr. Ted..." Abiba was out of her chair. "Look."

Ted squinted at the computer screen. "What the hell?" An animated cartoon of a crying baby splashed across the screen. Over and over the baby rocked in its cradle and made an annoying high-pitched wail. After each scream a pop-up box appeared demanding three hundred dollars in Bitcoin.

Holy shit! It can't be. The CryBaby virus. He heard crying from every computer in the office.

"Ted, what's happening?" A dozen voices called for his attention.

His brain kicked into high gear. "Shut your computers off. Everybody! Now!"

Ted sat in Abiba's chair. He felt like a little kid whose feet didn't reach the ground, he was at least six inches shorter than she.

He did the math quickly in his head. *Forty-two times three hundred. That's, let's see. Three times two... twelve thousand six hundred dollars. And we don't have any guarantee that they'll keep their word, and they're free to do it again.* "I'll be damned if I'm going to pay a ransom."

The cacophony began to subside as, one by one, his staff shut down the power to their computers.

He rubbed his head. *What do I know about CryBaby? It spread all over the globe in a couple a days. Millions of computers got infected. It shut down the British health care system. How in the hell did it get past our firewalls?*

He leapt up and ran towards the computer room.

He looked through the thick glass walls that allowed people on the outside to see what was going on inside. Two rows of servers filled the room, while a countertop with pull-out keyboard trays ran along one wall. On shelves above the counter, flat-screen monitors blinked and flashed. Four workstations allowed operators to control all aspects of the network.

He put his ID card up to the reader and waited for it to beep. Then he put his palm to the scanner to be verified. Next it asked him for a passcode, then the door beeped, and he opened it. He stepped up onto the raised floor of the man-trap in a tempered-glass room, eight-feet square. No one was in the computer room to buzz him through, so he reached for his smart phone and brought up the security app. With a few touches on the keypad, a loud buzzer sounded, and Ted pulled the door to the computer room open.

The computer room was freezing. He heard the hollow ring of his footsteps as he dashed across the raised floor. Cool air flowed up through the perforations.

He slid into the swivel chair in front of the master console and clicked away on the keyboard. *Shut the whole fuckin' thing down.* The control center menu came up on the screen in front of him.

Ted considered himself an expert in computer security. So did a lot of other people. Since he came on board Flaherty & Associates, he'd built a substantial business protecting other companies' data.

How did this happen? How did the virus get into our network?

Ted believed in the Boy Scout motto: "Be prepared." He clicked on a red button marked "Emergency" in bold black letters on the console screen. He had long ago anticipated this kind of incident.

A pop-up box asked him if he really wanted to disconnect from the Internet. He clicked on "Yes."

They were safe, for the moment. Without Internet access, nothing else could come in or get out. They already had the virus, but at least they wouldn't spread it.

His thoughts were interrupted by the sound of "La Cucaracha" on his cell phone.

"Mr. Ted," Abiba's voice said. "I know you have a three o'clock, but I can't remember who it's with. What do you want me to do?"

Ted pulled the phone from the holster on his belt. "Abiba, when they get here, whoever they are, explain that we have an emergency and that you'll have to call them to reschedule. All of our computers are locked up and we can't get to our calendars."

He paused to think. *Are our clients safe? If this can hit us, it can hit them.*

"Get everyone on the phones. Have them use their cell phones, our land lines won't work. Call all our clients. Tell them to shut down Internet access. We built secure firewalls for them, but if the virus can get to us, it can get to them. They should all have red "Emergency" buttons on their network dashboard. They need to protect themselves from this virus."

The buzzer over the door sounded. Ted looked up at the monitor to see Marilyn Faulkner in the man-trap. He pushed the button on the desk and the inner lock clicked open.

A petite woman with neatly trimmed gray hair, Marilyn had come to Catrina after a career in computer programming. Catrina helped her daughter with a messy divorce and Marilyn lent her somewhat out-of-date technical expertise where ever she could. She was smart, thorough, and easily accepted Ted when he came aboard.

"What's going on, boss?" She practically ran across the room to Ted's desk. "My beeper went off."

"We've got the CryBaby virus. I don't know how it got here, but I've shut off all Internet access."

Marilyn sat in the chair next to Ted and turned the large flat-screen monitor so they could both see it. She brought up the Network Operating System window. "Looks bad, boss. Everyone has it."

Ted pushed back the lock of black hair that always seemed to fall into his left eye at moments like this. "I'll check out backups. I want you to locate where the virus came from, how it got in."

They went to work.

At about 10:00 pm, Abiba pushed the man-trap button. Ted buzzed her through. Her arms were full of take-out containers.

"You two have been locked in here for hours. I thought you needed a dinner break."

Ted ground the heels of his hands into his eyes. "Abiba, what are you still doing here?" His stomach growled

"If you're here, I'm here," she answered.

"Don't put that stuff down in here." Ted turned towards Marilyn. "You hungry?"

Marilyn leaned back in her chair and stretched her arms. "Mmmm hmmm." She let out a deep breath. "Oh my, I had no idea it was so late. I better give Bill a call."

"Let's move to the break room." Ted stood from his chair and helped Abiba with some of the boxes. "What you got for us?"

"The Kao Kao Barbeque. General Tsao's, almond chicken, pork fried rice, chicken chow fun, and honey garlic shrimp. Oh, and of course, barbequed pork."

"Sounds wonderful." Marilyn held the door open for the other two. Ted touched the screen of his phone and the outer door clicked open.

———

TED NEVER FIGURED out chop sticks. While Marilyn and Abiba deftly picked up pieces of chicken and lumps of rice, he used a fork.

"I taught my kids to use chop sticks by picking up peanuts," Marilyn said between bites.

Ted's cell phone buzzed. *Who the hell?* He looked at his phone. It was after midnight.

"Well, I'll be damned." He answered. "Bear, that you?" Bear had been Ted's mentor at his first job out of college at YTS Security. They hadn't kept in close contact in the years since Ted left YTS Security to work with Catrina.

"That's right, Hero. I suspect I'm working on the same thing you are."

"So, you got it too." Ted smiled and stuck his fork into the container of noodles. "We're just taking a dinner break. You makin' any progress?"

He heard the sullenness in Bear's voice. "Nothing. We're rebuilding servers. We've got no idea how it got in." Of course, sullenness was a daily habit of the stocky little man. "It's everywhere."

"We're lookin' for computer zero. So far, we got nothin'. I'm strippin' down and rebuildin' the servers. We lost about half a day's worth of data."

"You should keep up with the times, Hero."

Bear was the only one who still called him that. He hated it. He earned the nickname when he and Chris stopped a terrorist attack on a cruise ship on the Canada's Inside Passage a decade earlier.

"We're doing hourly backups off our mirrored SAN network now," Bear continued. "We never lose more than a few keystrokes."

"So you don't know how it got into your system?"

Ted heard Bear's yawn on the other end of the line. "Don't have a clue. As far as we can tell, it didn't come in through email. We're still tracking back all the websites anyone in the company visited, but so far haven't found squat."

"Listen, Bear, if you come up with anything, let me know. You'll have to call. I've shut down all external access to our systems."

"You, too? I doubt you'll find it before I do, but there's always a first time."

"Like the time I beat you in findin' a way to hack into Justin's personal files?" Ted grinned. "Poor, little ol' me is always followin' in your footsteps."

Ted turned the conversation back to business. "I haven't tried to reverse engineer the code yet. It would help if we knew who wrote this thing. Whoever it was, they're bordering on genius."

"GOOD EVENING. I'm Janet Petersen, welcome to *News Front*." The theme song crescendoed and the camera panned out to show the anchor sitting behind her ebony desk. "Our story tonight: The CryBaby virus."

The entire Microsoft campus was in a hushed state. None of the usual bustle or people running around waving tablets at one another.

"Shh ..." Sam waved his arms at the room full of engineers. "Quiet, everybody, It's on." He pointed to the giant TV on the wall.

"If you haven't heard yet about the CryBaby virus, you've been living in a cave," the blonde reporter said. "Hundreds of millions of computers world-wide running the Windows operating system have been infected. Billions of dollars in ransoms have been paid. I have special authorization to reveal that even this network paid the ransom so we could stay on the air."

A murmur filled the room.

"We have reports that Microsoft is in full panic mode. They deal with viruses and other malware daily, but this is different. CryBaby is popping up all over the world. It started in Australia, but by the end of the day, Asia, Europe, the Americas, Hawaii, and the Pacific Islands were infected."

"Shit." A young man dressed entirely in black with midnight-black hair and matching lip stick and mascara, shook his head. "That's all we need. More pressure, more publicity."

"Shh ... watch," Sam responded.

"The biggest crisis is currently in Great Britain," Petersen went on, "where the medical systems have shut down. Hospitals can't administer care and life-saving procedures were postponed. The British Minister of Health made the decision to pay the ransom to keep these vital systems online. We'll have a full report on that in a minute."

"Come on, get to the root causes ..." Sam whispered.

"In Germany, the train system shut down." Petersen spit the words out like machine gun fire. "In China, universities were hacked. There are reports of data held hostage in Australia, Turkey, India, Italy, Taiwan, the Philippines, Japan, Mexico, and more. Estimates of the economic impact are still being tabulated, but they could easily run into the tens of billions of dollars." The images on the big TV screen followed her narrative.

"You're not going to believe this," a young man with a Surface tablet on his lap shouted. "The virus isn't coming from the outside. It's not being spread over the Internet."

"Wha ..." Sam couldn't get the words out as the whole group fell silent.

"According to the pop-up screen telling you that you're infected," Petersen went on, "the ransom is going to double tomorrow and will double every day for the next week. At the end of that time, the data will be lost forever."

Sam turned off the TV. No one at the Windows security work group in Redmond cared about *News Front* anymore. Everyone sprinted for their desks.

TED HADN'T BEEN HOME, showered, or slept for two days. He could smell his own BO and was sure Marilyn moved her chair a little further away from him in the Flaherty & Associates network control room.

Marilyn managed to step out, shower, and dress in the clean clothes her husband, Bill, brought to the office for her. Aside from Abiba, Ted didn't have anyone to take care of him.

Abiba, fresh as a spring flower, brought them food and coffee. Ted wasn't sure if his stomach would survive any more coffee, no matter how good it was.

"Mr. Ted," Abiba said, and handed Ted a card. "You have a postcard from Mrs. Flaherty."

Ted looked at the picture. It was a busy street scene with the caption Hong Kong in bright yellow letters. He turned over the card.

"Having fun. Wish you were here," was all that was written on the back.

"Well, at least she's not having to worry about any viruses." He handed the card to Marilyn.

"Hmmm … looks exotic." Marilyn fanned herself with the postcard.

"Okay, that's server number sixteen," Ted told Marilyn and pushed his rolling chair back from the desk.

"How many do you have left?" Marilyn asked.

"Four more and we're up and running."

Marilyn sighed. "Ted, I went through every email we received. I searched hundreds of websites we visited. I don't think the virus came from the outside."

"Then where could it have come from?" Ted scratched his head with a ballpoint pen.

"You remember Sherlock Holmes?"

Ted knocked on his temple with the palm of his hand. "I was never a big mystery reader."

"Mr. Holmes said that when you have eliminated the impossible, whatever remains, no matter how improbable, must be the truth."

Ted shook his head. He longed for sleep. He couldn't quite put two and two together and understand what Marilyn told him. "Huh? I don't get it. What are you saying?"

"Think about it, boss. If it didn't come from the outside, it must have come from the inside."

"Yeah?"

"But it's infected millions of computers all over the world. What do they all have in common?"

Ted leapt from his chair. It clicked in his head. "Marilyn, you're a genius." He grabbed her face in both hands and planted a kiss on her forehead.

"Oh, my." Marilyn was so flustered she sank back in her chair.

"When was the last Windows update? Look it up. I want to see that code."

CHAPTER SIX

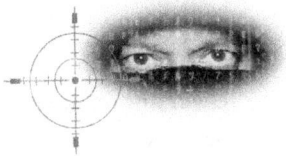

T ed looked around the rundown tavern. It was more than a decade since he hung out here during his university days. The walls were still adorned with Dave Horsey cartoons. The old ones from the days Horsey worked for the now-defunct *Seattle Post-Intelligencer*. These pictures all depicted scenes from the University of Washington's glory football days, under coach Don James.

It was a whole new world.

The Northlake Tavern was still packed with college students and still served the best pizza in the world, but times changed.

Bear looked worse than Ted. "When was the last time you went home, dude?" Ted asked.

Bear lifted his Arnold Palmer and quaffed a long drink. "I don't remember having a home."

"You guys makin' any progress?" Ted asked.

"We've cleaned up our systems," Bear said. "We're back online. We've checked all our clients, and they're either clean or we scrubbed them. We still don't know where the virus came from, or how it got in."

"I know where it came from." Ted paused as the server brought their Lumberjack pizza. It was loaded with meat, grease, calories, and trans-fats; a school boy's dream.

"Okay, smart guy." Bear reached for the first piece. "Where did it come from? How did it get in?"

Ted looked around to make sure no one was listening to them. "You're not gonna believe this." Ted slid a slice of pizza onto his plate. "There's a reason I asked you to meet me in a safe place. This may be the biggest news in a decade." He paused. "It's embedded in the operating system. Think about it. If the ransomware didn't come in through email and didn't come in through the Web, where did it come from?"

Bear sat up and his eyes cleared. "No way." He wiped the grease off his red beard. "You have proof of this?"

Ted shook his head. "We're working on it. But, I mean, how else did it get in millions of computers all over the world on the same day?"

"How?" Bear asked. "I mean, those guys are the best. How could they let something like that though?"

Ted sat back and took a sip of his beer. "I don't know. I need someone to help me figure it out. I need the best white-hat hacker in the world to find this for me. Do you have any ideas who I can talk to?"

"Holly crap, Ted. You don't need the best white-hat, you need the best black-hat. This is big. It may be the biggest hack in history. Whoever figures this out is going to be famous."

A smile spread across Ted's tired face. "Like I said, any ideas who can help me?"

Bear glared into Ted's eyes for a moment. "You offering me a job?"

"I hear rumors." Ted paused to let that sink in. "I heard you might not be too happy at YTS."

"Mmmm ..." Bear brushed the crumbs from his crimson beard as he polished off a piece of pizza.

"Look, Bear, let's not fool around. I need help. Ever since Cat left, I can't keep up. I have more business than I can handle. I have a couple of assistants, but they're not world-class. I hafta run a business with two departments. I need you to run the cyber-security part for me."

Bear took another bite of pizza and rolled his eyes. "Hmmmm ..."

"There's gonna be complications," Ted said. "You were my mentor. I used to work for you. How's that gonna work?"

"The only way it can work," Bear said, "is if I don't work *for* you. I'll work *with* you, but I need independence in my department."

Ted nodded. "I get that. I agree. But there's something you need to be honest about. We're working with a lot of women. Catrina built the business by rescuing displaced women, giving them jobs, and letting them excel at what they're good at. You have two self-trained hackers in your group who are just such women."

Bear nodded.

"I can't emphasize this too much. They've all been misused by men. They've been beaten, raped, threatened. They're all wounded birds clinging together for mutual safety."

"So?"

"So, you're a world-class asshole. One might even say a misogynist."

Bear winced at the accusation but kept quiet.

"You're grumpy, short with people, and have no patience with anyone who you think isn't smart. You're going to be surrounded by those kinds of people. You're going to have to work with them and not scare them off. I won't have anyone destroy Catrina's business. I'm just a placeholder until she comes back."

Bear contemplated that for a moment. "This Catrina, I've heard of her. Never met her. We don't exactly run in the same circles. Who is she? Why did she leave her business with you?"

Ted helped himself to another slice of Heaven. "That's a long story. She was a police woman. Her husband, also a cop, badly abused her. When she left him, he started a campaign of harassment against her in the department."

Ted thought for a moment. *How much of this story is pertinent to your question?* "She sued the Port of Seattle Police Department for sexual harassment; won the biggest settlement in history."

"Hmmm ..."

Ted knew Bear wasn't particularly in tune with women's issues. As far as Bear was concerned, women should stay home and take care of the kids, as witnessed by his harried wife and their six offspring.

"She set up Flaherty & Associates to help women in the same predicament she was in. She's saved hundreds of women. She's kind of a legend in the women's movement in Seattle."

"So, what's that got to do with your situation?"

"A couple of months ago she broke a case. Remember the Chinatown Killer?"

"Ah ... yeah." Bear sprinkled Parmesan cheese on his last bite of pizza.

"The serial killer turned out to be her boyfriend. The man she thought was her true love."

"Oh my God." Bear's brow scrunched up.

"Yeah." Ted took a breath. "When it was all wrapped up, she just left. Took off to who-knows-where and left me to run the business. Honestly, Bear, I'm in over my head. I need help. I need you to run the cyber-security business, and I need to find someone to run the investigative department."

Bear put down his fork and wiped his beard again. "You gave me a lot to think about. How about salary? Benefits?"

"Decide if you're interested, then we can talk details."

THE FOG DIDN'T CREEP in on cat's paws. It roared in like a charging lion. Within moments, the visibility was near zero from the bridge of the U.S.S. Douglass Roberts, DDG-157, an Arleigh Burke class guided missile destroyer cruising along the eastern half of the Formosa Straits.

"It's lookin' pretty ugly out there," the helmsman said over the console to LTJG Emily Thompson, the Officer of the Deck.

"Boatswain, stand the foul-weather watch and sound for fog," she called, a note of an apology there. He had to wake the watch.

"Aye, Ma'am."

"Conn, how're we doing?" the lieutenant asked.

"Forty contacts, ma'am," Ensign Bishop at the radar station answered. "I see thirty-eight. AIS lists thirty."

Lieutenant Thompson walked to the starboard bridge wing. She only had about a hundred yards of visibility.

She turned to the other officer on the bridge. "Make five knots, Conn."

Ensign Bishop hesitated. He was still new and had to think about his orders.

"Helm, make turns for five knots."

"Make five knots, aye," the helmsman echoed.

The quartermaster made a note in the navigation log.

"Ma'am, something funny just happened," Bishop said.

Lieutenant Thompson moved to the radar station. "What?" she asked, looking over the con's shoulder. The screen looked perfectly normal to her.

"The screen went dark for an instant, then came back up. Like it was rebooting or something."

"Sir, we're making five knots," shouted the helm.

"Very well," said Ensign Bishop.

Thompson yawned and looked around to see where she left her cup of coffee. "Restart it. Quartermaster, note it in the log." The hair on her arms tingled.

It was a horrible time to be on watch. At 1:23 a.m. the night chill cut through her pea jacket, even though the temperatures would reach towards three digits at the height of the day. The fog seemed to seep into her every joint. How long had she been on duty?

The captain had fired the navigation officer on the previous day when the destroyer went dangerously off course. The navigational team stood half and halfs—two teams taking six hours shifts. Lieutenant Thompson now stood her second day in a row.

"I've got a contact two thousand yards off the port stern, ma'am," Ensign Bishop said. "He's CBDR."

Ugh. Collision course. "Do you have an AIS contact for him?" She wanted to talk to this guy.

Ensign Bishop scrolled to select the vessel on the console. "No, ma'am."

Thompson grabbed a pair of binoculars, went to the port bridge wing, and had a look back on her port quarter. Nothing. *Damned fog.*

She stomped back into the bridge. "Probably a fishing boat."

Thompson picked up the handheld mic and checked to see if the VHF radio was on channel 16, the international destress frequency all vessels were required to monitor. She keyed the mic.

"Unknown vessel on course one-seventy-five at twenty knots approximately twenty miles east of the Pescadores Islands, this is US warship one-five-seven. Identify yourself."

There was no response.

"Combat, bridge, we have an unknown contact on course one-seventy-five at twenty knots. Likely a Russian or Chinese fishing boat."

"Bridge, we're tracking him."

The lieutenant sighed. The Formosa Strait was known for its traffic congestion. A hundred miles wide, the strait between mainland China and Taiwan was one of the busiest ocean superhighways in the world. All the traffic going from China's factories transited the straits before heading into open waters and courses to the American coasts or around Africa to Europe. The fact that a fishing boat either didn't have AIS, the international ship tracking system, on board or turned it off, wasn't surprising.

There were forbidden fishing grounds off the islands, and any pirate fishing captain taking the chance to fish there wasn't going to broadcast his position, and he sure didn't want to meet a U.S. warship.

She glanced at the radar screen where Ensign Bishop watched the ship nervously. They had twenty minutes, and she wasn't sweating it. She just didn't want to call the captain and wake him. "Any change?" she asked.

"No, ma'am."

"Conn, come to course zero-two-zero."

Ensign Bishop looked up to check his instruments. "Helm, right five-degree rudder. Steady on course zero two zero."

The helmsman piped up, "Right five-degree rudder. Steady on course zero two zero, aye." He paused to turn his small black plastic wheel to the right. "My rudder is right five-degrees, coming to course zero-two-zero." The ship swayed lazily to the right. Driving one of America's most powerful war ships was more like a lazy game of cricket than a hot soccer match.

"Sir, my course is now zero-two-zero."

"Very well," Ensign Bishop acknowledged.

Time passed slowly. Thompson checked on the radar from time to time, but felt they were safe. She heard the reassuring blast of the fog horn.

The quartermaster made an entry in the logbook every three minutes since they were within thirty kilometers of land.

The navigation system kept the ship on a steady course. The automatic pilot was off, but the ship followed near the line charting its course.

Butterflies fluttered in Lieutenant Thompson's stomach. Something didn't feel right. She double checked the radar and the nav system. Everything looked good. Putting binoculars to her eyes, she scanned the waters around the ship, but with the fog, couldn't see anything.

ASSAD SAT BACK in his chair and watched the big screen TV on the wall. The eyes of his Islamic brothers were glaring at the screen.

"Are we in?" Assad asked.

"Allah be praised," the tall thin hacker answered. "If they didn't notice the reset when we took over, we're ready to go."

Assad thought about it. Another test, one of so many. This time they had to get it right. The last time they took control of a Navy ship, they botched it. They left a trail for the Navy to follow, although the fools hadn't found it yet. This time had to be perfect.

When they launched their attack on the United States, everything had to be perfect.

"Where are we?" he asked his tall comrade.

"All is going according to schedule. We placed a ghost fishing boat, moving the target into the path of the container ship. Their radar does not show the container ship, and we've shut down the AIS on the container ship. The destroyer can't see it."

"It's just a matter of time." Assad asked.

"Yes. It is inevitable."

LIEUTENANT THOMPSON RUBBED her eyes and drained the last of the nasty liquid in her coffee mug. Her hair itched. No, it was more like a tingle.

"Quartermaster are we on course?"

"Yes, ma'am."

Something feels funny. The lieutenant thought. *I don't know ... something's just not right.*

"Ma'am," the boatswain shouted. "There, off the starboard bow."

Thompson ran to the bridge wing. She looked into the fog. She could see nothing.

"What did you see?"

"Lights. Red and green. They were pretty far apart."

She strained her eyes, peering into the fog. *Wait.* Did she see something. Maybe a green flash?

"Conn, come here," she shouted. "There," she pointed. "Do you see that?"

The conning officer put his binoculars to his eyes. "I don't know … maybe … oh my God! Ship off starboard bow."

"Sound collision," Thompson yelled. "Right full rudder."

"Right full rudder," the helmsman echoed back.

"Don't you mean left rudder?" the conning officer asked.

"Engines back full." Thompson glared at her junior officer. *Really?* They were about to fight the ship, and then she would lose her job.

From out of the fog, she saw the huge bow of a container ship looming over the destroyer's side. "Brace for impact."

CAPTAIN RICHARD GORDON didn't so much wake as suddenly come to life. A giant metal object sliced through his cabin. He slammed against the bulkhead and grabbed on to a loose pipe. *Where the hell did that pipe come from?*

The ship rolled over on her side. She hung there for a moment as if deciding whether to live or die.

The giant metal object slowly receded from his stateroom. The deck was gone. His hands felt wet and slippery as he held onto the pipe over the rushing sea.

He heard the inflow of water. What happened? Had they shut the watertight doors?

LIEUTENANT THOMPSON STAGGERED to her feet. "Rig for collision. Shut all watertight doors." The claxon alarm thundered over her head.

"Damage report."

"We're taking on water in compartment four. All doors shut. All pumps working."

The executive officer charged onto the bridge. "What in the hell just happened?"

"We were rammed, Sir. It looks like a big container ship from what I saw."

"Holy shit! Were you guys asleep up here?"

"Sir," the damage control officer shouted, "compartment four is completely flooded."

"Oh God! That's where the captain's quarters are."

CHAPTER SEVEN

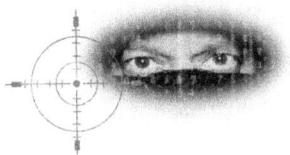

T ed waited at the corner of First and Pike, where he expected to meet the star reporter for *The Seattle Times.* Above him the red neon sign said Public Market, and behind him was a labyrinth of small stores, open-air green grocers, meat and fish markets, and rows upon rows of flower vendors.

Ted admired Dan Rider. Dan had just returned from a trip to the Middle East where he broke a story about how ISIS was developing the capabilities for cyberwarfare.

"Dan, glad you're back in Seattle in one piece," Ted said, reaching out his hand.

Ted first met Dan when Dan interviewed him and Chris after they foiled the terrorist plot to blow up a cruise ship on Canada's Inside Passage years ago. Dan had written several stories on Ted's adventures in the intervening years.

"There were times when I thought I'd be coming home in a box." A couple of decades older than Ted, Dan's gray hair and blue eyes reminded Ted of an eagle. He was taller than Ted, but then again, who wasn't?

"I'm glad you could meet." Ted led Dan towards the Pike Place Market. "I'm dying to hear what you learned about ISIS's capabilities."

"This isn't altruistic, Ted." Dan patted Ted on the shoulder. "I need some background information for my story. You're the best IT guy I know. I want to pick your brain."

They entered the Pike Place Market and walked to the staircase in back. Down a couple of flights and they were on the mid-level, between the market above and the waterfront below, home of Ted's favorite lunch spot, El Puerco Lloron.

"You're not going to believe what I found." Dan got in line to order. "What they're doing is frightening. They've learned how to hack cars, home and business electrical systems, appliances. It's not a matter of if they'll attack, it's when."

Ted whistled. "Man. It's like science fiction. I know this kinda stuff can be done, but I always expected the threat would come from China, or Russia, or North Korea. To have a terrorist organization have that power in their hands. They might as well have nuclear weapons. They could bring down our economy."

A startled look came over Dan's face. He cried out, grabbed at his chest, and fell to the ground.

The people in the outdoor café screamed. Some ran, some crowded close to see what happened.

Ted dropped to his knees. His friend's face turned pale then faded to blue. "Someone call nine-one-one. He's having a heart attack."

"My pacemaker." Dan gasped.

Ted felt for his pulse. Fast and weak. *Oh, God, I need help.*

"Is anyone a medical professional?" Ted shouted.

A woman in blue scrubs came forward. "I can help."

Ted undid Dan's tie and pulled his shirt open. While he was measuring the distance from his clavicle, the nurse cleared Dan's throat. She gave him five breaths.

Ted started CPR. He heard sirens in the distance.

C'mon, Dan, stay with me.

TAMIKA ADAMS WASHINGTON, mayor of Atlanta, called the meeting to order. A middle-aged black woman, she looked half her age with smooth skin and a delightful figure. She sat in the middle of a curved array of desks at the head of the City Council Chamber.

"Mr. Johnson, can you tell us what happened?"

Jackson Johnson, Atlanta 's Chief Information Officer, picked up a piece of paper and leaned into the microphone. "Thank you, Madam Mayor." He cleared his throat. "We have been hit by a ransomware attack."

"Could you explain ransomware for those of us technically challenged?"

"Yes, ma'am. Ransomware is a piece of malicious computer code that infects your systems. It typically encrypts your files, so you can't open them without a password. It pops up a screen telling you that to fix your computers you must pay the hackers a certain amount of money."

"Thank you, Mr. Johnson. Go ahead with your report."

"It's bad. To date we have identified the virus in our court systems, our police systems, and Internet and Wi-Fi connections are down throughout the city. Nine-one-one doesn't work. The airports systems are down. People can't pay their water bills or court fines. All court cases have been postponed. No one can do any business with the DMV." Johnson looked up from his paper. "In effect, the entire City of Atlanta is shut down."

Mayor Washington shook her head. "And how did this get into our systems?"

Johnson harrumphed. "It found a security flaw in our firewall."

The mayor already knew the answer but asked the question to get it on the public record. "Mr. Johnson, why did we have a security flaw?"

Johnson looked down at his paper and spoke in a monotone voice. "We didn't apply the Microsoft patches in a timely manner."

"How long has it been since you received the last release?"

"Over a month." Johnson was sweating.

"And this last release would have plugged the firewall hole?"

"Ah... yes, ma'am."

"Explain to me," her voice rose an octave, along with the volume. "How you could have let this go so long?"

"Madam Mayor, it's a matter of budget. We just don't have the budget to apply all patches in a timely manner."

"Are you telling me you left us unprotected because of a few measly dollars? That's like not responding to a fire because the fire department is short on funds. If it's a critical patch, you find the dollars. Am I clear?"

"Yes, ma'am."

"Okay, people what are we going to do about it?

The city treasurer spoke up. "Ma'am, they are asking fifty-one-thousand dollars in ransom. Do we pay it or fight it?"

"It has always been our policy not to negotiate with terrorists. Mr. Johnson, how long will it take you to fix this problem?"

Jackson Johnson wiped the sweat from his forehead and squirmed in his chair. "I can't really tell you. It could be a couple of weeks or a couple of months."

"A couple of months?" Mayor Washington almost came out of her chair. "You mean the City of Atlanta won't be able to do any business for a couple of months?"

"It could take longer, ma'am."

"Ms. Williams, pay the ransom."

MARY BETH HENDERSON cruised the parking garage for ten minutes looking for an empty space. Kaiser Permanente's Bellevue hospital certainly was popular. There were acres of handicapped parking, right in front of the main entrance, but the higher ups must have wanted able-bodied patients to get more exercise.

Finally, Mary Beth found an SUV pulling out and waited, holding up traffic. Her blue Toyota Sienna mini-van fit easily into the space.

She always wore sensible walking shoes, so the quarter mile or so to the coffee stand in front of the building was no problem. Taking a page from Catrina's book, she wore a flower print dress to appear less threatening. She had taken over the closet in Catrina's office and kept several changes of clothes handy, so she would be ready for anything.

Mary Beth found her client sitting at a table in a corner by herself wearing standard green scrubs, "Jane, nice to see you. Sorry I'm so late."

"Hi." Jane kept her voice down and glanced around nervously. "I'm on a break, so we have to make this quick."

Mary Beth looked up at the sun in the clear blue sky. It was too glorious for anyone to have marital problems. They sat at concrete tables in the middle of a sea of concrete. Interstate 405 was only feet away on their west side and the noise was incessant, but somehow, trees poked through cut outs in the pavement, birds sang, and the world seemed wonderful.

Mary Beth slipped into the seat across from Jane. "I'm glad you called me. What's going on?"

Jane shook her head. "I don't know why I called. I mean, he's being his usual self, but there's nothing anyone can do about it."

"What happened?" Mary Beth reached for Jane's hand, but Jane pulled away.

"He blew up at my daughter. It's always the same. She wore a cute little mini-skirt with a tank top to school today. He asked her—no, demanded—she change her clothes. If she didn't, she was a whore. He said that when she came home pregnant, he would throw her out of the house. I can't stand the way he treats her."

"I'm so sorry." Mary Beth shook her head and looked into Jane's teary brown eyes. "This seems like a common pattern in your house."

Jane merely nodded and stared into her paper coffee cup.

"I told my daughter to dress for him when leaving the house, then she could change into what she wanted when she got to school." She shook her head. "I can't believe I'm doing this, undermining my husband's authority, but he's living in the Dark Ages."

"What else does he do?" Mary Beth needed her to open up. She couldn't help Jane if she didn't know the whole story.

"He has good days and bad days. When everything goes well at work, he's the nicest man in the world. When he has problems, he takes it out on us."

"Go on …"

"He mostly picks on me." Tears ran down Jane's cheeks. "He thinks the fact that I work outside the home is unforgiveable. His religion tells him wives should stay at home and take care of the kids. We have a never-ending battle over my daughter and me not wearing hijabs. He makes me call him when I get home, so he knows where I am. I have to keep a log of where I go and when. If I'm the least bit late, he thinks I'm with someone."

Jane paused. She fingered the edge of the table and bit her lips.

"Are you?"

"No!" Jane's head perked up and her eyes flashed anger. "Of course not. I'm faithful. I made my vows and I stick to them."

"I didn't mean to insult you. I just need to know everything."

Jane nodded.

"What else has he done?"

"He never goes off on my ... our ... son, who can't do anything wrong." Jane took a sip from her cup. "Don't get me wrong. He's a great kid. It's just that his father thinks he walks on water and his sister is worthless. He has a college fund going for our son but won't put a dime away for our daughter. He thinks women don't need an education because they're just going to become someone's wife. I opened a secret account for her and have money deducted from my paycheck before he sees it."

"You're strong. So will your daughter be." Mary Beth wrote in a spiral notebook.

"Thanks." Jane looked up from her coffee. "We have our worst arguments because he wants a large family. I had a horrible time with my son's birth. The doctor said if I got pregnant again, I could lose the baby, maybe my own life. I had my tubes tied. There I was in the hospital, so weak, with my new baby, and I feared he would kill me."

"Did he hit you?"

"No." Jane looked off towards the Cascade Mountains to the east. "He belittled me. Said I had no faith. He said that if God willed that we would have more children, then it would be safe. If not, then it was God's will that I come to him."

"Did you discuss the problem with him before you had the surgery?"

"No ... I ... ah, I know I should have. I know I should have let him be part of the decision, but I knew what his answer would be. I needed to take charge of my body, my life. I couldn't let him stop me." She sniffled, then blew her nose in a napkin. "Mary Beth, I screwed up. This is all my fault."

"It is not your fault. Don't take the blame for his bad behavior." Mary Beth reached back into her memory to understand Jane's feelings.

"That was the start. From then on, he devalued me. Treated me like a piece of property. He thinks he owns me. He won't let me have any friends or call my parents. He checks my cell phone and email. He does the same thing to my daughter."

What do I do? She's not in any physical danger, but this abuse is intolerable. I have to get her out.

"Jane, when you're ready, I'll be here to help you."

"I ... I ... don't know." Jane looked at her watch. "I have to get back to work. Thank you for talking to me."

CHAPTER EIGHT

The lunch rush ended. Hope Higuera collected her purse and jacket. El Nuevo Chaparral ran with clock-like precision. She really didn't need to be there most of the time, but she wanted to meet the guests, build a personal relationship with them. Like Papa always said, love was the secret to success in the restaurant business. She had just enough time to go to her meeting and get back for the dinner rush.

Hope grew up poor in the barrios of East L.A. Mama was a maid in some bigshot Hollywood producer's Bel Air home and Papa cooked in a Mexican restaurant. Hope never had money and never learned how to manage it.

Her classes at UC Davis put her on the right track, and she had Papa's values. She saved every penny she could get her hands on and rarely spent money on anything extravagant.

Her five-year-old Subaru Outback waited for her in the back of the parking lot off Eastlake Avenue. The Subaru was the ideal car for her. It was small, which fit her tiny size, it had lots of cargo room and was inexpensive to drive. Papa would have been proud of her choice.

The lot sloped down the hill and a fringe of mature trees cut off her view of Lake Union. She would drive down to South Seattle to pick up her liquor order for the week, then back to Seattle to see her advisor.

From Eastlake, she made her way to the Denny Way on-ramp and merged into traffic on Interstate 5 South. As the radio played her Stratus channel, she set the cruise control and rocked out with Brianna as she headed on down the road.

The car accelerated. She didn't notice at first, but soon found herself zipping from lane to lane to avoid traffic. She tapped on the brakes.

The cruise control didn't turn off. She tapped the brake pedal several times. Nothing happened. She stomped on the brakes. The car didn't slow.

The needle on her speedometer climbed steadily. Eighty, eighty-five, ninety. She was flying past traffic. The car in front of her was moving too slowly, and there was no room to change lanes.

She stomped on the brake again, then held down her horn. The car moved over just before she rear ended it.

"Mama!" she cried out.

She tried to shift out of gear, but the lever wouldn't budge no matter how hard she tried. She pulled on the emergency brake handle, but nothing happened.

Ninety-five. One hundred.

Red lights flashed in her rear-view mirror. The sirens screamed in her ears.

A patrol car pulled alongside her, and the officer waved her to the side. She tried to indicate that she couldn't stop to him.

The officer understood. The patrol car shot ahead of her. *How fast must he be going?* The other cars on the road moved to the right.

Hope's speedometer was pegged. Two more police cars joined the cavalcade. Through her open sun roof, she spotted News Chopper 7.

She reached down and turned off the ignition. The car kept running.

"Holy Mary, Mother of God ..."

Exit after exit flashed by. She was well past South Seattle. Next up was the Federal Way exit.

She pushed the phone button on her steering wheel and said "nine-one-one."

"Nine-one-one, what is your emergency?"

"I'm in the blue Subaru headed southbound on I-5. My car's out of control. I can't stop it."

"May I get your name and location please?"

"Hope Higuera. I just blew past the Federal Way exit. You have three cop cars with me."

"Please stay on the line."

Hope's heart tried to break out of her chest. Her breathing came in short gasps.

"Ms. Higuera, this is Officer Keith." The voice came over the speakers in her dashboard. "I'm riding alongside of you."

Hope snuck a quick glance to her right. The officer in the car next to her smiled.

"I understand you have a situation. You can't control your car. Is that correct?"

"Yes, I can't make it stop."

"Okay, stay with me. Don't panic. I'm right here. We're going to get you out of this."

The cell phone went silent. The next exit was Tacoma. As they blew by, Hope noticed a patrol car with its lights flashing, blocking the on-ramp from traffic.

"How are you going to stop me?"

"Don't panic. We're working on an idea. The State Patrol is taking over the situation. They have cars lining up to help you south of Tacoma."

As he spoke the words, Hope noticed a State Patrol sedan joining in the chase.

"Miss, I'm sorry, we have traffic ahead that we can't clear in time. I'm going to ease you into the guard rail to slow you down and use my car to steady you. Do you have your seat belt on?"

"Yes." Hope was breathless.

"Keep trying the brakes and emergency brake. I'll be ready in a few moments."

Hope pumped her brakes, crossed herself and said another Hail Mary. The landscape flew by so fast she couldn't tell where she was. The highway signs flashed by her in instants.

"We're ready, Miss." Officer Keith said. "Hold on. Cross your hands in front of your face and wait for the impact. It should be over in a second. Do you hear me?"

"Y ... Yes."

The patrol car inched closer and closer to her. Hope held the wheel until the last possible instant, then crossed her fists over her face and closed her eyes.

She heard the horrible screech of metal-on-metal. The devil scratched his claws against Heaven's gates. The cop pushed her into the concrete Jersey barrier. Her car screamed in protest. The airbag exploded in her face. It seemed to take five minutes for it to inflate; everything happened in slow-motion. The bag slammed into her face. The airbags on the side burst opened.

She felt the car leave the ground but couldn't see anything, her face buried in the airbag. She felt a rolling motion. Her stomach let go on her. She spewed her lunch into the airbag.

After what felt like an hour, the car came down on its roof. The crash was deafening. She felt the roof cave in on her head. The car skidded forever, spinning on its top, before smashing into a concrete road barrier and coming to a stop. The engine still screamed in her ears.

Before she had a chance to take another breath, foam filled her world.

She saw Chris's face in a flash of light, then everything went black.

TED DRUMMED his fingertip on his desk. Bear, across from him, squirmed in his chair. Late afternoon sun filtered through the window, highlighting the dust motes in the air.

"I just heard from my contact at SPD," Ted said. "Dan's heart attack was due to a run-away pacemaker. Grab onto your chair." He paused for effect. "This is the weird part. They think someone took over his pacemaker by cell phone and deliberately made it go haywire."

"That's murder." Bear wrinkled his brow. "They have to investigate it."

Ted sat back and twirled an ink pen in his fingers. "My contact says they don't have a clue. They don't even know where to start. They're bringing in the FBI."

Bear stood and turned towards the door, then he turned back. "What are *we* going to do about this? He was your friend, Ted."

"Yeah." Ted dropped the pen and cupped his chin with this hand. "We have to do something. To help. I'm going to research pacemakers. See how this could have happened."

"Me too." Bear stood in the open doorway. "The Fibbies don't have much of a cyber-intelligence program. I can run circles around them. We need to step in."

"Who would do this?" Ted asked.

Bear scratched his head. "I dunno. Maybe Russia. China. North Korea. They all have the technology and motive. But why Dan Rider?"

"He just got back from the Middle East. He was writing a story about ISIS's technical abilities. He was convinced that they were going to launch a cyber-attack against us."

"There it is. They needed to stop him from publishing the story."

"Okay, that's where we're gonna start. I'll call the *Times*, talk to the editor, see if I can get a copy of his notes."

CHRIS HARDWICK DASHED out of court, leaving his second chair, Kathy Nguyen, to cross examine the witness. He had to get to Hope. Nothing else mattered. Disregarding stop signs and speed limits, he pulled his Porsche into the Harbor View Hospital emergency room parking and ran to the emergency room desk. "Hope Higuera. Where is she? I'm Chris Hardwick. They're expecting me."

The heavy woman behind the counter typed a few strokes and looked at her computer screen. "She's in operating room three. If you'll go down this hallway, turn left, then right, you'll find the waiting room. I think there are some others there already."

Chris didn't bother to thank the woman. He dashed down the hallway, blond ponytail flapping with each step. As he ran he smelled the antiseptic scent of the hospital, and felt the cold air on his skin.

A left, a right, then an open area with an aquarium, chairs, tables, and a TV on the wall. The afternoon news was on the set.

"I-5 southbound is closed from South Tacoma to Olympia. Police don't know yet what caused the crash. An officer who wished to remain unnamed told me that the car went out of control. The driver, who has not yet been identified, was airlifted to Harbor View Medical Center, where she is undergoing surgery now."

The scene behind the red-haired reporter showed a foam-covered blue car smashed into the center barrier of the road. A patrol car sat with its driver-side wheels on the jersey barrier.

"Chris!" Ted yelled and jumped to his feet.

Mama was faster. She wrapped her arms around Chris before he took a breath.

"How ... how is she?" All Ted told him on the phone was that Hope had been in an accident and to get to the emergency room right away.

"We don't know anything." Ted placed a hand on Chris's shoulder. "She's in surgery. They'll tell us as soon as they have an update."

Mama released her hug and Chris felt his body flush with heat. A tingle ran all the way down to his feet. He expected to melt into the floor at any second.

"Chris, Ted, how is she?" Chris's stepmother and business partner, Candice Hardwick, came running into the room on clicking heels.

She wrapped her arms around Chris and pulled him tight.

"We don't know anything yet," Ted said. "She's in surgery."

Chris's world spun around him. *No. Not again. I can't lose someone I love again. Why is it everyone I love dies?* Chris staggered towards a chair, grabbed the seat back and lowered himself into it.

Ted sat next to him. "Hey, hermano. She's gonna be okay. You know that don't you?"

Chris stared at the floor.

"She's seen worse. Higuera's are remarkably tough."

Chris thought back to their last trip to Mexico. He, Cat, and Hope went south to help Ted rescue his fiancée who had been kidnapped by a drug lord. Hope was shot up so badly, no one thought she'd live. Now this.

Why her? Hasn't she already suffered enough?

Candace squatted down on her heels in front of Chris and Ted. "I heard something about her car going out of control?"

Ted looked at her. "We don't know anything for sure yet. I know my sister though. She would never be doing over a hundred. Something must a gone wrong."

Chris watched his stepmom. Just having her there was like having a little bit of Dad. Seeing her brought a measure of calm like lying on a warm, sandy beach.

"Mrs. Higuera," a short, dark doctor entered the waiting room and removed her cap.

Mama stood. "That's me."

"She's out of surgery and doing well. She has a broken clavicle and some broken ribs, and a rib punctured her lung, but she should heal. She'll be off her feet for some time, but she'll be all right in the long run."

Tears flowed from Mama's eyes. Candace grabbed her in a big hug. Chris cracked a smile at the two women. In her heels, Candace was more than a foot taller than Mama.

"I've got to see her. Can we talk to her?" Chris asked the doctor.

"One person can go in now. For only a few minutes. Then she needs to rest. You can all see her tomorrow."

The family looked at each other. "I'm going," Chris said in a voice that brooked no disagreement.

"Can you give us a minute?" Chris asked the assembly. "I need to talk to Ted." He led Ted to a corner of the waiting room.

"What's up?" Ted asked.

Chris swallowed. "I've been trying to get up the nerve to have this discussion for some time." He stared off into space.

"And?"

Chris turned back to Ted. "You know how I feel about your sister ..." More silence. "I, uh, Ted, you're my best friend. You're like a brother to me."

Ted furrowed his eye brows.

"There's nothing I would do to mess that up. I mean, I know family comes first for you."

"What are you getting at? Stop beating around the bush," Ted demanded.

Chris took a deep breath. "I want to ask Hope to marry me. I mean ..."

"Woo-hoo!" Ted leapt and pumped his fist in the air. He grabbed Chris by the wrists and looked into his blue eyes. "I've been wondering when you'd ask her."

"I ... I ... don't know. I mean, with the wreck and all. Do you think she'll think I'm taking advantage of the situation?"

"You're an idiot. She's been wanting you to ask forever. Do you know how hurt she was when you gave her a bracelet for her birthday? She thought for sure it was going to be an engagement ring."

"Really? I mean, I didn't know. I mean, I wanted to square things with you first."

"Hey, brother." Ted pulled his tall friend into a big *abrazo*. "They're more than square with me."

Chris had his fill of hospital rooms when recovering from being shot by terrorists in Canada. He wasn't happy about being in another one, but he was happy to see his soul-mate on the bed. She had a cover pulled up to her chin with tubes going in and coming out from under it. Her shiny black hair was pulled back in a ponytail.

He'd never seen the olive-skinned girl look so pale. Her deep-brown eyes were open but had no fire in them.

"Hey, love, can you hear me?" He pulled a chair close to the bed.

"*Corazon.*" She made a barely audible sound.

"The doc says you're going to be all right. What happened?"

She closed her eyes for a moment. "I don't know. My car went out of control. It's like it wanted to kill me ..."

Chris struggled with whether or not he should hug her, hold her close. He finally settled on taking her hand.

She winced at the touch.

"Listen, I don't have much time. They said I could only be here a couple minutes."

Hope turned her head and looked into his eyes, then let out a little groan.

"This wasn't how I planned it. I mean, I wanted to go to some romantic restaurant and ask you between dinner and dessert. I wanted all the diners to applaud you."

Hope wrinkled her nose.

"I mean, uh ... what I mean is ... I've been wanting to do this for a while. The time never seemed right. Then, with the accident and all, I realized I have to ask you now. We never know if we'll have a tomorrow."

"Chris, you big *babaso*, what're you talking about?" Her voice was barely above a whisper.

Chris slid from his chair to one knee, reached into his jacket pocket and produced a tiny, velvet-covered box. "Hope Higuera, will you marry me?"

"Ohhh." She let out a little gasp. She wriggled her fingers to indicate she wanted him to give her the ring.

He handed her the box.

She stared at a huge diamond in a gold setting. Dozens of smaller diamonds surrounded the central stone.

"Oh, my."

Chris felt her pain as the words came out.

"Well, what do you think?" he asked.

Tears flowed down Hope's face. "Chris, I do want to marry you. To make you happy, but..."

Chris creased his brow. "But what?"

"I can't give you children. I can't give you a son. When I took those bullets down in Mexico, one of them ripped through my uterus. The doctor said I couldn't ever have babies."

Chris smiled. "I know that. Ted told me."

"That miserable little turkey-butt .... He wasn't supposed to tell anyone. When I told him, I swore him to silence. I didn't even tell Mama."

"There's not much we don't talk about." Chris smiled at his girl. "We're kind of like, you know, joined at the souls."

CHAPTER NINE

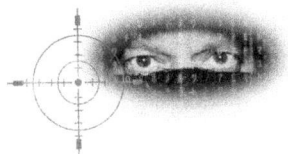

"Mary Beth, may I see you a moment?" Ted stood at the entrance to her cubicle and motioned for her to follow him to his office.

As he seated himself in his swivel chair, Mary Beth reached his door. "Yes?"

"Come in." He waved her in. "Close the door. Sit down."

He watched the petite woman take a leather-covered chair opposite his desk. She had on her "Catrina outfit." Tight black jeans that complemented her slim figure, a tight black T-shirt, and boots with three-inch heels. He could smell the leather from the new boots. Catrina used to have her "work" boots custom made. These looked more like something from the Shoe Warehouse.

"You wanted to see me?" She had the look of a whipped dog in her eyes.

Ted wasn't used to people seeing him as a man of power. "Relax. You want a bottle of water?"

"No thanks." Mary Beth swallowed.

"Here's another card from Cat." Ted tossed the card across his desk.

This one had a picture of Machu Picchu in Peru on the front. On the back were the words "Having a great time. Wish you were here."

"She's sure getting around," Mary Beth said. "First Hong Kong, now South America."

Ted turned to the refrigerator under his credenza and grabbed a bottle for himself. "Yeah. I'm glad someone is having a good time. As for me, I have a problem. You can help me with it."

Mary Beth let out a huge breath and rolled her eyes to the side. "What kind of problem?"

Ted twisted the top off his bottle. "Since Cat left, I've been in over my head. I can't do everything she did and all the stuff I did, much less all the stuff we never got around to. Since she left me in charge, I want to run F&A in a more professional way. Like a business."

"What does that have to do with me?"

Ted leaned back in his chair and put his hands behind his head. "I've given this a lot of thought. I've talked to Chris and Candace about it. They don't agree with me, but, what the hell, I'm in charge here."

The words hung in the room.

"What don't they agree with?"

"Chris started me thinking about it. I told him I'm in trouble, and he suggested I split the company up; hire a consultant to help me figure out where we're going. He thinks we should have an Investigative Department and a Cyber Security Department." Ted leaned forward in his chair and scooted himself closer to his desk. "He's right. I need two strong people I can count on. People I can trust. People with the same values this company was built on."

"So ..." Mary Beth tapped her right index finger on the arm rest. "What does all this have to do with me?"

Ted stopped to think. *This is it.*

"I want you to head up the investigative department."

Mary Beth sucked in a breath.

Ted continued. "I know you're still new to this, but hell, so am I. You're smart, strong and have common sense. You're going to have to hire at least one more detective to fill your spot, then you need to bring your co-workers along. Get them experience in the field. Get them licensed."

"I ... I ... I don't know anything about this. I can't run a department. I barely make it through the day as it is."

"You're gonna have to trust me on this one, MB. I know you can do it. You know how I'm always telling you to trust your intuition, your Spidey sense? Well, my Spidey sense is telling me you're the man for the job."

He could see the confusion in her eyes. *How hard do I push?*

"Chris and Candace disagree with me. They've got nothing against you, but they think you're too inexperienced. They want me to hire someone with a solid background. I don't agree. I think you're the best person because you worked so closely with Cat. She rescued you and your kids from your abusive husband. She taught you the trade. You'll think like her and, more importantly, your heart thinks like her."

"What would I do? I mean, how is the job different than what I'm doing now?"

Ted pulled a file folder out of his desk drawer. It was labeled "Head of Investigations."

"I've been working with the business consultant to help plan this all out. Here's the job description she put together for you."

He handed her the folder.

"Aside from what you're already doing, you need to lead the team. You need to delegate authority to someone to head up the Background Check group. That group has always run by itself, but each employee always reported to Cat. We think you need a subordinate who can do the handholding and report to you."

"Ah ... okay ... probably Susan. She's been there the longest and knows all the ins and outs. But Marilyn is always there to take care of the systems problems. Our rickety old database is always going down."

Ted got up and walked around his desk, sitting in the chair next to Mary Beth. "We need people with special talents. You need to develop people who are good at surveillance, at deep background checks, at working undercover. Cat used to do all of that, but if we're going to grow we need to handle multiple clients at the same time. You can't do it all."

Tears streamed down Mary Beth's cheeks. "Oh, Ted. I can't do any of this. I'm not Catrina. I can never replace Catrina."

"Nobody will ever replace Catrina. I just need someone to do her job. I need a Number Two."

Mary Beth flipped the page in the folder. "Holy crap! I mean, I'm sorry. I mean, wow! Is this true? Is this salary right?"

Ted flashed a big smile. "Yep. We thought we should be competitive.

Actually, I'm starting you at the low end of the pay-scale, so you have room to increase as you grow in the job."

"I can't believe it." She turned a serious eye towards Ted. "Who do I have to kill?"

Ted laughed. "That's the first light-hearted thing you've said since Cat left. Maybe there is hope for you." The smile left his face.

"There is one other thing." He studied her as he spoke. "I hired a head of the cyber security department. His name is David Jones. Everybody calls him Bear because of his surly temperament and grumpy moods. He's the best there is at what he does, but he isn't real good at handling people ..." *How can I put this?* "He ... ah ... doesn't get along well with women."

Mary Beth's eyes widened, and her mouth formed a little "o."

"Don't get me wrong. He's not a misogynist or anything. It's just his religious views, I mean, he thinks women should stay home and take care of the family."

"You're out of your mind." Mary Beth jumped to her feet. You're not going to bring a person like that into the firm, are you?"

"It's not as bad as it sounds. I just wanted to prepare you ..."

"Prepare me! Ted, look out your window. What do you see?" She didn't give him time to respond. "Twenty-six women. All of them are here because they were abused or mistreated by men. I won't let you turn a bull, or a bear or whatever, loose in this China shop."

ABIBA SIPPED on her strong coffee and stirred the pot of oatmeal, her daughter, Aida's, favorite breakfast.

The kitchen in the First Hill apartment was small, but efficient. A new refrigerator and stove gleamed between the cabinets. Abiba wasn't happy that she had to buy a countertop microwave with such little counter space, but that was life.

And life was good. With her job at Flaherty & Associates, she could put a little away each month for Aida's college fund. With today's prices, it would never be enough. Aida had to win the Miss Washington pageant and get that scholarship.

With her looks, slender body and copious talent, Abiba thought she had a chance.

"Morning, Mom." The perky seventeen-year-old flounced into the kitchen.

"*Indemin adersh.*" Abiba smiled. "And how is my precious gift this morning?"

"Oh, Mom ..." Aida opened the refrigerator and rooted around inside. "I'm going to Jarucia's after school today." She pulled a bottle of orange juice from the fridge and gulped it down.

"Aida!" Abiba waved a spoon at her. "And just what are you two planning to do this afternoon? I'm sure it doesn't involve boys."

Before she could answer, the microwave oven turned on.

Huh? I wasn't using that, Abiba thought.

She took a couple of steps to the appliance and pushed the stop button. It didn't shut off. She pushed the button to open the door. It wouldn't open.

"That's really strange." She randomly pushed buttons on the keypad, but nothing changed. The microwave continued to buzz, the turntable inside continued to spin. She could feel the appliance getting hot to the touch.

What's going on?

"Mom," Aida asked. "What's happening?"

"I don't know, my precious. The microwave just went on by itself. It won't shut off."

"Just unplug it," the long-legged girl said.

Abiba did. *I'll have to call Panasonic when I get to work.*

On the bus, Abiba scanned the news on her cell phone. *There it is.*

The headline read "Hundreds of microwaves go crazy across the country."

Microwaves all over the city sparked fires, the article said. Every piece of firefighting equipment on the East Side was engaged in fires and the calls were still coming in.

RODNEY JACOBSON (R–AL) looked out over the many empty seats in the Senate chamber. *Where's everyone? This is the most important bill that'll be introduced this year.*

73

"And so, my fellow senators, I place this important piece of legislation before you. The Secure Our Borders Act will not only stop this shameful influx of illegal immigration, it will secure our great nation from the threat of Islamic terrorists seeping into our country."

There was a quorum of senators sitting in the seats, but not enough to get a truly emotional rally going. Senator Jacobson finished his speech and closed the folder on the lectern.

We should pass this with no problem. At least we'll keep those sand niggers out.

His chief of staff handed him a tablet as they exited the Senate Chamber. "You have a lunch with Senators George and Kelly at the Rotunda, then a meeting with the chairman of General Motors at four."

"Is the car ready?" the senator asked.

"Yes, sir. Standing by."

"Then let's go."

He didn't need to be led. He made his way down the long hallway to the elevators and pushed the button for the parking garage. Two U.S. marshals waited at the exit from the elevator. They walked the senator to his car.

The chauffer jumped from his seat when he saw the senator coming. He stood holding the door before the senator was within ten steps of the car.

"Mornin', Senator," the driver said.

"Mornin', Charles." Senator Jacobson bent his long, thin body into the stretch Lincoln limo. "We're headed to the Rotunda for lunch."

"Yes, sir." Charles held the door for the chief of staff to enter, then closed it and got into the driver's seat. He fired up the engine and headed out of the parking structure.

Turning onto the busy street, he headed for Georgetown.

As they moved into traffic, the limo sped up.

"Holy shit!" Charles exclaimed. He slammed on the breaks. Nothing happened.

The street curved to the right. Charles yanked the wheel to keep on the road. The two left tires lifted off the pavement.

"Jesus Christ," the senator screamed. "Charles, slow down."

"Something's wrong with the car," Charles yelled. "It's doing this by itself."

Senator Jacobson pulled out his cell phone and hit speed dial. "George,

Listen. I'm in the limo. I may not have much time. The car's gone out of control. You know that hack the NSA presented to our last Intelligence committee briefing? I think we've got it ..."

The transmission stopped when the car hit a curb and went airborne, slamming into a glass-fronted coffee shop. People, tables, and chairs were tossed about as if in a hurricane as the heavy car plowed through. The car hit a reinforced-concrete wall at the back of the shop and smashed up like an accordion.

There were no survivors.

CHAPTER TEN

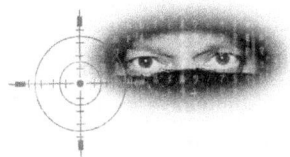

"Mr. Ted," Abiba was out of breath as she ran to Ted's office with a coffee cup in each hand. "Have you heard the news?"

"What news?" Ted looked up from his monitor. *She looks like a kid looking for the bathroom.*

The last employees had long since left Flaherty & Associates, leaving only Abiba, Bear, and Ted. The lights in the investigative area were out, leaving a ghost town like feeling to the offices.

"Microwaves all over the country are catching fire."

"Huh..."

"At home, my microwave turned on this morning and wouldn't turn off. It's brand new."

Ted leaned back in his chair, folded his hands across this stomach, and thought a minute. "There's a known security flaw in all Haier microwaves. I read about it a few months ago."

"How can a microwave have a security flaw? It's an appliance." She lowered her bulk into one of Ted's cherrywood chairs."

"Here's the thing. These new microwaves, and I'd bet Whirlpool is the same, have an Internet connection. It allows you to turn it on or off from your cell phone. No one ever expected anyone to want to hack a microwave, so they didn't put in any firewalls to block outside interference." Ted reached for his coffee cup. "I'd bet that someone exploited that flaw to cause these fires."

Abiba shook her head. "But why? Why would anyone want to start a bunch of fires? What purpose would it serve?"

Ted put his cup down and held his fist to his lips and tapped his thumb on his cheek bone. "Let's see … What purpose … Okay, how about this, someone is a pyromaniac with hacking skills. He did it to watch the fires."

"No, Mr. Ted, I'm not buying that. It's happening all over the country, he couldn't possibly watch all the fires. I have a feeling …" she paused, and her eyes rolled up and in. "There is a hand behind this." Her voice sounded far away. "Yes … A black man, someone very evil. Oh!" She jumped in her seat. "I see your friend having the heart attack. They're both the same man."

Ted sat up straight and crinkled his whole face. "What the hell are you talking about? A black man, Dan's heart attack."

Abiba was pale beneath her ebony skin. Her breath came in shallow gasps. "I don't know, Mr. Ted. They're connected. Somehow."

"Abiba, go home." Ted said in a firm tone. "Let me worry about this. You know that Bear and I might be here all night."

"No, Mr. Ted. If you're here, I'm here." She said in her clipped British accent.

"What about your family? You don't want to stay through till morning."

Abiba took the coffee cup from Ted's hand. "My daughter knows my work. I'll call and let her know I'm not coming home and not to worry." She looked in the empty cup. "Would you like a refill, sir?"

"No." Ted stomped his foot. "And you're impossible." He rose and walked towards Bear's little huddle of cubicles.

"You or Mr. Bear need anything, you let me know," Abiba said to Ted's back.

"Humph." Ted shrugged as he walked.

A black man. Did she mean race or soul? Microwaves, heart attacks, the CryBaby virus. How are they connected?

The cyber security department took up only a small percentage of the total floor space. A group of four desks, surrounded by cloth cubicle walls, created a bull pen for its inhabitants. At the present time, the inhabitants consisted of Bear. His helpers had long since gone home.

"You makin' any progress?" Ted asked as he plopped down in front of a workstation. "Do you know how they did it?"

"This is impossible," Bear growled. "This is the third time I've gone over this code line-by-line, and I don't see anything. Either this guy is really good or I'm going blind."

Ted sat at a workstation, beads of sweat forming on his forehead, and opened a window filled with computer code. "I don't discount the second possibility at all." He searched on "Ted, you stopped here." He always left a marker when he got up from his desk so that he would know where to go back to work. The cursor moved to the yellow highlighted string. Ted removed the comment. "It's in here somewhere. We just have to keep looking."

"You know the definition of insanity, don't you, Hero?" Bear ran his paw through his mass of unkept red hair. "We need to try something new."

Ted swiveled in his chair to face Bear. "What you got in mind?"

"I'm thinking we need a little help."

"Okay."

Bear's face lit up in a grin. The first Ted saw since Bear moved in. "I have a friend. You ever heard of the Iceman?"

Ted furrowed his brow. "Yeah. Some kind of super hacker. He's in Europe somewhere. Often works with Interpol on their cyber cases. Isn't he the guy who cracked the mañana virus."

"Yep. I met him once. In person."

"You're shitting me. No one even knows what he looks like."

Bear smirked at Ted and rolled back from his keyboard. "Nope. Just me. He gave me his card."

"Wow! You have the Iceman's card?" Ted flipped both of his hands up and out. "Can you bring him in on this?"

Bear held his hands together in front of him as if in prayer. "I can try. If this hack doesn't interest him, he's dead."

"Great, get in touch." Ted frowned. "Call him right now."

Bear dug through his backpack until he found a slender wallet case. "All my important business cards." He waved the wallet at Ted. "I happen to have his email address at the Eide Prolytechnique de Lusanne."

"The what?"

"It's the MIT of Switzerland. Our boy's a professor there."

"How do you know these people?" Ted asked as he rolled back to his workstation.

"That's not all. I have the Joker's address, too."

"The Joker?" Ted turned back to his friend. "You're shittin' me. He's the world's most infamous hacker."

Bear gave Ted and "ah, shucks" grin. "Yeah. During the elections, he hacked the Russian Foreign Ministry's website and put up a notice that if they continued interfering in the American election, he'd launch an all-out cyberattack against them. The leaks of DNC emails to wikileaks.com stopped."

"You know the Joker?"

A smug look crossed Bear's face. "Yeah. He used to be in the Army, in their cyber security division. He got frustrated because his superiors wouldn't let him strike back when he found another country attacking us, so he quit. Now he runs a group of vigilante hackers who strike back any time they find another country hacking us. He probably set China's hacking program back five years."

Ted smiled, twirled in his chair and high-fived Bear. "Can you bring him in on this too?"

"I can try."

The hours went by. Ted crawled through the operating system patch code line by line. His vision blurred, and he ran to the bathroom every half-hour or so to relieve himself of Abiba's potent coffee.

He made notes on a yellow legal pad as he scrolled through the lines. His eyes refused to stay open. His head lolled to the side.

"Hey, buddy," Bear said. "You falling asleep? Maybe you should take a break."

"Nah, I'm fine." Ted stretched his eyelids and bulged out his eyes to clear his focus.

"You know, when you're so groggy, you probably missed something. You have to stay sharp to do this."

Ted shook his head. "Yeah, yeah, yeah. I'm good."

He went back to his computer screen. *Hmm ... what's this?*

He found an RPC (Remote Program Call) to an application he had never heard of. He tracked down the application on his hard drive. It was a very small, compiled .exe file with a hexadecimal name. *Where did that come from?*

With so many downloads, emails, and other ways to infect a computer, there was no way to know when or how the file got there. But it was there, and he didn't know what it was.

"Bear, look at this." He turned his screen so Bear could see. "What do you make of that?"

Bear rolled over to Ted's screen. "Don't know. Have you decompiled it yet?

"Just found it. I found an RPC from our Windows patch to it. I don't know how long it's been sitting on my computer. The time/date stamp is six months old."

"Yeah, but in hacking 101 they teach you how to manipulate the time stamp."

Bear slid back to his computer and typed a few keystrokes. He opened his File Explorer and typed the file name into the search box. He waited. The little blue progress bar at the top of the screen moved slowly to the right.

Ted knew the value of patience. He closed his eyes and leaned back in his chair as the operating system searched for the file in Bear's system.

He opened his eyes when Bear spoke. "Yeah, I got it, too. Let's check some other computers."

They moved from desk to desk, logging in as admins on each desktop, and searching for the executable. They found it on every computer.

"Okay," Ted said. "This is the virus. We don't know how it got here, but it's on every computer. There's a call in Windows that opens the file on a certain date, then they're off to the races."

Bear stood up from the computer he was working on. "You got that decompile done yet?"

"I dunno, let's see." Ted got up and headed back to his workstation.

"Yeah, here it is." He opened the file. "Man, it's gonna take some time to look through this. I'll send you the file. I think I need breakfast. How about you?"

"Abiba," Bear yelled. "We need food."

Abiba appeared at the workstations, looking fresh and ready to go. "What do you want, Mr. Bear?"

"I don't know, Ted?"

"Pancakes. Sausage or ham. Eggs."

Abiba smiled at them as if she was house mother to a couple of out-of-control frat boys. "You want Glo's? You want me to order in, or do you want to go see Glo?"

Ted and Bear exchanged glances. "Let's go," they said at the same time.

"You wanna come?" Ted asked.

"No, Mr. Ted. I think I'll just go home."

Both Ted and Bear grabbed their jackets and pocketed their cell phones. As they started towards the door with triumphant swaggers, Abiba stopped them.

"Mr. Ted. There's something you should know."

Ted stopped and turned around.

"Huh?"

"I know you don't believe in me like Mrs. Flaherty did, but I have to tell you." There was a long silence. "Your man, your hacker. He's here, close by somewhere. He lives a normal life, has a normal job, but he's evil. He has a band of evil followers, and they are going to cause a great disruption to all of our lives."

"What the heck?" Bear asked. "How could you possibly know that?"

"I just do."

Bear looked at Ted.

Catrina believed in Abiba's extraordinary powers of perception. *We've solved more than one case based on her intuition. But how much do I trust her?*

"How did you get this insight, Abiba?" Ted asked.

"I sat there, in front of my computer, and all of a sudden, I felt his presence. If I had something that he touched, I could tell you more."

"Something he touched?" Ted asked. "Fuck. He's a ghost. He hasn't touched anything."

"Do you really believe this mumbo jumbo?" Bear asked.

Ted looked from Abiba to Bear and back again. He stared hard into Abiba's eyes. "Yes. I don't know what it is, but Abiba has a gift. She's been right more times I can count. If she says it, I believe it's true. We just need to decode her message."

CHAPTER ELEVEN

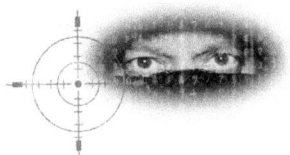

Hope sat naked on her bed, looking at her bruised and battered body. Tears flowed from her eyes as she fingered the scars left from her surgeries. *Will Chris even want me now?* There were five scars from the bullet wounds she got in Mexico and a long white line where the surgeons had gone in to repair her lung.

Well, I guess this means the end of my bikini days.

"Ezperanza, honey, there's someone here to see you," Mama shouted from the living room, using her Spanish name.

Hope dragged on a pink robe and stumbled to the door. *Who?*

As she emerged to the living room, a short Latino man in a Men's Warehouse suit extended his hand.

"Miss Higuera, I'm Oscar del Toro,." He flashed a badge. "Special agent for the FBI."

"The FBI?"

"Please Mr. del Toro, sit." Mama waved her hand towards an overstuffed chair. "Can I get you some coffee, maybe Mexican chocolate?"

Del Toro took a seat. "Mexican chocolate? I haven't had that since I was a kid."

Hope let out a small groan as she sat on the sofa. "What can I help you with, Mr. del Toro?"

"I'm here about your accident. I just have a few questions."

Hope wrinkled her brow. "Why would the FBI be interested in a traffic accident?"

Del Toro took out his note book. "There have been a series of similar accidents around the country. You may have heard about Senator Jacobson."

Hope nodded her head.

He looked up at her from his notebook. "When did you know your car was out of control?"

She answered the questions until Mama entered the room with a tray with three steaming mugs and a plate of pastries. "Señor del Toro, I hope you like *pan dulce.*"

"That smells like home."

Mama served each of them a cup of chocolate and seated herself on the sofa next to Hope.

Hope sniffed her mug. It had the rich aroma of spices and chocolate. The frothy mixture was topped with cinnamon sprinklings.

"Why are you so interested in my accident?" Hope asked.

"We think these accidents are all related. Our investigation shows that the computers in the cars went crazy."

"I understand that, but why the FBI? Why not the National Traffic Safety Board? What interests the FBI?"

Del Toro took a sip of the chocolate. "Miss Higuera, I'm really not at liberty to discuss an on-going investigation."

"That's not fair." The color rose in Hope's cheeks. "You come in here and ask me all sorts of questions, then don't even have the courtesy to tell me what it's all about."

Del Toro put down his mug and patted the air with both hands. "I'm sorry, Miss, but the Bureau has procedures that I can't break . . ."

Hope took in a breath of air, ready to start a new harangue.

"But let me just say that we think that someone took over the cars' computers and caused these crashes. That's all I can tell you."

ABIBA WAS at the end of her tether. On the short drive from Flaherty &

Associates to her apartment on First Hill, she was surprised that she hadn't melted into a blob. She shook herself awake several times.

She took the elevator to the third floor and slid her key into the lock. The door opened smoothly. Abiba stepped inside and dropped her purse on the hallway table. *Hmm ...* there was a piece of paper, folded in half, with "Mom" written on the outside. She took off her jacket and hung it on a wooden peg behind the door.

She picked up the paper and unfolded it. It read: Mom, I'm at the UW performance center practicing with Kim and D'Anthony. Be home for dinner.

Abiba tossed the paper back on the table and headed straight for her bedroom. Wooden masks and spears adorned the hallway walls. Her bedroom centered around a king-size bed. A small nightstand was on one side, a large carved armoire stood at the foot of the bed with a flat-screen TV on top of it. Over the head of the bed hung a colorful picture of an African woman walking down a road with a basket on her head.

Abiba kicked her shoes towards the mirrored closet doors and pulled her bright orange dress over her head. She couldn't wait to claw her bra off. As she unclipped it and slipped it off her shoulders, she said, "There you go girls. Freedom." Her huge breasts fell free.

Without stopping to put on night clothes, she pulled off her panties and crawled under the covers.

The night was dark. Her alarm clock on the nightstand was blank. She stirred and looked down the hallway. It was dark. No night light. She flipped the switch on the light on the nightstand. Nothing.

We having a power outage?

She got up and wandered into the living room. The lights there didn't work either. She opened the drapes on her million-dollar view. She might live in a cheesy neighborhood, but the view of Elliot Bay and Puget Sound were magnificent.

Everything was dark. All the street lights were out, no buildings had any power. The ship yards and unloading docks were blank. They never shut down, any day, any time.

What's going on?

She felt a presence behind her and spun around.

"Good evening, Abiba," the shadowy form said.

She clutched her arms over her breasts and backed up to the wall.

"I'm not going to hurt you – this time." The figure had a slight accent. Was it Middle Eastern? "I'm here to warn you. Stop snooping around in my business. You already know too much about me. Stay away."

"Who are you? How did you get in here?"

"You don't need to know who I am. And how did I get here? You brought me here. You summoned me."

Abiba sat up with a start. Sweat ran down her face. It was broad daylight, mid-day.

THE MINUTE HAND on the wall clock ticked over another mark. How many of those minutes ticked by since the ordeal started?

Ted wiped his hand over his eyes. It didn't help. The world still looked fuzzy. He scratched at the three-day old beard. *Man, I gotta get outta here and take a shower. A couple hours sleep would be nice.*

"What time is it?" Ted asked without looking up.

"You gone blind, Hero," Bear responded. "You got clocks all around you."

Ted mumbled and looked at the lower right-hand corner of his computer screen. *4:23 a.m. Christ.* They'd done it again. Worked through the night.

He looked over at his partner. Bear's orange hair was wilder than usual. It stuck out at all angles as if he were electrically charged.

"We gotta take a break. I'm not even reading the code anymore."

"Go ahead," Bear said. "I want to finish this piece before I lose track of what I'm doing."

Ted stumbled out to the reception area and lay down on the couch.

When he opened his eyes, he felt as if days had passed. He leapt up and ran to the work area. Bear was gone. Sunlight peeked in the windows.

He picked up the pizza box and napkins and threw them in the trash. As he reached for his coffee cup, a thought struck him.

He jumped into his rolling chair and looked at his screen. The cursor flashed on a line of code. He read it and frowned.

The command went to a website and returned a yes or no.

Why the hell are they going out to a website?

Ted opened a browser on his other screen and typed in the URL. He got a 404 message. Website not found.

Hmm ... If the website isn't found, it returns a no. What happens if it returns a yes?

Ted pulled up a new browser window and registered the name of the site the program called for. Then he quickly created a single web page that answered yes when it was called up.

He went back to his other screen and started the code in debug mode. He stepped through line by line until it came to the call. This time, the website answered with a yes.

The program jumped to a module that Ted hadn't seen before. It unlocked all files, erased all the virus files from the hard drive, and shut down.

Ted blinked his eyes. Could it be? He searched his file system. No sign of the virus, no locked files. The bug just committed suicide.

That was it? It's too easy. The programmer who built this put in a kill switch. Why? Why would a black-hat hacker put a way to kill his own virus in the code?

I've got to check this out. Who's still infected?

He reached for his phone and dialed the Law Offices of Hardwick & Hardwick. The phone rang several times before he got a "Hello?"

"Kathy, this is Ted."

"Ted? Ted who?" the female voice replied.

"Ted Higuera. Chris's friend. Your investigator."

A momentary pause, then "Oh, yes. I'm sorry, Ted. I wasn't expecting anyone to call this early in the morning."

Ted smiled. "The reason I called is that you're the only person in the world who'd be at work this early." Kathy Nguyen was the third attorney at Chris's firm. He and his stepmom, Candace, hired Kathy to help with the murder case against Ted's little brother.

"I need you to do something for me." Ted's heartbeat sped up. "There's a laptop in Chris's office. It's infected with the CryBaby virus. I haven't had time to clean it yet."

"Uh-huh?"

"I need you to get it and turn it on for me."

"Ted, are you sure we should be doing this? I mean, it's Chris's laptop. I'm not going into my boss's office when he's not here and get into his personal files."

"It's okay. He won't mind. Listen, I think I've solved the CryBaby virus. I need to verify it. I need an answer fast, that's why I called you."

"Can't we just wait until Chris gets in?"

Ted shook his head. "No. Listen, I need you to do this. NOW."

"Ah ... okay. I guess. Hold on."

He could hear movement on the other end of the phone line, then silence. He drummed his fingers on the desk, waiting.

C'mon, c'mon.

It seemed like a life time. Finally, Kathy came back on the phone. "All right, Ted. I have his laptop."

"Open it, turn it on." He heard movement on Kathy's side. There was a pronounced click. He waited.

"Okay, it's coming up. We're at the Windows splash screen ... It wants me to log in. I don't know Chris's password."

"Try Defiant4 with a capital D."

He heard the clicking of keys on the other end.

"Oh, that worked."

Ted smiled. The *Defiant* was Chris's dad's sailboat that got blown up on their little adventure in Canada.

"I've got the CryBaby pop-up window."

"Good." Ted's heart threatened to break out of his chest. "Click on the 'submit' button."

"Okay. I've got the little blue circle going around. It's gone. The pop-up disappeared."

"Great. Try to open a file. Any file."

"Ted, I shouldn't ..."

"Just do it," he screamed.

"It works. I can get to our document management system."

Ted let out a deep breath and slumped in his chair. "That's great, Kathy. Thank you. I'll ... ah ... talk to you later."

JUSTIN MCCORMACK, CEO of YTS security and a legend in the cyber world stood behind the lectern in the main auditorium at the Las Vegas Convention Center. He brushed back his long brown hair and spoke.

"I hardly need to introduce you to Bill Ogilvie. He is one of the NSA's top scientists. He has been involved in cyber-security since before there was cyber-security. His department has headed off attacks from foreign governments as well as black hat hackers. So please help me welcome Dr. William Scott Ogilvie!"

The short, stocky man adjusted his glasses and took the lectern. The National Security Conference was his favorite venue.

The attendees were the crème de la crème, the elite of the computer-security industry. He loved the adulation showered on him by these intelligent, educated people.

"Thank you, Justin." He shook the moderator's hand, then turned to the audience. "And thank you to all of you who took time out of your busy schedules to be here with me today." He looked out into the blackness. The stage lights blinded him. He'd played this game before. With more than two thousand seats in the auditorium filled, he could hear their breathing, feel their presence.

"I want to start today's talk by emphasizing the seriousness of cyber-security. This week's ransomware attack in Atlanta shows just how vulnerable our country is. The hack virtually shut the city down. The 9-1-1 system and the whole police department, city systems, and the Atlanta airport were all compromised. You can't pay a parking ticket or apply for a job in Atlanta. The city finally agreed to pay fifty-one thousand dollars in Bit-Coin to get their systems back up and running. This is unacceptable."

He felt a tingling in his left arm. He couldn't catch his breath and his heart rate began to accelerate.

Oh, God! Not now, not here.

He had a heart attack before. *This can't be happening.*

He clutched his chest. A loud gasp arose from the audience. Ogilvie's knees went slack, and he collapsed.

Justin was there in a second, flipped him onto his back, and felt for a pulse. "Somebody call nine-one-one. Is there a doctor here?"

CHAPTER TWELVE

"Mama, Chris asked me to marry him." Hope stood in front of her mother, seated on a flower-patterned sofa in their living room.

"Mija!" Mama jumped up and wrapped her arms around her oldest daughter.

"I couldn't ask her father for her hand," Chris, dressed in his best suit said, "so I asked Ted instead."

"Mija, I'm so happy for you." She released Hope and wrapped her arms around Chris. "And Christopher, I'm so glad. You will make a wonderful son and a better husband."

Hope looked around the room. It was so different from the place she'd grown up in East LA. The Queen Anne neighborhood said "money." There was no fence with broken glass around the house to discourage visitors. The colonial-style-four-bedroom shouted "middle-America."

Mama let go of Chris and reached for her daughter's hand. "Esperanza, when is the wedding?" Esperanza was Hope's name in Spanish. She reached for Chris's hand, too.

"We're thinking next June," Hope said.

"June! But that's ten months away."

Chris smiled down at the little woman. "That gives us lots of time to plan the wedding."

"Oh, my." Mama gasped.

"I'm going to ask Candace to help me," Hope said. "She has the most perfect taste."

Mama sucked in a little air. "Oh, Hope, I hope you're not going to have an Anglo wedding?"

"No, Mama. It will be traditional."

MARY BETH STOOD up from her swivel chair, placed her hands on the small of her back, and stretched. She'd spent hours combing through the Internet in search of information about Jane's husband.

Jane still wouldn't tell Mary Beth her real name, but with basic sleuthing skills, Mary Beth followed her home, got her address, and the license plate number of her car.

It was child's play to find the name of the owners of the home and the car. Mary Beth had never heard of these people. They were totally normal.

She looked at their credit score and records for their children. Nothing stood out. They were model citizens.

She thought it odd that Jane never mentioned her husband was an immigrant. He had come to America on a student visa and stayed to contribute to the country's growth and prosperity. That didn't make him an abuser.

Coffee. Must find coffee.

Mary Beth didn't work the long hours some of her co-workers did. She was a single mom with responsibilities at home. But in the forty hours she did work, she threw herself into the job and often did her research at home after the kids were in bed.

She grabbed her coffee mug and headed for the break room.

She hesitated at the door. *He* was there. She didn't know why she didn't like him, but her feminine instinct warned her to be cautious.

"Hi, Bear." She put on her best fake smile.

Bear looked up from his magazine, gave her the once over, and said, "Hi."

Mary Beth felt as if he was undressing her with his eyes. She went over to the coffee machine and loaded a packet of French Vanilla. She placed her cup under the spout and pushed the button.

On the refrigerator next to the coffee machine, she spied a postcard.

She slid it out from under a black cat magnet. It was from Cat. This time, the picture was of the Sydney Opera House. As usual, the message on the back was brief.

I'd love to see Australia. That girl's sure getting around.

"You guys have that virus thing under control?" She didn't really want to talk to Bear, but it was rude to seem as if she was avoiding him.

What was it? His unkept red hair? His short, powerful body. He looked like some sort of caveman who might club her over the head and drag her back to his cave by her hair.

"Mmmmm ..." Bear mumbled something unintelligible.

Her coffee done, she set the cup on the counter next to the refrigerator and opened the door. While she poked around inside looking for her chestnut-flavored creamer, she heard a low, rumbling sound behind her.

"I don't mean to pry, but you have two kids, right?"

Mary Beth turned to face him. "Ah ... yes. Bob and Dorothy."

"That's great." Bear looked up at her. "I love kids. We have six."

Mary Beth let out a breath. Maybe he wasn't so bad. "Wow. Six is a lot these days."

"Julie and I always wanted a big family." He smiled at her and waved to an empty chair at the table. "Why don't you sit down. We should really get to know each other better, being that we're going to be working together."

Mary Beth took the chair. "How does your wife feel about so many kids?"

"She loves it. She's a stay-at-home mom and home schools them. She's a smart woman, but has a hard time keeping ahead of the oldest two."

"Mmmm ..." Mary Beth sipped her coffee.

"How about your kids, how old are they?"

"Bobby's the oldest; he's nine. Dorothy is seven."

Bear looked her over carefully. She felt as if she was being X-rayed. There was that feeling again, she should be wary of this man.

"Those are nice ages. Old enough to be interested in the world, but still innocent. I think I like those years the best."

Maybe I'm judging him too harshly. "How old are your kids?"

"They range from thirteen to six months."

She sipped her coffee and tried to feel the camaraderie.

"May I ask you something personal?" Bear asked.

"Sure." She was beginning to feel a little trust for this man.

"Why do you hate your kids?"

"Wha...?" Mary Beth's mouth dropped open.

Bear leaned towards her and took her hand. "I mean, at this age, they need their mom more than ever. Why did you leave your husband? He needs to support your family and you need to be at home with your children."

Mary Beth sat and stared at this strange man.

THE INTERCOM on Ted's desk sprang to life. "Ted, get in here! *Now.*" It was Bear.

"What's happenin', Bear?"

"You gotta see this. Holy crap, there's another one."

Ted rushed down the hall from his office to the computer room. He logged in at the security door and Bear buzzed him in from the man-trap. He glanced at Bear's work area. Typical. Three empty Diet Coke cans littered the desk, along with five Thai take out boxes. Piles of paper were scattered across the worksurface. Bear was nothing if not sloppy, but, man, could the boy code.

"What's goin' on, oh Great One." Ted dropped into a swivel chair and sent himself rolling across the floor to Bear's workstation.

"Check this out." Bear highlighted a line of code on his screen.

Ted leaned forward and squinted at the screen. "It's a call to a module called 'daisy chain.' What's that?"

"You're not going to believe this." Bear clicked on his screen. The debugger jumped to another piece of code. "This is well hidden. I don't think I'd have ever found it if I didn't see the call."

Ted read through the code. "This is in the original Microsoft code?"

"You betcha." Bear beamed as if he had won first place in a beauty pageant. "It creates zombies, then sends them out to infect every Windows computer it can contact."

He clicked on another button on the screen. Once again it jumped.

"This is outside the operating system. The hackers must have thought it was too dangerous to embed their code. The infected computer downloads the executable, then starts a DOS attack on … wait for it … wait for it … here it comes … the Fed."

"Huh?" Ted scooted closer to the screen. "The Fed. Like in the Federal Reserve System?"

"Bingo." Bear held his right index finger to his nose as if a bullet were piercing it. "Then it attacks the New York Stock Exchange."

"A Denial of Service attack?" Ted thought for a moment, then scratched his head. "That would take down our whole financial system. It'd be chaos. It'd be worse than the crash of 2008."

"Now you're catching on, Hero." Bear sat back in his chair and swiveled three-hundred-sixty degrees. "This thing will create millions of zombies. They'll spread the attack all over the world. The servers at the Fed and the Stock Exchange won't be able to handle the volume and they'll shut down."

"Is this part of the CryBaby attack?" Ted asked.

Bear shook his head. "Nope, something entirely different, but it's spread the same way."

"That means it's probably the same hacker. How the hell could he get the code into Windows?"

Ted read through the code. "Hey, did you see this?" He pointed to a line of code on his screen. "The attack isn't automated. It starts when the computers get a message from this website."

Bear typed in some characters on his keyboard, then turned his second monitor to face Ted. "Hmm … this is buried pretty deep. It has to be here somewhere."

After about ten minutes, Bear smiled. "Got it. Look at this sucker. It's hidden so deep in the Dark Web, its own mother couldn't find it."

Ted looked at the webpage Bear displayed. It had only one button on the page. "Open the source code. Let's see what makes this bad boy tick."

Bear clicked on the ellipsis in the upper right-hand corner of the page to drop down a tools menu. He clicked on Developer Tools and the screen split, with the web-page in the upper pane and the code in the lower pane.

Bear read through the code as Ted looked over his shoulder.

"There's lots of remote calls," Ted said.

"Right. The developers covered their tracks really well. They created objects for everything, then made them each their own executables. It's going to take days to work through this maze."

Ted breathed heavily and lowered his head. "Do we really want to invest the time in this? We could alert Microsoft and let them deal with it."

Bear opened a new can of Diet Coke and drank deeply. He wiped his lips. "We can't do that. If they know we have access to their source code, they're going to shut us down. We either deal with this ourselves or stand back and let it happen."

Sweat appeared on Ted's brow, despite the cool temperature of the computer room. "We can't just let the economy collapse if we can do something about it. Should we notify the Feds? We could do it anonymously."

"Same answer." Bear reached in a desk drawer and pulled out a bag of Lay's Sour Cream and Onion potato chips. "There's no such thing as anonymous with the Feds. They'd track us down, then they'll want to know how we found this. I'd be surprised if they didn't arrest us, in the name of national security, and hold us until the whole thing was over."

"Shit! Shit, shit, shit." Ted put the palms of his hands to his forehead as if he knew a tsunami of a headache was coming. "We can't let this happen. Do we have a chance to figure out a way of stopping it ourselves?"

Bear shook his head. "Why should we care? We're not being paid to fix it. It's going to take a lot of time and effort. I'll have to bring in a couple of contractors. That's out-of-pocket cash. I don't think my budget can handle it. And even if we did, we couldn't take credit. There's no win for us on this one."

Ted got up and began to pace. "How much money do you have socked away in your 401(k)? How much do you have invested in the stock market?" He turned back to face Bear

Bear popped a chip in his mouth. "I think we should figure out how to benefit from it. Maybe move all our stocks and securities into gold, or government bonds. We could short a bunch of stock, so when the value dropped, we'd rake in the cash."

Ted stood quietly for a moment, then shook his head as if trying to clear away some thoughts. "People lost billions in 2008. Working people. People like you and me. We can't let that happen again."

"Okay, we've got to find a way to insert killer code into every Windows OS in the world. How do you plan to do that?"

"Maybe we don't have to. I met a guy from Microsoft at the last developer's conference. He's in charge of the Windows security team. I'll bet he can sneak it in for us. If we can develop a vaccination, I'll bet he'd be willing to distribute it for us. He'd get the credit for stopping the attack. He'll be a hero. No way he's gonna say no."

"What's in it for us?" Bear looked into Ted's eyes. "What do we get for saving the world?"

"Sometimes, saving the world is its own reward."

Bear shook his head and turned back to his computer. "So, what do you suggest? How are we going to defeat this virus?"

Ted stepped over to the white board and wiped it clean. "How about if we create an army of zombies. They'd spread to every Windows computer in the world. They can insert the killer code so when the bad guys release it, nothing happens."

"You're a genius." Bear finished the last gulp of his Diet Coke, crushed the can and tossed it back with the others. "Now tell me, how are we going to do this? We don't even understand how this code works yet. It may take weeks to figure it out. In the meantime, the bad guys could release the virus anytime. What happens if they release it before we kill it?"

"Then it's a race. The clock starts now."

CHAPTER THIRTEEN

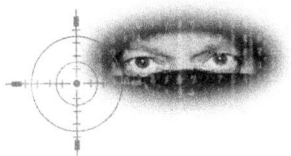

"Hackers have broken into our files," the voice said over the cell phone. "The CryBaby virus, it was one of ours."

Dr. Elaine Jefferson's heart pounded. Her agency worked year-round devising new weapons for the coming cyber-war, but there had only been one previous leak. The nefarious Edward Snowden. Now this.

The Tailored Access Operations (TAO), came to public awareness as the result of the Edward Snowden incident. Prior to the contractor leaking thousands of documents that revealed the U.S. government's spying operation on dozens of foreign leaders, the TAO operated in relative obscurity. Of course, the Senate Oversight Committee was aware of it, but the public didn't even know it existed. It was much easier that way. Back then she didn't have to worry about press scrutiny or public opinion.

Elaine's team was the world's elite cyber-spy agency. They created such tools as ExtraBacon, EpicBanana and EligibleBachelor that could breach the firewalls of virtually any system. Now she had a leak.

She was at her office in thirty minutes, dressed in a sweat suit, hair pulled back into a ponytail. The middle-aged brunette pulled the glass door at the NSA's Fort Meade, Maryland facility open with such force she was afraid she tore it off its hinges.

John Archer, her second-in-command waited for her. The high-tech office had glass walls that could darken on command, providing privacy, or lighten to allow her to view her troops working on the floor below.

"We knew this would happen someday," Archer said as she took off her coat.

"Not on my watch," Elaine said. "What do we know?"

Archer opened a folder on his laptop. "So far, a group calling themselves the Shadow Brokers released about three hundred megs of files for free." He pushed a few keys on his keyboard and a website appeared on Elaine's big screen on the wall. "They say these are the least innocuous executables. Tech confirmed they're ours."

Elaine settled back into her leather chair. "How do we know that?"

"So far, we identified three hundred and forty-seven algorithms that have never been used by anyone but the NSA. They use RC5 and RC6 encryption. We've done file compares with the files we have here and they're exact matches."

"Oh my God." She closed her eyes. "I suppose the press got wind of this?"

"If they haven't they're blind."

"So, what's the bottom line?"

Archer closed the file and gulped. "Shadow Brokers set up an auction. When they're paid one hundred million in Bitcoin, they're going to release the rest of the files."

"So, one of our enemies is going to get their hands on everything?"

"It's worse than that. When they reach one hundred million Bitcoins, they're going to release the code to everybody. They have diverse groups already contributing to the auction. If each group puts up part of the ransom, they'll all get the code."

"I suppose the Chinese and Russians are leading the charge."

"So far, we can't tie any of the bidders to them. The North Koreans are right up front. They're bidding with no attempt at secrecy. I think the Chinese and Ruskies will channel money to cover organizations to keep their participation secret."

Elaine opened a bottle of Glacier water and poured half of it into a glass. "Do we know how they got the data?" She dropped two Alka Seltzer tablets into the glass, stirred, and slugged it down.

"I'd say there's a fifty/fifty chance there wasn't a hack." Archer looked at his screen. "You know how hard it is to break into our systems. It's virtually impossible. I think it's probably a Snowden-style leak. Someone walked out of here with a flash drive."

"Christ, John." She shook her head. "Okay, recommendations. Where do we go from here?"

TED DROVE his BMW Z4 Roadster onto the Microsoft complex. He was always awed at the size of the campus. Comprised of more than two hundred and sixty acres, eight million square feet of office space, and room for thirty to forty thousand employees, it blended in with the terrain. The buildings were low, and the grounds were covered in lawns and mini-forests. It abutted a green belt and it was hard to tell where the campus ended, and the green belt began. It even contained a shopping mall, the Commons, with upscale retail stores, restaurants, and gyms. It was a self-contained city.

Parking was not a problem. Hundreds of acres of striped blacktop surrounded the buildings. Every other space seemed to be filled with a Mercedes, BMW, or Porsche. Ted's midnight-blue roadster fit right in.

Following his GPS, Ted easily located building nineteen. He parked and walked a few paces to the green area outside the main entrance. He'd been to Microsoft many times, but it never failed to amaze him. The green area was filled with healthy-looking young people strolling, playing ultimate Frisbee or soccer, or just sitting on the concrete benches playing with their laptops, tablets, or cell phones. Didn't these people ever work?

"Mr. Higuera, so nice to see you again." Samir Hussaini reached out his hand. Ted recognized him from the conference he had attended the previous year where Samir gave a talk on cyber security.

"Mr. Hussaini." Ted took his hand. "I'm glad you could meet me."

Samir was the head of the Windows security team. If anyone could help Ted, he was the man.

"Let's walk, Mr. Higuera." Samir made a gesture with his hand towards the concrete paths. "It's such a nice day."

"Ted, please. Everyone calls me Ted."

Samir flashed his million-watt smile. "Okay, Ted. But only if you call me Sam. It seems so much more ... ah ... American."

"You got it. Sam."

"You said you found something hidden in our OS?"

"Yeah. Look, I know this is delicate. I called you because you seemed like the kind of guy who would understand."

The path led them through a grove of trees, and eventually, alongside a small creek.

"Tell me what I would understand."

Ted looked about as if checking to see if anyone was listening. "Uh ... what I'm going to tell you is confidential; it could destroy my company. I expect that you'll keep it that way. I don't want to experience any repercussions."

Samir stopped and looked at Ted. "I have no idea where you're going with this."

"Okay, here it is. At Flaherty & Associates, we have the capability to reverse engineer Windows. We can decompile virtually any executable. We can see your code and know how it operates."

Samir just stared at Ted.

"What I've come here to tell you today is that you have a problem. A big problem."

"Ummm ...hmmm ..."

"You'll want to check it out for yourselves." Ted stopped while a couple of women strolled by hand-in-hand. "We've found something that shouldn't be there."

"Like what?" Samir pulled his head back and narrowed his eyes.

"Someone inserted an Easter Egg into your system."

"No. That's not possible."

"It's true." Ted handed Samir a flash drive. "Look at it for yourself. It's activated remotely from a website hidden deep in the Dark Net. When it goes off, it'll cripple the nation's financial systems."

"Mr. Higuera, I have a hard time believing this ..."

"Just look at it. You've got it all there. My notes, the commented code, everything. There's also an inoculation on the drive. It will root out the code and kill it. You can stop this attack before it happens."

Samir took the flash drive and put it in his pocket as if it was a vial of acid.

"Why are you coming to me with this? Why didn't you go public? You could be a hero."

Ted laughed. "I've already been down that road. Don't like it very much." He scratched behind his ear. "Listen, if we went public, Microsoft would have a cow. They'd want to know how we found this. They'd find ways to block our access to your code. That would severely damage our ability to serve our clients."

Samir motioned towards a bench along the path. "I did a little research on you and your company when you first contacted me. You intrigued me." He sat down on the bench. "You've done some amazing things. Foiling a terrorist attack on a cruise ship. Breaking up a couple of Mexican drug cartels. Unraveling the scandal at Millennium Systems. You've built an impressive list of clients and quite a reputation. That's why I agreed to talk to you, to see the man behind the legend. But I must tell you, I can hardly believe your story. It just goes beyond the realm of possibility."

Ted sat and shook his head. "I wanted to give this to you because it's not my problem. I don't get paid to save the world. When this attack happens and when it gets traced back to your code, Microsoft is gonna look bad, worse than bad."

Sam pulled the flash drive from his pocket and stared at it. He flipped it into the air and caught it several times. "Okay, Ted, I'll look at it. I'll have my people go over it and see if it is as you say. If it is, we'll take the appropriate action to remove the harmful code."

MARY BETH PUT down her coffee cup and took stock of her surroundings. It was like every other Starbucks she'd been in, yet it had its own unique touches. This store had a long, thick wooden table down the middle of the store, anchored to the concrete floor with steel pipe legs. It was a large space, with coffee tables and chairs on one side and the barista stand on the other. The walls, as expected, were covered with displays of coffee and merchandise. The aroma of coffee filled the air and reminded Mary Beth of growing up in her parents' home.

Why did she call me? Mary Beth looked across the coffee table to her client. Jane had dark circles under eyes that were dull and listless. She slumped in her seat and the hand holding her cup shook. *She needs a counselor, not a detective. Unless she wants me to help her get out of this situation, there's nothing I can do for her.*

"He won't let me have any friends. There was a get-together with some of my sorority sisters and he wouldn't let me go."

"Did he hit you? Lock you up?" Mary Beth leaned forward.

"No ... not really ... he ... ah ... told me I was fat. That I would be embarrassed to be around my college friends. He said my dress was so out of style they'd laugh at me ..." Jane hung her head and sniffled.

"I see." Mary Beth reached for Jane's hand, but Jane pulled it back. "This just keeps going on. Do you want to get away from him?"

Jane closed her eyes for a moment, then went on as if Mary Beth had not spoken. "He won't let me see my parents. He's convinced they're prejudiced against him and think our children are half-breeds. My mom can't even spend any time with her grandchildren." Jane broke down crying.

Mary Beth reached into her purse, handed Jane a tissue, and patiently waited for her to recover herself. She knew Jane's husband was Syrian but found no evidence that he didn't fit into American society. What were her parents prejudiced about? That he was raising their grandchildren as Muslims?

"He checks my cell phone, my messages, my email. I have no privacy. No sense of my own place. He thinks I live to serve him. If I didn't have my work, I think I'd go nuts." She wiped her nose. "He doesn't even want me to work. We fight at least once a week about it. He says Allah wants me to stay home and take care of the family."

Mary Beth reached over and lifted Jane's chin. She spoke directly into Jane's brown eyes. "You've got to take control of your life. You can't continue to let him devalue you. This is where I can help, if you want. We can work out a plan to extract you from that house. I have contacts. I can get you into a safe house, get a restraining order, help you find a place to stay. You can start your life over. You don't have to live with someone bullying you from seeing your friends and family."

Jane stared into space. Her hands trembled, and her body wracked with heavy sobs.

Mary Beth became aware other people in the coffee shop were watching them. *To hell with them. I have a job to do here. I know I can save this woman.* "Jane, you have to make the decision. No one else can do it for you."

Jane spoke again in a monotone. "He does the same stuff to my daughter. He checks her cell phone, controls how she dresses, who she hangs out with. He won't let her go out with her friends if there's any possibility that they might run into boys." Jane shook her head and a quiver ran down her entire body. "She told me she was going to leave home. That she was going to move in with a friend." Jane took both of Mary Beth's hands and looked into her eyes. "I can't allow that. If she tries it, he'll kill her. He says it would be an honor killing, that he couldn't let her dishonor the family."

CHAPTER FOURTEEN

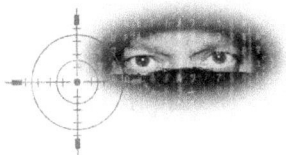

T he end of another long day. They were all long days. Ever since Maria left him and fled to Mexico with his unborn child, Ted did little but work and sleep.

He slipped into the driver's seat of his BMW Z4. He always liked to think of it as the cockpit. When he drove the sleek dark-blue roadster, which he nicknamed the Blue Bomber, he felt as if he were flying a jet fighter.

The engine turned over and he sat and listened to the throaty purr of the turbo-charged six-cylinder engine for a moment. Pushing the button to retract the hard top, Ted sat back in the white leather seat and took a deep breath. Driving the Blue Bomber always brought him a sense of peace. It was his own personal status symbol. It told him that he had made it.

For a kid born and raised in the barrios of East L.A., he wasn't doing too bad. He didn't like the fact that Catrina dropped the business in his lap, but he liked the idea of being his own boss, and the business was doing well.

But he still had a hole in his soul. It wasn't just that Maria left him. He could understand that … well not really. They were the ideal match. She was his soul-mate.

It was the fact that Maria took over her father's drug cartel when he was killed by El Pozolero, a rival drug lord. That Maria hit back hard, led a war against El Pozolero's organization and cold bloodedly killed all who opposed her. She even plunged the knife into El Pozolero's heart.

She was a changed person, and she was carrying his baby. He had to find a way to see his son. He may not be able to rebuild his relationship with Maria, but he had to have a relationship with his own offspring.

He pulled out of the parking lot and took the Sixth Street on ramp to I-5 north.

He had to go to Mexico. He had to see Maria in person, to explain his desperate need to be part of the boy's life, to bring him into the family.

As soon as he reached freeway speed, he knew something was wrong. The Blue Bomber took off like a cheetah. He touched the brake to slow it down. Nothing happened.

The speedometer clicked past sixty, seventy, eighty. He stood on the brakes. Nothing. He pulled the handle on the emergency brake. Still nothing. He tried to take the car out of gear, but the gear-shift lever wouldn't move. He tried to turn off the ignition, but nothing happened.

Fortunately, it was late at night and not many cars were on the road. He pushed the talk button on his steering wheel.

"Dial nine-one-one."

"Nine-one-one, what is your emergency?"

"Hi, my name is Ted Higuera. My car is running out of control. I'm on I-5 northbound. I just passed the Dearborn off ramp."

"Have you tried shutting off the ignition?" the operator asked.

"I've tried everything. It just won't respond. I'm doing a hundred miles an hour and accelerating."

"Stand by please. I'll get the State Patrol on the line."

The city swept past him at a speed he couldn't have imagined. His hair stood out stiff in the breeze as he flew past the baseball and football stadiums. Speeding through the tunnel under the convention center gave him the feeling he was exiting the mothership like on *Battle Star Galactica*. He came up out of the tunnel and saw the Ship Canal Bridge in front of him.

"Oh God," he gasped. Two lanes were shut down for construction.

He pulled his cell phone out of its cradle and swiped the screen. After Hope's incident, he had prepared for this moment. He found the app called Kill It and tapped on it. The engine of his powerful sports car died.

The car flew towards the bridge. He stood on the brakes. Tires screeched, and the speedometer dropped from one-sixty to one hundred. He was trapped in his capsule like an astronaut returning to earth.

The speedometer said eighty as Ted said a Hail Mary and turned the steering wheel to the stops. The Beemer skidded into a spin as the speed bled off. It slammed sideways into a dump truck. Ted's head banged into the airbag. The car continued on and glanced off a police car, going airborne. It flew over the side of the bridge and launched into space.

The events that took only seconds seemed to last forever. Ted was aware of flying through the black night, then the nose of the car dove, and he saw the black water of the ship canal one hundred and fifty feet below him. He braced himself for impact.

The car slammed into the frigid water and plunged below the surface. Ted held his breath while he was knocked around. The car took most of the force of the impact, and his seat belt kept him tightly secured to the leather seat.

The BMW bobbed back to the surface, but rapidly filled with water. Ted was stunned. He couldn't quite take in what was happening around him. Water rose around his chest. The cold water snapped him back to reality, and he realized his peril.

He punched the button on his seat belt. It wouldn't release. God spoke to him. He remembered the letter opener he picked up at a fabric store he went to with Maria.

Holding his breath, he fumbled around until he got the console open, found the razor-sharp letter opener and cut the belt.

He pushed up with his legs and floated free of the sinking car.

———

THE GOOD-LOOKING young reporter stood at the side of I-5 with a microphone in one hand and a tablet in the other. His wavy brown hair ruffled in the breeze as the sun climbed over the Cascade Mountains painting Seattle pink. The morning news anchor handed the story off to him. He stared at the camera a moment and nodded.

"Thank you, Todd. As you can see, the freeway is still closed." He swept his hand towards the mass of flashing red and blue lights behind him. The camera followed to show a pack of police cars clogging the bridge.

"As far as we can tell, no one was hurt in this late-night accident. A source who doesn't want to reveal his name told me the runaway car was doing well over a hundred miles an hour when it hit the construction equipment and went airborne over the railing. The driver was recovered and taken to Harbor View Hospital for observation. So far there's no word of whether alcohol or drugs were involved."

"NOOOOOO," Assad al Allah shouted to his empty kitchen. "How did that infidel survive the accident?"

———

TED'S HEAD rang and his vision was blurry. When Abiba picked him up at the hospital, he couldn't walk in a straight line. She offered to stay the night with him. He tried to shoo her home, but she would have none of it.

"The doctor said you should stay awake, that you should not be alone."

And that was that. He and Abiba stayed up playing rummy all night.

This morning he sat at his desk, sipped coffee, and stared off into infinity. There had been several reports of cars going out of control all over the country. Senator Jacobson died in such a crash. As far as he knew, Hope's accident was the first.

Was there some kind of connection? It seemed too coincidental that both he and his sister should have their cars go bat-shit crazy. The police were optimistic that they'd be able to get some good clues from his car. It wasn't destroyed like Hope's and the Senator's.

A strange, disjointed thought floated around in his head. Could this be on purpose? He'd read some doomsayers claim that modern cars could be hacked. He hadn't thought about it too much. Was it really possible?

"Morning, Hero." Bear stood in his doorway with a box of doughnuts in his hand. "Am I early?"

Ted stood, overcome by dizziness. He grabbed the back of his chair to steady himself. "No. No come in. Whatcha got?"

"I stopped by Top Pot on the way in."

Ted craned his head. "You got a chocolate in there?"

"Does a bear go in the woods?" Bear set the box down on the coffee table on the far side of the office. "What's this emergency meeting about?"

"Mary Beth'll be here in a few minutes. I'd like to tell you both at the same time."

Abiba arrived with her silver tray filled with the coffee service. "Morning, Mr. Ted. I must say you look like you've been in the wars."

Ted took the offered cup of coffee. Abiba made the best coffee in Seattle. "I'm doin' better. Thank you for stayin' with me last night." Abiba gave him a motherly smile. "Don't worry. I'm all right. I just got banged around a little bit. I'm going to be fine."

"Morning, everybody." Mary Beth walked through the door.

Dressed in a flower-print dress, pumps with two-inch heels, and her short brown hair pinned up behind one ear, she looked ready for a shift at Nordstrom.

"Morning, MB." Ted waved towards the chairs around the coffee table. "Now that you're here, we can get started." He took a chair himself and nibbled his doughnut.

"Doughnut?" Bear asked, as he flashed a half-smile at her. "Top Pot only makes the best doughnuts in the universe."

She glanced back at Bear with a frown on her face. "No, thanks."

"The reason I called the meeting this morning, is that something's come up. I have to leave town for a couple days. I want to make sure everything runs smoothly in my absence."

Bear had a sparkle in his eye; Mary Beth turned down the edges of her lips.

"We don't have anything major going on right now." Ted looked at Mary Beth's sour face. "MB, you have the Williams case. I'm sure you can handle it. Bear, you've got a penetration test coming up. I assume you're ready for it?"

Bear mumbled and polished off a crueller.

"I turned our findings over to Microsoft. They'll take care of the Wall Street Virus. I think I can take a couple personal days."

"You want me to make reservations for a flight to Cabo?" Abiba asked.

Ted's mouth flew open. "How did you know ...?"

Abiba shook her head. "You're going after the girl, aren't you?"

"Ah ... yes ..."

She flashed him The Look. "I wouldn't do it, Mr. Ted. Nothing good's going to come of it. You go after that girl, it's going to come a cropper."

Ted shook his head to clear it. How did Abiba know these things? "Yeah. Alright. I'm going to be gone a couple of days, that's all. You all know how to get a hold of me. I'll have my phone on and answer all my emails and texts. There shouldn't be any big decisions to make; each of you will continue to run your departments. I'm still not comfortable with this hacking stuff. Bear, keep following up on that. And while you're at it, see what you can find out about hacking cars. Somethings going on that we don't understand yet."

His head swam for a moment. With a giant force of will, he brought his mind back into focus. "MB, do you think you'll have to do an extraction for Jane?"

"It's her only chance. I just hope she'll see that and get her and her kids out of that house."

Ted forced himself to concentrate. "You'll need backup. If you do the extraction before I get back, call Chris. I've already briefed him on this."

"A lawyer? You're giving me a lawyer for backup?"

"Yeah." Ted smiled. "Lawyers are pretty scary. Besides, he can handle himself in a tough situation."

Mary Beth slumped back in her chair and didn't respond.

TED SAT in the plush first-class seat on the Alaska Airlines 737 and dialed the ranch's number for perhaps the hundredth time. Maria's phone hadn't been in service for months.

After about ten rings, Theresa's phone went to voicemail.

"Hi Theresa, this is Ted. Please listen to this message. I'm on an airplane now. I'm flying down to talk to you and Maria. I know this is my baby and I want to be part of his life. I'll contact you in a few hours when I'm on the ground."

What am I doing? This is insane. There's no way Theresa will let me near Maria. They lived on a huge ranch with hundreds of employees and their families. There were dozens of armed guards and most of the employees were armed. The only way in was through the front door.

———

THE PLANE STOPPED in San Diego to take on extra passengers, then was off again. The flight attendants barely had time to roll out the beverage carts when it happened.

"Chuck, we got a problem," the pilot said to her copilot who was reading his Kindle.

The copilot dropped the Kindle and focused on the control panel. It was blank. System by system all the electronics had shut down.

"San Diego Control, this is Alaska 314, do you read me?" the pilot said into her microphone. There was no response.

"What're you thinking, Chuck?"

The young copilot flipped switches and turned dials. "Nothing. All our systems are down. No radios. No GPS. We're in a heap of trouble."

"I'm taking her back to Brown Field; there's less traffic there. We're doing this by the seats of our pants, so stay alert."

Chuck pulled the emergency checklist from its receptacle. "Let's see. Emergency landings – no systems."

He began to go over the items one by one. The pilot meticulously followed the instructions.

———

A MURMUR FILLED the cabin when the lights went out. The passengers were uncomfortable, but not panicked.

The panic came when the plane dove suddenly, and the oxygen masks dropped from the overheads.

Above the din of screams, the head flight attendant reached for the microphone. "Ladies and gentlemen," she said in a normal voice. The intercom was out.

Ted fought the urge to panic. *There's nothing I can do one way or the other.* One minute he was looking out his window at endless tracks of ocean.

The next time he saw the coastline and land out his window. *What's going on?*

"Excuse me, Miss," Ted yelled to the flight attendant. "It looks like we've turned around. What's happening?"

The lovely Asian woman looked out the window. Her eyes widened, and her brow furrowed. "Um ... I don't know, sir. Let me check with the pilot."

CHAPTER FIFTEEN

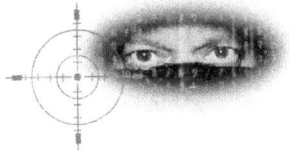

The flight attendant stepped to the cabin door and knocked. There was no answer. She knocked again.

"Hello. Lydia, Chuck, are you there?"

The door cracked open. "We have an emergency," a female voice responded. "All systems are down. We're heading back to Brown Field."

"Should I tell the passengers?"

"Uh ... Yeah. The intercom's down, so you'll have to talk loudly to them. Keep them calm. Prepare them for an emergency landing. We're going in without radio contact. I'm not sure what's going to happen."

The flight attendant took a deep breath and turned back to the cabin. She hustled aft and huddled with the other attendants in the galley. In a few moments, she made her way back to the front of the craft.

"Ladies and gentlemen, may I have your attention please?" She waited a minute for the noise in the cabin to die down. "The captain has informed me that we have an in-flight emergency." She almost shouted so that the people in the back row could hear her. She knew a co-worker was shouting the same message in coach. "It's nothing to worry about. We train for these kinds of emergencies all the time. She's turning the plane around and going back to Brown Field in San Diego. I'm sorry for any inconvenience this may cause you, but it is our policy to always put safety first. Thank you."

There were cries and moans in the cabin. An older man got up and opened the overhead compartment.

"Sir, please. You must remain in your seat."

"I need to get my cell phone."

THE OLDER WOMAN seated next to Ted reached for his arm. "What's happening?"

"I have no idea." He didn't want to scare the lady. "We're turning around. We'll be fine." Ted looked out the window, his stomach twisted in knots. *The lights are all out, the stewardess didn't use the PA system. Is this another hack?*

"I was on my way to see my grandchildren in Cabo." The woman dug her wizened fingers into Ted's arm. "Are we going to crash?"

Ted winced at the firm grip. "Let's do like the lady said and stay calm."

The plane hit an updraft and the noise level in the cabin rose.

The jet settled on a northeasterly course and headed back to the safety of land and the airport.

Ted called the flight attendant over. "Miss, I'm Ted Higuera." He handed her his card. "I'm a cyber security expert."

She turned his card in her hands.

"I believe that the plane has been hacked. I think the bad guys are trying to kill me. They don't care if they take down a whole plane-load of people with them."

The flight attendant's face whitened. "I'll tell the captain," she said, and hurried away.

Well, that's that. I'm in this up to my neck now.

The clock seemed to stop. The heat in the cabin increased. The air was stagnant. Ted fiddled with the vent controls over his head, but nothing helped. It stank like a locker room.

Ted wiped the sweat from his brow. *Is this how it's going to end? I'll never get to know my son.*

THE PILOT ENTERED the landing pattern with all caution. Her co-pilot craned his neck looking for traffic.

Both pilots scanned the control tower for any acknowledgement of their presence. A green light flashed at them.

"We're cleared to land," the pilot said. "Landing checklist."

Chuck began the landing process.

THE PASSENGERS HELD their collective breath. The flight attendants did a final cabin check, asked passengers to assume the crash position, and belted themselves into their seats. The big jet settled closer and closer to the runway.

The wheels kissed the runway with a squeak and a cloud of dust. The pilots reversed the thrust to slow the plane down. They slowed and pulled off the runway onto a taxiway that took them to the maintenance hangars.

Inside the plane, people clapped and cheered. They had just been given their lives back.

The plane taxied up to the terminal and a boarding ladder was wheeled up to the door. As the flight attendant opened the door, two men in suits entered the plane and talked with the pilot.

"Will everyone please keep theirs seats," the flight attendants yelled over the din. "We will begin de-planing in a few minutes."

The two men came down the aisle.

"Mr. Higuera? Will you come with us please?"

ASSAD AL ALLAH, the Lion of God, paced back and forth in the safe house. His compatriots cowered at his show of temper.

"How does he do it?" the Lion roared. "That's the second time. How does this infidel, Higuera, manage to cheat death? It's almost as if Allah himself was looking out for him."

"OKAY, Mr. Higuera, why do you think that you're the target?"

Ted sat in a plain conference room inside the tiny Brown Field terminal. A cup of vending machine coffee in a paper cup covered with pictures of playing cards sat untouched in front of him. *I wouldn't drink that swill if my life depended on it.*

"I don't know that for a fact, but it makes sense to me."

"How so?" The tall man with closely cropped gray hair asked.

"I'll bet you anything that you find that the planes computers were hacked. I'm an expert in this field. I can smell it. Give me some time and I'll figure out how they did it."

The black man with a shaved head leaned back in his chair. "Mr. Higuera, leave the solving of crimes to us. Just answer the questions."

Ted stared at the picture of a P-51 Mustang in flight on the opposite wall for a moment. "All right, here it is. First of all, there's the CryBaby virus. I found the fix to disable it. Then there was a time bomb left in the Windows operating system to shut down Wall Street. I gave the cure to Microsoft. Kinda a coincidence, don't you think? There have been a series of hacks on cars, killing and injuring people. My car was one of those hacked. Then I'm on an airplane that loses its electrical systems. You startin' to see the pattern?"

"Umm ..." the gray-haired man mumbled.

"Think about it. I find a cure for CryBaby, then the Wall Street Virus, and suddenly I'm attacked. This smells to me. I'm guessing someone somewhere is cooking up a major attack on the U.S. and they think I'm in their way. What do you think?"

The questioning lasted two hours before the Homeland Security agents released Ted. *What did those babosos want with me? I sure as hell didn't hack a plane I was on.*

Madre de Dios. Ted made his way to the boarding gate and listened to the announcement. The Department of Homeland Security shut down all flights in the United States. This hadn't happened since 9/11. He was stuck in San Diego.

What do I do? Rent a car and drive home? Drive to La Paz? No, they don't let rentals cross the border. What if I cross the border and try to catch a flight from Tijuana?

He pulled his cell phone from his pocket and tapped the screen. He brought up the web page for Volaris Airlines, a Mexican commuter airline that had flights to La Paz.

Ted almost lost his lunch, if he'd eaten lunch, at the thought of getting on another airplane. Then he thought of Maria and his son. In a few moments, he had a ticket on the next flight. But he had to get to the Tijuana airport.

Ted hustled across the Brown Field facility to the bus station and took the 992 to the City College trolley station, then took the blue line to the border crossing.

Paying the twelve bucks for the new foot bridge across the frontier looked like the best option. After clearing customs, Ted caught a taxi to the airport and touched down in La Paz a couple of hours later, still pale and shaking.

He took the EcoTourBaja bus from the San Jose del Cabo airport to La Paz. After a two-hour ride, he walked from the terminal to El Dolfin, his favorite hotel. It was right on the *Malecón*, the wide sidewalk along the water front.

He walked a couple of blocks to the rental car agency and left in a red Jeep Wrangler. The vehicle had a surrey top to shield him from the sun, but it couldn't protect Ted from the hundred degree plus heat. He headed out of town to the Los Santos Ranch.

What do I say? Will they even let me in?

Ted drove the familiar highway, turned off on a dirt road and continued through the scorched countryside. After about an hour, he came to a locked gate.

When he got out of the Jeep, two *campesinos* carrying AK-47s appeared from nowhere.

"What is your business here?" the taller one asked in Spanish.

"I'm Ted Higuera." Ted thought he recognized the man. He may have fought with him against El Pozolero's *narcos*. "You're Santos, sí?"

"I remember you, Señor Higuera, but you cannot come in. The señora forbids it."

"But I've—"

"The señora forbids it." Santos waved the barrel of his gun at Ted.

Ted sized up the two men. Could he take them? If he did, what would it accomplish? Either he or one or both of them might get hurt, even killed. For what? So he could talk to Maria? The equation didn't add up.

Ted got into his Jeep without another word and turned back to the city.

THE OPEN-AIR BAR in El Dolfin looked out over the *Malecon* to La Paz Bay. A white sandy beach stretched for miles in either direction. To his right, a couple dozen blue-and-white pangas, the boat of choice for local fishermen, lay beached in the sand.

Ted nursed a Margarita and glanced at his watch. *What is it about this country? Can't anyone ever be on time?*

It was early evening and a *ranchero* band tuned up in the back of the restaurant. Dressed like cowboys, in jeans and plaid shirts with white cowboy hats, the band would soon belt out their raucous *rancheros*.

A lean man, about Ted's height, with dark hair, a bushy mustache and a scar on his cheek walked in from the street. He looked around for an instant, then made a straight line to Ted.

"Señor Higuera, I presume," he said in accented English.

"Sí," Ted replied in Spanish. "They call me Ted Higuera."

The man extended his hand, Ted appreciated his firm grip.

The man sat on the stool next to Ted. "*Negro Modelo, por favor,*" he called to the bartender.

Turning his attention back to Ted, he reached in his pocket and produced a business card. "They call me Hector Rodriquez. You called me?"

Ted looked at the private investigator for a moment. *He seems competent. Looks pretty tough to me.* "I need help. My fiancée left me, came to Mexico, and is hiding on her family's rancho. She won't talk to me; refuses to see me."

Hector smiled a knowing smile. "The course of true love never did run smooth."

Ted laughed. "A PI who quotes Shakespeare. What's next?"

"You know, Señor Higuera, yours is an old story."

The bartender set a bottle at Hector's hand.

Ted raised his glass and said, "*Salud, dinero y amor.*"

"Health, money, and love," Hector snickered. "Some things never change." He took a sip of his beer. "Now, tell me how I may be of service to you."

Ted looked around the bar and thought for a moment. "Okay, here's the thing. She's pregnant. It's my kid. I know it is. She insists it isn't and won't talk to me. I know it isn't anyone else's; it couldn't be." He sighed. "I can handle losing her. I don't like it, but I can handle it. But never seeing, never knowing my son. That I can't handle. I need you to get proof for me that it's my boy. I can confront her and convince her to let me be part of the boy's life."

Hector pulled a notebook from his pocket. "And what is the young lady's name?"

"Maria Gonzales."

Hector folded up his notebook, put it back in his pocket, and whistled. "You are serious? La Reina? The queen of the drug cartels in Baja?" He stared at Ted for a moment. When Ted didn't respond, he continued, "You're out of your mind. Get back on a plane and return north. There's nothing for you here."

Ted swirled the remains of his drink in its glass. "Do you have children, Hector?"

"Sí, two boys."

"Would you go off and abandon them? Would you walk out of their lives and never see them again?"

"I see what you mean." Hector raised two fingers and motioned to the bartender. "But what can I do for you? And what good will it do if I can provide the documentation you seek?"

The brass thundered the opening of the band's first set. The sounds of *Rancho Grande* blasted through the bar.

"I don't know, but I need something. I have to find some way to get in touch with her. She's due soon. See if you can find proof. See what she puts on the birth certificate. Get hospital or doctor's records. Find a way to get the baby's DNA. Put your ear to the ground; see what people are saying. Find anything you can. I need to get a leg up. I'm desperate."

Hector leaned over and put a hand on Ted's shoulder. "I will do what I can, my friend. It's not going to be easy, it's not going to be cheap, and it will be dangerous."

"Look, do whatever it takes. I have money. Just let me know what you need."

Hector shook his head. "Money isn't the problem. Who will be the father to my children, the husband to my wife, if this goes badly?"

Half an hour later, Ted sat on the edge of the hotel bed and stared at his cell phone. He hated to lean on Chris again, but he had to make the call.

He pushed the speed-dial buttons on the phone and listened to the ring.

"Ted. Where are you?" his friend answered. "What's going on?"

"Hey, amigo. I'm in La Paz." He heard a little intake of air on Chris's side. "I'm trying to get in contact with Maria."

"Ted ..."

"I know. I know." Ted let out a breath. "I'm not going to try to get back together with her. I've given up on that. I need to work out some kind of arrangement so I can see my son." He could picture Chris rolling his eyes and shaking his head. "Can you help me?"

"Ted, how the hell do you think I'm going to help you? You're a couple thousand miles away in a foreign country. What can I do?"

"You can find me a Mexican lawyer. Someone I can trust. I know that you can't practice law in Mexico. I need to start some kind of proceedings to allow me visitation with my son."

CHAPTER SIXTEEN

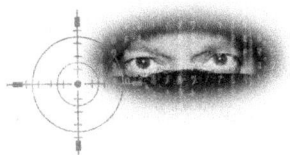

The safe-house buzzed with excitement. This was it. Assad al Allah and his minions stood ready to test their full-scale assault on the Great Satan.

Twenty men sat at computer workstations throughout the five rooms in the house. Soft voices filled with anticipation floated throughout the building.

"My brothers." Assad stood and shouted loud enough to be heard in all the rooms. "This is it. Today is the first day of the beginning of the Caliphate. Today, we bring The Great Satan to its knees." He closed his eyes and took a deep breath. "Are you ready?"

Nods and murmurs of assent were his reply.

"Muhammed, we start with you. Take down the sewage plants."

A man at a workstation began typing furiously on his keyboard.

"Caleb, kill Air Traffic Control."

"Emir, take down the power grid."

One by one, Assad dictated to his minions to launch the attack.

MORNING WAS Mary Beth's favorite part of the day. Every day started with new promise, new challenges to conquer. Coffee was her top priority. Then came fixing breakfast for the kids.

Her daughter, Dorothy, wandered into the kitchen half asleep.

"Good morning, sweetie," Mary Beth said.

"Uhnnn ..." Dorothy replied.

Mary Beth stood at the sink in her Kent home. The house was located at the bottom of the valley, surrounded by urban sprawl.

She never complained, but it was all she could do to pay the rent. Then came the big promotion. She finally had the chance to save for the kids' college and maybe even do the remodel she wanted.

A gurgling sound rumbled in the bathroom. She hurried to the door and watched as a spray of brown water erupted from the toilet.

"Aeeeek ..." She screamed as the sewage spilled over the edge.

She reached in the cupboard and pulled out a handful of towels. She built a dam at the door to keep the disgusting water from spreading.

She dashed to the bedroom, grabbed her cell phone, and dialed her cousin, the plumber.

"Tommy, you have to come over here," she shrieked. "The toilet's backing up all over the floor."

"I can't." Tommy seemed more panicked than Mary Beth. "My toilets are overflowing; the neighbors just came over with the same problem. Anita says the drains and man-hole covers in the street are backing up with sewage."

"What do I do?" Mary Beth screamed into her phone. "How do I stop this?"

"I don't know. The shit is hitting the fan all over the city. Get out of your apartment. Get to high ground; you don't want to be stuck in this shit. The kids are in school, right? The school'll take care of them."

The phone went silent.

———

CANDACE LOVED SEATTLE. After growing up in rural Idaho, she loved the hustle and bustle of the city. She loved the cosmopolitan atmosphere. She loved the diversity.

However driving in the city was a suicide mission. Like most Seattleites, she drove to work each day. It took anywhere from a half hour to two hours, depending on traffic. Fortunately, she could afford a nice car. The sound system on her Escalade was amazing.

She was supposed to pick up her parents at the airport after work. They had tickets on an Alaska Airlines flight from Boise, but the flight had been canceled. They had to drive the twelve hours to reach Seattle. She looked forward to seeing her parents. She hadn't seen them since the previous Thanksgiving and was anxious to hear how her sisters and nieces and nephews were doing.

The traffic signal ahead of her turned yellow. The car in the other lane sped up to beat the red, but Candace slowed and stopped.

The light was red for an instant before it turned green. She started into the intersection when she noticed a car speeding at her on the left. She slammed on her brakes.

The other car blew its horn and tried to stop, but it was too late. It T-boned Candace's Cadillac and pushed her into the other lane. The car in the next lane swerved to miss Candace and slammed into a cargo van.

Horns blared from the three collisions in the intersection. Cars backed up. Police sirens wailed.

ANNIE LINDBERG SAT in her beat-up Chevy waiting for traffic to move. The radio switched from soft rock to a news announcement.

"We bring you a special traffic report now from Chopper 7. Dianne, what's going on?"

Annie listened to the broadcast over the thump-thump-thump of the helicopter's blades.

"Well, Jodie, traffic is at a standstill throughout the city. It seems that the traffic control system has gone down, putting all traffic signals on green. There have been multiple crashes around the city. Most intersections are blocked, and traffic is not moving."

Annie looked at her watch. 3:00 pm. She was stuck. Nothing moved in any direction. A blue bank bag sat on the floor on the passenger side. *What do I do?* She was on the way to the bank with yesterday's deposit from her restaurant, Aunt Annie's Pancake House.

Obviously she was going nowhere. Should she leave her car and walk back to the restaurant? Could she make it back in time for the dinner rush? Would there even be a dinner rush with the streets clogged? And how about the money? Did she dare walk around carrying three thousand dollars?

"Asiana flight one-three-four-one, this is SFX Approach Control."

Huang Hua, a Chinese man with short cropped black hair and a tiny mustache picked up the microphone and replied. "Approach Control, Asiana thirteen-forty-one."

"Thirteen-forty-one, maintain flight level thirty-five and come to a heading of ..."

"Approach Control, thirteen-forty-one. Please repeat." Huang held the microphone in his hand, close to his lips.

There was no reply.

He waited a few seconds.

"San Francisco Approach Control, this is Asiana flight thirteen-forty-one. Do you read me?"

Silence.

He turned to his co-pilot. "Padma, check the backup radio."

"Already done. No response from ATC."

"Could they be off the air?"

Moments before, Huang was the happiest man in China. His first trans-Pacific flight in a new Boeing 747. What could go wrong?

"All aircraft on San Francisco Approach Control, this is Asiana flight thirteen-forty-one. Can you make contact with Approach Control?"

More silence.

"What's going on?" Padma asked. "Maybe we should try another frequency."

"Good idea." Huang switched the radio frequency to the San Francisco Tower.

"San Francisco Tower, this is Asiana flight thirteen-forty-one. I've lost contact with Approach Control. Do you read me?"

Silence.

"What the hell's going on?" Huang turned to his co-pilot. He felt a herd of butterflies attacking his stomach.

"I'm not sure," she said. "But we can't monkey around here for long. With those headwinds, we're running short on fuel."

Huang tried San Francisco Ground Control and got no response. He tried the channels for other nearby airports with the same results.

"Okay, here's what I know." He felt the moistness in the palms of his hands. "We have no radio contact anywhere. We're low on fuel and have to land. I'm thinking we need to continue our approach to San Francisco."

Padma closed her eyes and said a prayer to her ancestors. "I concur. I'll plot a course that brings us in on downwind for runway 10R."

Huang began the big plane's descent and informed the flight crew of the issue.

"Ladies and gentlemen," Huang spoke into the intercom. "We are beginning our descent into San Francisco International Airport. Please return to your seats and follow the fight crew's instructions."

Both Huang and Padma's heads were on swivels, looking out their cockpit windows for other traffic.

"I've got a 737 on the starboard side," Padma said. "He's slightly above us on a parallel course."

"Thank you. Keep an eye on him."

The altimeter showed them descending through twenty-thousand feet. The coastline was clear in their windshield.

Huang took a deep breath. *It's beautiful. Will this be the last time I see it?*

"This takes me back to primary flight training," Padma said. "We'll enter downwind at twelve hundred feet."

"Roger that. Maintain speed of one-six-oh knots."

The plane continued its descent. It seemed as if time was flashing by on one hand and frozen on the other. Huang was drenched in sweat.

"Descending through ten thousand," Padma said.

Below them, Huang could see the white waves breaking on the rocky coast-line. He could feel each beat of his pulse.

There was no such thing as seat of the pants flying in China. There was no private aviation. You went to school, you studied, you trained, and eventually

127

you won your license. No one grew up flying small planes out of grass-roots air strips. This was the first time Huang had attempted a landing without communications with the tower. He felt an overwhelming urge to urinate.

"I've got an Airbus A380 on the port side," Huang said.

"Five thousand."

Huang took a deep gulp and throttled back on the engines. He saw San Francisco International Airport with its crossing sets of parallel runways ahead of him.

"Begin landing checklist."

Padma held the laminated check list in her hand. She began going over the items as Huang performed them.

"Two thousand feet." Padma sounded as nervous as Huang felt.

"Lowering flaps. Lowering landing gear."

They were approaching runway ten from a forty-five-degree angle.

"Twelve hundred feet."

Huang spoke into the microphone. "This is Asiana Flight thirteen-forty-one entering downwind for runway 10R." He only hoped that someone out there could hear him.

Their rate of descent slowed, and the plane pitched up. Huang trimmed the nose back to level, so he didn't frighten the passengers.

At eight hundred feet, he turned onto cross wind. Airliners just didn't do this kind of stuff. They normally approached the runway from straight in.

He stepped on the left rudder pedal and turned the yoke slightly to the left. The plane turned onto final approach and settled in.

Huang silently said a quick prayer to his ancestors and kept his eye on the runway. The four white stripes perpendicular to the runway flashed beneath him. The plane continued to settle. He pulled back tenderly on the yoke and slowed the rate of descent.

There was a slight jolt as the wheels touched the runway. "Reverse thrust," said to Padma.

Before Padma could move, the plane burst into a fireball as the Airbus A380 dropped on top of them.

Los Angeles's Koreatown is the most densely populated three square miles in the United States. From a decaying urban center, the area lifted itself up to become *the* place to go and be seen amid funky art deco buildings and modern steel and glass.

Kathy Nugyen's father, Chun, owned his own little piece of paradise. Rocky's Beer and Liquor stood at the corner of Eighth and Wilshire. His father opened the store shortly after arriving from Vietnam and Chun wasn't going to let it go down. Rocky's had paid Kathy's way through the University of San Francisco and law school.

The day started out as normal as any other day. Chun rolled up the steel gate guarding the store front and unlocked the doors. Almost immediately, customers dragged in.

The afternoon was its usual slow self. Chun took inventory and restocked shelves in anticipation of a busy night. By nightfall, his wife, Seong, joined him behind the register. Customers flowed into the store and the cash register rang.

Then the power went out.

"Damn. I'm tired of this cheap old building with bad electricity." Chun fumbled under the counter for a large Maglite flashlight. He kept it there as much for a weapon as a light.

He lit his way to the back room and checked the fuse box. None of the fuses were burned out.

"Chun," Seong, his Korean wife, called back to him in her sing-song voice. "I no think it our problem. All lights on street are out."

He stepped out onto Wilshire Boulevard. Horns blasted in the night. People walked around with stunned looks on their faces. "It like zombie movie," Chun tossed back over his shoulder to his wife.

The city was plunged into darkness. As far as he could see in either direction, the only illumination came from auto headlights.

Chun stepped back inside and took a key from the drawer below the cash register. He returned to the back room and inserted the key into his Honda 3500 generator. It sprang to life and the lights came back on in his shop.

"Don't know if this good or bad for business," he said as he returned to the sales floor. He checked under the counter for his sawed-off pump-action shot gun. It was loaded. He made sure a box of shells was handy. "We be ready for anything."

Sirens filled the night. Police cars and ambulances tried to make their way through the jammed-up streets. In many places, they had to drive on the sidewalk to make any progress.

Traffic signals were out, and there were collisions at nearly every intersection.

The small TV screen on the wall opposite the cash registers went to a special report. "The mayor declared a state of emergency," the good-looking young Latino man said on the screen. "A curfew has been imposed. He urges everyone to return to their homes or shelter in place. Do not go out on the streets."

Chun looked out his front windows. Obviously, no one was paying attention to the mayor's order.

Chun watched a group of young Hispanic men swagger down the middle of the street. They stopped at a Lexus driven by a good-looking blonde woman.

"Hey, mama, you wanna come out and play?" one of the men shouted.

The man pulled on the handle and found it locked.

He and his friends began to push on the car, rocking it back and forth on its springs. "C'mon out, little bird," the man cooed.

Chun saw the woman grab her cell phone. She screamed and threw the phone across the car.

The men continued rocking the car. It rose higher on each push.

Chun retrieved his sawed-off shotgun.

"You come out now," the Latino shouted, "or we'll make you sorry you didn't."

She didn't respond.

"Okay, Chico, torch this muthafucka."

A slight man popped open the gas tank cover and unscrewed the cap. He pulled off his T-shirt and stuffed it down the hole.

"You come out or we'll burn you out." The man pounded on the windows.

The woman screamed in panic.

"Torch it!"

The slight man pulled a lighter from his pocket and lit the shirt. It smoldered as the flame caught.

The gang retreated from the car. The woman popped open her door and began to run. She didn't get far.

"Whoa there, mamacita." The Latino man grabbed her wrist and pulled her towards him. "Let's see what we got here."

"Let her go!" Chun stepped out from the safety of his store into the street.

"Huh?" The Latino turned to see the source of the interruption.

Chun brandished his shotgun. "Let her go or I shoot."

"You're gonna hit her too, with that scatter gun."

"Maybe. But you'll hurt her if I don't shoot. Maybe it's better for her if I make it quick for her?"

"We can take him, Tony," one of the gang members said.

Tony was quiet for a second. "Nah, let her go. That skinny bitch ain't worth it."

The man released his grip. The woman stumbled forward, falling to her knees. Chun moved to her and helped her up.

"You come with me. Be safe in my shop."

He backed towards his door with the woman tightly in his grasp.

The gang members slowly turned away.

Seong waited breathlessly at the door. "Why you do that? You put us in danger."

"I can't stand by and watch," Chun said as he ushered the woman into the shop.

"You no think. They remember. They come back and burn store."

A pained look spread across Chun's face. "I didn't think of that."

The Lexus in the street exploded, the fireball reaching high into the dark sky.

The gang found some bricks and threw them through an electronics store window. Gang members broke away the glass still in the frame and jumped through the window.

From nowhere, people off the street followed. A woman reached for a box with a big-screen TV. A man shoved her to the floor and took the box himself.

Fire broke out in a building down the street.

Chun retrieved a chair from the back room and settled himself in front of his door, shot gun in lap.

Looters piled up in front of his store.

"You stay back. I'll shoot," Chun shouted.

Someone threw a brick through his window. The shattered glass was everywhere. Chun felt the cuts on his arms and face.

He reacted instantly and fired into the crowd. People screamed. Some ran in panic, trampling others in the crowd. Several more bricks flew towards Chun. He was hit in the shoulder.

He fired rapidly into the crowd, pumping after each shot to eject the spent shell and load the next. He felt no fear. If he could stand up to a column of North Vietnamese tanks, he could handle this.

The crowd ran in panic. He reached in his pocket to insert another shell into the magazine. A brick hit him square in the chest. The shell went clattering along the sidewalk.

Another brick hit him in the head and he went down. The crowd surged forward. He felt with his hands for his shotgun. He couldn't find it in the mass of running feet.

He heard Seong scream from inside the store.

CHAPTER SEVENTEEN

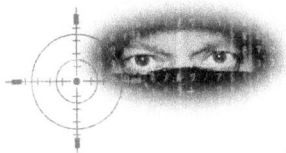

Jennifer Hussaini sat in the dark on the sofa with her legs up and back turned so she could look out the window. It was the second night she hadn't slept.

A light rain pattered against the glass. She held a half-empty glass of chardonnay in her hand and tears stained her cheeks.

Where is he? How could he not get in touch with us for two days? The kids were asleep. They didn't feel the absence of their father as acutely as she did. Something was wrong.

She picked up her cell phone and dialed 9-1-1.

"I'm sorry, but all circuits are busy. Please hang up and try again later."

Shit!

Devi, her next-door neighbor, told her traffic was impossible. With all the electricity out and the traffic signals not functioning, travel was a nightmare. Policemen were stationed under every traffic signal with their flashlights, but the flow was painfully slow.

Maybe Sam's caught in traffic somehow. But that doesn't make sense. He could walk to work, but why was his car gone? Did he have a meeting somewhere he had to drive to? Could it be that he couldn't get home?

Why hasn't he called? She shook her head. *Of course, he can't call. The cell towers aren't working. How many times have I tried to call him and couldn't get through?*

The sky to the east was turning a soft pink with the dawn's light. The start of a new day.

School was closed, so the kids would be home by themselves. No big deal. They'd done that a hundred times before. She had to get ready for her shift at the Kaiser hospital, but how would she get there?

It was in downtown Bellevue. She couldn't walk the twelve miles. Did she dare drive? Would she even be able to get close?

Her fear instantly turned to anger when she heard the lock on the door click.

She leapt to her feet and ran to the door as Sam opened it. Anger melted to relief.

"You're safe! Thank God. I was so worried." She threw her arms around his neck and clung on to him like a sailor to a life jacket. "Where have you been? Why didn't you call us?"

Sam pulled her arms from around himself and took off his jacket. "I was at work. We had an emergency with the power outage. I couldn't leave until it was resolved."

He looks so tired.

Sam tossed his jacket onto the sofa and went into the kitchen. "The phones were all down. We didn't have time to find a solution."

Jennifer felt a lump of ice in her gut. "Ari's home. Devi told me he came home last night, and he's home tonight. Doesn't he work in your group?"

Sam's eyes flared, and he stared at her for a moment. "Why do you question me? If I tell you I was at work, I was at work." He reached in the refrigerator for a bottle of water. The light did not come on.

"Sam, I'm not questioning you. I just want to understand." She placed both of her hands on his chest. "We were so worried. Not hearing from you for two days."

"That is my work. That is how I put this roof over your head, how I put food on your table, how I buy obscene American clothes for you and your daughter." He shoved her away from him. "I'm tired. Exhausted. I need to rest."

He walked towards the bedroom. She followed.

"Can't you at least explain to me? To us?"

He turned on her with fire in his eyes. "You need to know what I tell you. Nothing more. You are a woman. Allah says to be subservient to me. You don't ask questions; you obey orders."

She froze, her eyes opened wide. "Sam ... Samir ... I thought we worked through that before we got married. I'm an American woman. I converted to your religion, but I'm not your chattel."

Sam flung his water bottle across the room. "You whore!" he shouted. "You decadent American. We will follow the Quran in this house. 'Men are the protectors and maintainers of women, because Allah has made one of them to excel the other.' You will all do what I say. You will not question me."

Jennifer took a deep gulp and stood toe to toe with him. "Get those ideas out of your head. Neither Amira or I are second-class citizens. Get over it. You treat us as full-blown people or you get out. I can't stand this anymore."

His backhand sent her crashing into the bureau, sending small perfume bottles and combs flying.

"You will follow Allah's will. Don't even think about leaving. If you leave me, I'll hunt you down. I'll kill you both, you fat American cow and your slut daughter."

Jennifer slipped to the floor and fought back tears.

"When this is all over, we will go back to Syria. We will be welcomed as conquering heroes."

"Wh ... when ... what is over?"

"You'll see."

. WHITE HOUSE SITUATION ROOM: Everyone jumped to their feet as the President entered. Tall, with a full head of gray hair and piercing blue eyes, Jackson Ford was Hollywood's Central Casting's vision of the perfect President.

The President scanned the room. The white walls were down, hiding the array of high-tech equipment. His National Security Council stood around the mahogany table in front of their black swivel chairs. Aides for each of the principles stood around the perimeter of the room.

"Good morning, all," President Ford said as he took his seat at the head of the long, mahogany table. The back of his chair was six inches higher than the other seats in the room. "Let's skip the preliminaries and get right to business. What the hell's going on?"

The momentary silence was eerie. The whisper walls absorbed most of the sound, leaving an other-worldly hush in the room.

"Mr. President." Rebecca Clarke, the National Security Advisor, took the lead. "We have an unprecedented situation on the West Coast."

The President gave her a harsh glance.

"All power west of the Rockies went down. Power companies are working hard to find the source of the problem, but it appears to be a software glitch, not a hardware failure."

"And all of the other issues CNN is reporting?" the President asked.

"Sewage systems in five major cities have failed. All traffic control systems are down."

"Air Traffic Control is down over the entire country," General Robert Waldorf, Chairman of the Joints Chiefs of Staff, interrupted. "The military is up and running, but all civil aviation is grounded."

"And Atlanta?" The President drilled his National Security Advisor with his look.

"Ah ... As far as we know, the problems in Atlanta are not related to the West Coast events. It appears that an independent group of hackers took Atlanta down."

And so it went. Disaster after disaster plagued the struggling region.

"When are we going to be back up and running?" the President asked.

"There's no way of telling," The secretary of defense answered. "It could be a couple of days, it could be a few months. Until we find the problem, we won't know how to fix it."

The President shook his head and exhaled. "Okay, what are we doing about solving the problem?"

"We've got all of our best people working on it," the SecDef replied. "NSA and the Cyber Command have made it their number one priority."

The President thumbed through his Morning Book and looked to his right at The vice president. "Violet, let's turn to the bigger question. Why? Why did this happen? Is there a presence behind it?"

"I think that's a question for the DNI. Mr. Johnson?"

Hiram Johnson, the Director of National Intelligence, cleared his throat. The small man with wire-rim glasses and a bad combover flipped through the pages of the Morning Book. "We don't know yet. We don't have enough intel. We're scouring all of our sources, but we don't have enough facts yet to give a good opinion." He flipped his book closed.

"Whoever has the wherewithal to stage an attack like this, if it is indeed an attack, must be limited to a few players," the DNI continued. "No single hacker in his mom's basement could cause all of this damage. It could be Russia, China, or North Korea; they all have the capacity. The UK could, but they would never move to harm us. I can't believe Germany has developed its cyber-warfare capabilities enough to do this. Iran may or may not be on the list." He stopped to take a deep breath. "Then we have to look at non-government organizations. We've been getting reports on the growing capabilities of ISIS. We have bits and pieces, but nothing to indicate they're capable of this. There are private corporations with the technical knowledge to do such a thing, but I can't think of any way such an attack would benefit them."

"What about the Russian Mafia?" the Vice-President asked.

Johnson nodded and took a deep breath. "I suppose they might be on the list. They certainly have world-class hacking capabilities, but, once again, I ask what does this profit them? How do they make money by sending our country back to the stone age?"

"Well, dammit!" The President slammed his hand down on the table. "This is an act of war. We need to know who's behind it. This kind of attack warrants a military response. George?"

The secretary of defense straightened his tie. "Mr. President, the military stands ready to respond to any acts of war. As soon as we have identified a target, we can strike within twenty-four hours. Less if it's in the Middle East, Russia, or China. We have the capability to wreak havoc on their systems electronically, or we could respond militarily."

"Mr. President," the Veep interjected, "this could lead to all out warfare. It could be World War Three."

"I don't want a war any more than you do, but we can't allow anyone to attack us and let it go unchallenged."

"If I were a betting man," The secretary of defense cut in, "I would put my money on Iran. They have the capability and they hate us. They've sworn to destroy Israel and there is a substantial portion of their population who would love to see us on our knees."

"George, you can't be so cavalier with your opinions." The Secretary of State, a tall, thin, cadaverous man, answered. "The truth is, we just don't know at this point. We need more information. I strongly caution against making any threatening advances until we know for certain who this enemy is. I'm sure every other technologically advanced country on Earth is ramping up their defenses."

'I want answers and I want them now." The President's voice rose to an unusual level. "I want the military to go to DefCon 2. I want the terror threat level to be raised to red."

CANDLES LIT the courtyard and the smoke from incense was thick. Abiba knelt in front of the stone altar and placed corn, fruit, and a small dead bat on the ground-down stone. She placed straw on top of the food, then small pieces of kindling.

"Waaq, all powerful, father of all things. It is I, Abiba, daughter of Delilah, come to beseech your help." She lit a wooden match and set her offering smoking.

She looked up at the dark sky filled with stars. "Dearest Waaq, I know you are up there. I know you hear me. Your faithful servant begs succor and understanding of this suffering. I beg of you, show me he who would crush all but the daylight from our lives. Please, show me the man I seek."

A light breeze swirled around the courtyard. The smoke in the offering flared into a blaze of flame. Smoke filled the open space.

<The man you seek is here. He is near you.>

"Oh spirit-man. Come forward. Speak to me."

Abiba opened her eyes. In the twisting flame of her offering, she saw the form of a dark man.

<Why do you seek me out?>

"I need to know why. Why are you raining these pestilences on us? What have we done?"

The man grew in stature until he towered over Abiba. *<You are part of*

138

the Great Satan. You had a choice. You didn't need to be here, but you chose to come. You chose to forsake the religion of your fathers. You are as bad as any of the Americans. You do not follow the true path of Allah.>

The path of Allah? Was that what this is about? "Spirit from over the seas, where are you now. How can I find you?"

<Why do you want to find me?>

"I want to talk with you. To convince you that I have not forgotten the ways of my fathers. You must believe me. You are hurting many, many people. You must give me the key to stop the pain."

<Stop the pain? The pain has just started. Today, we ran a test, to prove we could bring the Great Satan to its knees. What we did to the West Coast, we will do to all of America. We will pull the entire decadent Western Civilization back to the Middle Ages. They will see that their only hope is Islam. Only when the world is one loyal caliphate, will peace come.>

The man faded into the smoke. Abiba stared into the diminishing flames. She saw the man walking up a concrete path towards a massive apartment complex. Grass and trees surrounded the buildings.

Then the smoke swirled away, and the courtyard was clear. Abiba rose from her knees, said one last prayer and departed.

DR. ELAINE JEFFERSON, the head of the National Security Agency's Tailored Access Operations (TAO), took a rare moment to sip her tea and enjoy the peace before the chaos of the day broke loose.

TAO, one of the world's elite cyberwarfare teams, never slept. Elaine pushed a button on her desktop and the glass walls of her office turned opaque to shut out the bustle of the office.

Her office was a blend of tradition and tech. Paneled in dark mahogany, the wall panels could slide up to reveal an array of flat-screen monitors. The monitor on her desk gave her instantaneous access to everything from spy-satellite images to the daily lunch menu at Ray's Diner on Twenty-seventh Street.

She needed to catch her breath. Too much was happening too fast. She put both elbows on her polished mahogany desk and held her head.

Someone hacked the country's most secure networks and unleashed chaos. It was her job to prevent this from ever happening. She had failed.

A jackhammer pounded in the back of her head. Her vision closed into a narrow tunnel. She took a hydrocodone pill from the bottle in her desk drawer, then started to put the bottle back. *Oh, what the hell?* She opened the bottle and withdrew another pill. She popped them into her mouth and chased them with hot tea.

"Elaine, got a minute?" John Archer, her number two, knocked softly at her door.

"Uh ... yeah, John. What you got?"

John entered the room and closed the door behind him. "You got the 'cone of silence' on?"

The Cone of Silence, an electronic jamming application, made it impossible for anyone outside the room to hear their conversation.

Just the sound of John's voice tore the growing crack in her brain apart. She pushed a button on her desktop. "Okay."

"We have a break." John took a chair opposite her desk. "We know who unleashed the CryBaby virus. These guys are good. Real good. It's taken us days, but we've finally managed to work our way through their maze of servers to locate the source."

"Well ...?" She knew her reply was curt, but she couldn't help herself.

"It came from Seattle." John sank back into his chair.

"Seattle? But ..."

"Yeah, I know." A big smirk spread across John's face. "I was sure it was a foreign terrorist, too. But it could be a domestic terrorist, or just a bunch of crooks trying to make an illegal buck."

The pain started to creep back into her head. "Uh ... so, who is it? Where did it come from?"

"That's the weird part." John shook his head. "It came from a company called Flaherty & Associates. They're a PI and cyber-security firm. They have a good reputation. We have a file on the principals. They're both clean as a virgin's dreams. Never any trouble up to now. As a matter of fact, they're both sort of vigilantes, crusading against the evil in the world."

Elaine rubbed at her temples. *Will this pain ever go away?* The only thing that helped was to lie down in a dark, quiet room. "So, why would two goodie-two-shoes go rogue?"

"I've got my contacts at the Bureau working on it. So far, we know that there are two registered owners of the company. A Catrina Flaherty and an Eduardo Higuera."

John pulled a paper from the folder in his hands. "Flaherty was a police woman, filed a major sexual harassment suit against the Port of Seattle Police Department. Won. Started her own detective agency."

He read down the page. "She brought Higuera on board about six years ago. He's a computer whiz. They opened a cyber-security department and have been doing pretty well. This Higuera's already on the Bureau's radar. Apparently, he was involved in a terrorist incident in Canada a few years ago and has been up to his ears in the drug wars in Mexico. Every time he goes down there, some drug lord or another ends up dead."

A steady tap-tap-tapping drove Elaine to the brink of madness. *Won't it ever stop?* She looked down and realized that her fingers were tapping the end of her ink pen on the desk. "So, I repeat, why would they go rogue?"

"We don't know … yet."

"Is the Bureau bringing them in?"

"They're gonna watch them for a while, see if anything else turns up. They'll tap their phones and monitor all their transmissions. They've got a twenty-four-hour tail on Higuera. They can't find Flaherty. We'll hack their network and examine every file on their system. Whatever they're up to, we're gonna know before they do."

CHAPTER EIGHTEEN

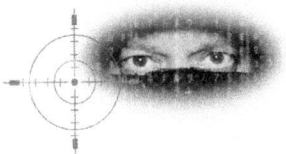

"He hit me!" Jane's face reddened with fear and indignation. "The bastard hit me. I'm done. I can't live like this anymore."

Two days after the massive power outage, life started to return to normal. Emergency power was on in necessary facilities. The police answered 9-1-1 calls and hospitals were up and running. Fires still smoldered throughout the city.

Mary Beth sat on the love seat across from Jane in Catrina's office. Jane's Dooney and Bourke purse sat on the glass-topped coffee table. Mary Beth looked at the woman. "Are you ready to get out?"

"He disappeared for two days. Then when I asked him where he'd been, he hit me. Then he took off again, and I haven't seen or heard from him since."

Mary Beth moved over and put an arm around Jane's shoulder. "I'm so sorry . . ."

"We can't stay there anymore." Tears flowed from Jane's eyes. "He's not the same man I married, and I have no idea what he might do next."

Mary Beth ran over Catrina's battered-woman checklist in her mind. "We can get you and the kids out. We can take you to a safe place."

Jane shook her head. "You don't understand. He has friends. They'll hunt us down. There's no such thing as a safe place."

The September sunshine filtered through the vertical blinds, throwing shadows that looked like prison bars on the wall. "Don't worry. We've done this before. We have a whole organization ..."

"That's it. He has an organization. I never thought of it before. I've seen him with these men. They're all tough-looking, Middle Eastern men. He says that if I ever leave, they will hunt me down and kill me."

"We have safe houses, Jane. Let me worry about that. We can even move you out of state if we need to, get you and your children new identities. We've been doing this a long time. We know how to handle it."

"WE HAVE another postcard from Mrs. Flaherty, Mr. Ted." Abiba danced into Ted's office with the mail. Nothing cheered her more than hearing from Catrina.

"Where is she this time?" Ted asked.

"This looks like Venice. That girl sure gets around."

Hmmm ... Ted thought, *Venice. Hong Kong. Australia. How far does she have to run to escape her ghosts?*

"GADZOOKS!" Bear's roar filled the office. "Hey, Hero, you gotta see this."

Ted sprang from his chair and ran to Bear's bullpen. "Whatcha got?"

"Look at this," the furry red man said. "We're being hacked."

"No shit."

Bear turned his monitor so Ted could see it. "I found this this morning. I've been working all day trying to find out where the hackers came from."

Ted knew that Bear enjoyed his moments, so he let him go on.

"Don't you want to know?" Bear asked.

"Hell, yeah."

Bear turned in his swivel chair to face Ted and crossed his arms. "The NSA."

Both men stared at each other for a long minute. Ted broke the silence. "The NSA? But ... why? Why would the NSA be interested in us?"

"I can't tell you, Kemosabe." A grin spread across Bear's face. "But we've got to shut them down."

Ted pondered that for a moment. "No ... I think ... I think we need to welcome them in."

"Huh?"

"Yeah, that's it." A big smile spread across Ted's face. "I want to know why they're hacking us. What they're up to."

"Are you talking about building a honey pot?"

Ted nodded. "Can you tell when they first hit us? How long they've had access to our system?"

Bear turned back to his keyboard and typed in a command. "Looks like last night, around eleven o'clock. This was just a first jab. They didn't get into much of anything."

"Perfect. Set up the honey pot. We'll build a whole virtual network for them to browse around in, we'll put the stuff there we want them to see. When we find out what they're looking at, we should be able to tell why they're hacking us."

Bear ran his hands through his bushy hair. "Gotcha. Jody and I'll start on it right away. You figure out what kind of stuff you want us to give 'em." Bear leaned back in his chair with his hands behind his head. "This is better than the movies."

Ted strolled back to his desk lost in thought. *Why us? What do we have that they want? Are they investigating an individual or are they just fishing? Don't they need a court order for this? Oh my God! Maria. I better call Chris.*

Ted reached for his smart phone, clicked on an icon and said, "Chris Hardwick." In a moment, Chris answered.

"What's up, amigo?" Chris's voice almost gave Ted a shred of hope.

"Hey, Chris. I got a problem. I need some legal advice."

"You know," Ted heard a tinge of irritation in Chris's voice, "anyone else I'd charge four hundred dollars an hour and tell them to make an appointment. So, what's the problem?"

"We're being hacked. The NSA broke into our system last night."

"The NSA? Holy shit. What have you guys been up to?"

Ted took a calming breath. "That's what I want to find out. I can't help but believe it has something to do with Maria. Don't they have to have a court order or a search warrant to do this?"

There was a momentary pause. "I'm not up on all the niceties of the Patriot Act, but if they say it's a matter of national security, they can do just about anything they want. I'll check with the courts in D.C. to see if they've issued a warrant, but I'll bet good money that there's no warrant. If I remember correctly, they can get the attorney general's approval to administer a search without informing the party to be searched. That allows them to get into your network, browse around, and not tell you they're there."

"What ever happened to the Land of the Free?" Ted leaned back in his chair and scratched his head with a pen.

"Nine/eleven happened."

"Crap. So they could have the legal authority to do this?"

"They could. Or they could be ignoring the legal system all together. Under certain circumstances, the NSA can conduct these searches without going to the courts."

Ted shook his head. "So, we're powerless to stop them?"

"Let me do some digging, Ted. I'll get back to you this afternoon or tomorrow."

Ted hung up his phone and nodded his head.

"How's the honey pot coming?" Ted asked as Bear walked past his office door.

Bear walked back and stood in the doorway. "Making progress. Jody's set up the virtual servers and is doing a great job with firewalls, proxy servers, and such. They won't know they're not in our real system. We need to get the list of files and applications that you want them to see."

"I'm working on it. I'll have it to you in an hour."

It was less than an hour when Ted heard, "Hey, Hero."

He hated it when Bear called him that.

"Look at this."

Ted ran back to Bear's desk.

"These guys got sloppy. Who do they think they're dealing with?" Bear turned his monitor again so that Ted could see it. "They left a key hole open for us."

"No way. No one's that stupid."

Bear swiveled to face Ted. "Yep, yep, yep. These idiots held the hole open so they could get back in easy. That means we can go through it to get at them."

"Well, stop wasting your time. Get in there." He waved a hand towards Bear's monitor.

It didn't take Bear long to start feeding Ted data.

After hours of pouring through meaningless documents, Ted had enough. He got up, stretched and headed for the break room. *Any of those bagels left from this morning?*

There were. He toasted a cinnamon-raisin bagel, slathered it with peanut butter, brewed himself a cup of coffee and headed back to his desk.

A new folder full of NSA files was on Ted's desktop. He clicked and opened File Explorer.

More useless trash, until he stumbled upon a file labeled "CryBaby Virus – Top Secret."

Oh well, in for a penny, in for a pound. He opened the file. It challenged him for a password.

He opened his Cracker application and let it hack the password for him. He'd been fine-tuning this password cracking app since he first wrote it all those years ago at YTS Security. In a few seconds the light on his dashboard turned green and the file opened.

"Holy shit." It was that day's report on the CryBaby virus. They still didn't know how it was spreading, but they knew where it came from. The NSA created the virus as one of many cyberwarfare tools they built. But someone got a hold of the code, modified it, and turned it loose on the world.

No way. According to the report, Ted Higuera unleashed the virus and was collecting millions of Bitcoins in his account.

CHAPTER NINETEEN

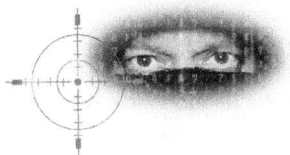

"Abiba, I need you to come with me." Mary Beth strode through the office with purpose. She entered Catrina's office—she still couldn't think of it as hers—and opened the locked desk drawer.

The ugly black Glock 17 semi-automatic pistol lay in the drawer, along with a box of cartridges, and an expandable steel night stick. Mary Beth stared at the contents. She'd never carried a weapon on a job before.

Do I really need it? Is there any possibility the husband will return?

She stood, dropped her head and ran her hand through her short, brown hair. *He's a man of habit. He never comes home during the day. But, on the other hand, he has broken all his usual patterns. Now staying out for days at a time, showing up at random in the middle of the day.*

"You wanted me, Mrs. Mary Beth?" Abiba asked.

Mary Beth looked at her hulking frame in the doorway. *I don't need a gun. I have Abiba.* "We're doing an extraction. Contact Jackie's House. Tell them we're bringing in a woman and two teenaged children. Tell them it's a priority one and the husband is violent with her and threatened her ... their lives."

"Yes, ma'am." Abiba turned back to her desk.

"And one more thing." Mary Beth shoved the drawer shut. "I need for you to go with me."

The dark-gray Land Rover that Ted nicknamed The Batmobile was covered in dust. It hadn't moved since Catrina disappeared four months earlier. Catrina had the gray beast built for her by the same company that builds presidential limousines. It would take an anti-tank missile to stop it.

Mary Beth pushed the button on the fob and the engine roared to life, a second push and the doors unlocked.

She opened the rear hatch and checked her supplies. The first aid kit, pillows, and blankets rested in plastic bins. Jane's kids were twelve and fifteen. No need for the teddy bears. She gulped and took a deep breath, then opened the secret compartment in the floor.

A sawed-off shotgun sat in the green velvet covered compartment along with a bandolier and two boxes of shells. *Catrina never went anywhere unprepared.*

Mary Beth shuddered and closed the compartment. *What if I get stopped by the police? That gun's illegal. I could get arrested.*

She shut the back hatch and opened the driver's door as Abiba arrived.

"I've never been on an extraction before." Abiba slid her considerable bulk into the passenger seat and the Batmobile settled onto its springs. "What do I have to do?"

Mary Beth checked the rear-view mirrors and put the SUV into reverse. The bumper camera showed her nothing was behind her. "Hopefully nothing. I'm praying the husband doesn't show up. If he does, you may have to intimidate him a little."

"I never fought a person before…"

"Don't worry about it." Mary Beth looked at Abiba from the corner of her eye. "Who, in their right mind, is going to mess with you?"

They took the I-90 floating bridge across Lake Washington and I-405 north towards Redmond.

"When we get there, get the kids into the car. I've already made all the arrangements. They should each have one bag packed. I'll get Jane, then we get the hell out of Dodge."

Abiba stared off towards Mount Rainier and hummed quietly to herself. "Yes, Mrs. I just hope you are right."

Traffic wasn't bad and in forty-five minutes they pulled into the massive apartment complex.

"With a car park this size, you'd think we could find a …" Abiba said. A strange look came across her face. "I know this place. I've seen it in a dream."

They drove the massive lot a couple of times before Mary Beth double parked in frustration. "We're not going to be here long. We'll be gone before a tow truck can get here."

Mary Beth led Abiba to apartment number 1601. Jane answered on the first knock.

"Mary Beth. Oh, Abiba, you came, too." She held her position in the door. "I think I've made a mistake. I don't think we should leave."

Mary Beth took a half-step back and her eyes widened. "You what? What's happened?"

"It's the kids. They don't want to go. They don't believe me about their dad. They don't think there's any danger."

"Do you want to let us in?" Mary Beth asked. "We'll attract attention standing out here."

Jane stepped aside, and they entered a picture-perfect apartment. No speck of dust would dare settle into this antiseptic environment.

"Where are the kids?" Mary Beth asked.

"Amed is in Amira's room. They both refuse to pack."

"Let me talk to them," the big black woman said.

"Are you packed?"

"Yes." Jane turned and lifted her one suitcase.

"Okay, here's what we're going to do. We don't have much time. Your husband could come back at any moment, and we don't want a confrontation." Mary Beth picked up the suitcase. "We're going to get the kids packed and get out of here. If they won't pack for themselves, then you grab a couple of bags and pack for them. We have to move fast."

Mary Beth followed Abiba to Amira's room. She found her friend standing in the doorway with the two young people sitting on the bed.

"We're not leaving," the girl said. "We're not leaving our friends. Amed is on the football team. He can't miss practice."

"You don't understand, child." Abiba's calm voice seemed to float across the room.

She took two steps and was beside the bed. She got down on one knee and held the girl's hand. "Your father is a good man, but he's done some bad things.

He hit your mother." Abiba pointed to the bruises on Jane's cheek. "Look at her face; she deserves better than that. We don't know if he will do it again, if he will hit you, or worse, but we're not going to wait around and find out."

"Who the fuck are you anyway?" Amed shouted.

"Amed. Language!" Jane jumped in.

"My name is Abiba Iskander. This is my boss, Mary Beth Henderson. We both have been in this situation. Mrs. Henderson's husband beat her and her children. My husband and mother-in-law wanted to have my daughter circumcised."

"Circumcised?" the girl asked.

"Yes. Female circumcision. The shaman cuts out her clitoris with a sharp stick. That way she will have no sexual desires and will never cheat on her husband."

Amira pulled her knees together. Her face went white. "Mom? Do people really do that?"

Jane sat on the bed next to the girl. "Yes, sweetie. Unfortunately, they do. In some tribes in Africa it's common practice."

"Yuk." Amira leaned close to her mother and Jane put her arm around her.

"Listen, you two. We don't have much time." Mary Beth picked up the duffle bag on the floor and tossed it to Amed. "We have to get going. We don't know when your father will be back."

"I'm not going anywhere. He's never been bad to me." Amed crossed his arms.

"Mom?" the girl looked at her mother with pleading eyes.

"Honey, both of you, listen. You know I work in the emergency room. I see this all the time. Women being brought in who have been severely injured by their husbands." She got up off the bed and took both of Amira's hands to pull her up. "I work with these people. As often as not, we see the same women come in again and again. Too many times, their last trip is to the morgue. We can't wait around for that to happen to us."

"But, Mom, he's never hit me."

"He never hit me either, until today, but he's been increasingly cruel. How do you feel when he calls you a whore? When he says he'll abandon you if you get pregnant? He's even threatened to kill you if you get pregnant."

Amed tossed the duffle bag aside. "That's too bad, but she's a girl. He's never been like that to me."

"Amed." Mary Beth sat on the bed next to him and looked in his eyes. "You're in even greater danger. Did you know that almost every man who killed his spouse came from a family where there was abuse?" She stopped to let that sink in.

"I know you're only twelve but look ahead if you can. Someday, you're going to meet a girl and get married. You'll have children and settle into a normal life. Do you want her to live in terror? Do you want your kids to be afraid of your touch? That's the kind of thing that happens to boys who grow up in an abusive home. We have to get you out of here now to break the cycle."

Amira picked up her duffle and, without a word, started packing it.

Amed glared at Mary Beth. She picked up his duffle off the bed and offered it to him.

He bit his lip and looked at her a moment, then took the bag.

"That's great. Jane is there anything else you need?"

Jane shook her head. "No. I've thought about this for months, and I know what we need. And by the way, my name isn't Jane."

"I know, Jennifer." Mary Beth smiled at her. "We're investigators. We know all about you and all about your husband."

"I don't think you know all about my husband." She looked into Mary Beth's soul. "He has friends. He meets with them. They seem dangerous. I can't prove anything, but my intuition tells me that they're up to something horrible."

They all froze when the door slammed shut. "I'm home, everybody," Sam shouted.

"Oh my God." Jennifer's hands went to her face. The children froze.

"Get everything together. We need to walk out of here as a group." Mary Beth grabbed Amira's bag. "Let's go."

Mary Beth led, followed by Jennifer, Amira and Amed, then Abiba.

"What's this?" Samir looked stunned. "Who are you? Where are you going?"

"I'm Mary Beth Henderson." She flashed her badge at him. "This is Abiba

Iskander. We're licensed private investigators. We're taking your family to a safe place."

"A safe place ..." Sam's eyebrows knit together, and his mouth dropped open. "Like hell. You're not taking them anyplace. They are my family. I say where they go."

"You don't seem to understand, Mr. Hussaini." Mary Beth's heartbeat took off like a drag racer. "They've asked for our help. They live in fear of you. We're taking them to a safe place. I suggest you consult a lawyer."

"Lawyer, hell!" Samir reached for his wife's arm.

From out of nowhere, Abiba's huge hand clapped over his wrist. "You do as Mrs. Henderson says, mate."

"Let go of me." Samir wrestled his hand free and looked up at the huge woman.

She was at least six inches taller and outweighed him by more than a hundred pounds.

Samir moved towards his children. "Amed, Amira, go to your rooms."

Abiba formed a wall between the man and his offspring. "I suggest you back off and leave us alone. If you persist in trying to interfere, it will be the biggest cockup of your life."

Mary Beth's eyes widened. Abiba was the kindest, gentlest person she'd ever met. Was she really threatening violence? Isn't that what she brought her for?

Samir's face turned red and his breathing sped up.

Jennifer grabbed Amed's hand and dragged him out the door. Mary Beth hustled Amira along while Abiba stood in the door, facing Samir until the family was clear.

Samir dashed around Abiba in a swift move and grabbed Amed.

"Abiba! Sit on him," Mary Beth screeched.

Abiba grabbed Samir by the shoulders, spun him around, and threw him on the couch.

"Keep your hands off of me, bitch." Samir tried to get up.

Abiba dropped her bulk on top of him, and he exhaled a great breath.

"You can't do this." He squirmed and tried unsuccessfully to break free.

"You stay where you are, mate. This'll only take a minute."

Mary Beth opened the tailgate and got the bags settled while the family climbed in the car. By the time Mary Beth slid into the driver's seat, Abiba jumped up and ran for the car.

"Let's get out of here." Mary Beth put the SUV in gear and pealed out of the lot. "I learned a big lesson today."

"What's that, Mrs. Mary Beth?"

"I thought about bringing my gun, then I knew that we had the shotgun in the car but didn't take it. I remember something Ted told me: It's better to have them and not need them than to need them and not have them." Her heart still raced, and her breath came in short gasps.

Abiba reached over and patted her hand.

"You did what you needed to do. I'm knackered. Let's get these lovely people to Jackie's House and go home."

CHAPTER TWENTY

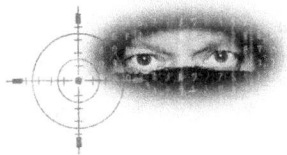

"NO!" Assad al Allah, the Lion of God, kicked the table, sending it and its contents flying.

The men in the safe house cowered. They'd never seen their leader in such a foul mood.

"I will not let it happen." Assad's fist clinched, and his eyes bulged. "I want to kill them all. Every last one of the infidels."

"But Assad." A small man with bright eyes stepped up to his leader. "Does not the Quran teach us that we are to convert the unbelievers? We are to kill only those who do not choose the way of God."

"No. Never. Not Now." Assad spat on the floor. "They have gone too far. I wish death to them all."

"We have opened a secure chat line with Syria, Assad," the tall, thin man said and got up from the computer workstation. They had a virtual private network that even the U.S. intelligence agencies couldn't penetrate.

Assad visibly shook as he attempted to get back under control.

"Why? What has happened?" the small man asked.

"It is nothing. We have a mission to complete." Assad sat at the workstation and typed on the keyboard:

<We have completed our testing. We are ready for the main event.>

He received an immediate reply. <*Congratulations on your great triumph.*>

Assad typed: <*Thank you. It is Allah's will.*>

He took a deep breath. He was under control now. He had to concentrate on this conversation. It would change the world.

Characters appeared on his screen. <*When will you be ready to launch your attack on the whole country?*>

<*We are ready now. We have just one item to fix.*>

<*Are you sure the Americans do not know of our plans?*>

Assad smiled. This was one of his proudest achievements. <*I'm not worried about the NSA or the FBI. I have given those fools a primrose path to follow. Our biggest threat now is an infidel called Higuera.*>

<*Who is this Higuera?*>

<*A very smart hacker. He knows how we imbedded the viruses and has written code to kill them. We must neutralize him before we launch Operation Sirocco.*>

<*Do we need to dispatch someone?*>

Assad shook his head slowly. <*No. We can take care of him ourselves.*>

He felt a glow of joy fill his insides as he pictured getting rid of the pesky American.

<*What about an American military response?*> the leader half-way around the world queried.

<*We have anticipated that.*>

There was a long pause.

<*And?*>

<*We have already run our live test.*>

<*???*>

<*When the Americans launched their attack on Sharyat airbase in Syria, they sent sixty missiles. Only fifty-nine reached their target. Number sixty was our test bed. We have trimmed the claws of the tiger.*>

Assad leaned back in his chair and accepted the cup of tea from his subordinate. He would repay the Great Satan for their mistreatment of him and all his kind.

PRESIDENT JACKSON FORD did not run for the office to sit underground with a group of military advisers and plan World War III. The Marine Corps helicopter ride across the Potomac River didn't do his aching head any good. He hadn't slept in two days. It would do him a world of good to snap a couple of generals' heads off.

The President looked around the room. Mahogany paneling went halfway up the walls, the upper half of the walls were painted white. The long table in the center of the room was dark mahogany to match the wainscoting. He closed his eyes and listened. The buzz of side conversations filled his ears.

He waited for the meeting to start, rubbed his forehead and squeezed his eyes shut, and for a moment tried to forget that he was in the underground The National Military Command Center, commonly called the War Room, located under the Pentagon and its parking lots in sub-urban Arlington County, Virginia. The president resented that his secretary of defense had an elevator in his office that brought him down to this level. Why did he get it so easy?

"Ladies and gentlemen, let's call this meeting to order." This was the SecDef's territory. The President was just an honored guest. "We're getting power back up in some parts of the West Coast power grid. Most of the sewage plants are back online. Now I want answers. Was this an act of war? Of intentional sabotage?"

CIA Director, Rebecca Wilson, a tall gray-haired woman, leaned back in her chair. "Mr. Secretary, our analyst believe that this could only have been caused by an outside entity. This catastrophe was not the result of system errors or mechanical malfunction. So, yes, the answer is it was an act of war."

"Okay, Becky, but who's the attacker?" the President asked.

"Our best theory is that it came from Iran." The CIA director bounced her heel on the floor under the table. "Since we decertified the non-nuclear pact with them and imposed new sanctions, they've been in a feisty mood. They have the capability to do this. They want to hurt us, cripple us so they can deal with the weak Brits and French. They know the Ruskies will be on their side."

The President stared at her for a moment. "But do we have one hundred percent rock solid evidence they're the perpetrators?"

"We're still working on that, sir. We have boots on the ground in Tehran running down leads."

"Let's not jump the gun, sir." The secretary of state cleared his throat. "Our sources say that North Korea most likely perpetrated this event."

"What do you have?" The President's head throbbed.

"Everyone knows that Kim Jong Un lost face when you backed him down on developing nuclear weapons. He's dying to strike back. They've been working on this capability for years. He even bragged they could take down our power grid."

Lots of theories but no evidence. What to do?

"Hiram, what's your opinion?" The SecDef asked the Director of National Intelligence. Who did it?"

The DNI took a deep breath. "We tend to agree with Becky, I'd put my money on Iran. They have the means and the motivation. I can't picture anyone else with the technical capabilities who'd benefit from this sort of attack."

The President held his eyes tight shut and bowed his head. Absolute silence held the room. "We need to do something. We need to show the world that we won't stand for this kind of an attack. After nine/eleven, Bush took decisive action that shut down Al-Qaeda. We can do no less."

An excited murmur swept the room.

"George," the President said to the secretary of defense. "I want a plan for a retaliatory attack on Iran first thing in the morning. Becky, I expect your report with incontrovertible evidence we can present to the UN."

MASTER SERGEANT BILL STOKES had the most boring job in the world. Day after day, hour after hour, he sat at his console in the Defense Information System Agency in Fort Meade, Maryland, and monitored the Department of Defense systems to make sure no one hacked in.

The DoD systems were, for the most part, cut off from the rest of the world. There were only a few closely guarded access points to the Internet to prevent outsiders from getting in. The firewalls and security around those access points were virtually impenetrable.

Sgt. Stokes sipped his coffee and worked on a sudoku puzzle. Nothing much ever happened. The best minds in the world constantly built and upgraded the security. The chances of him ever having to follow the emergency break-in protocol were practically nil.

The red light on his console flashed and a klaxon alarm sounded. He dropped his puzzle and focused on his monitors. Throughout the system, servers were shutting down due to overloading.

CAPTAIN TOM JENKINS'S back and shoulders ached from the responsibility he carried. His Burleigh-class destroyer carried enough ordinance on board to level a city the size of Manhattan. With the situation in the Middle East, he had been called upon to launch attacks before. His ship had participated in the attack on Syria a few months ago.

Tom was a devout Christian man. The fact that this order, even though he was carrying out a direct order from the President of the United States, would kill innocent people made his stomach feel like a grinder. He was a warrior and killed when necessary for his country but detested the loss of life.

He held in his hand the print-out of the coded message from the Commander in Chief. His ship and seven other U.S. Navy ships in the Persian Gulf received orders to attack Tehran.

Tom stood in his state room looking out over the waves. He was a career naval officer, a graduate of Annapolis. He would never consider not following an order. But this ...

He followed the news. He accepted that his superiors had access to intel he'd never know. But they were attacking a city of almost nine million people. The combined might of eight guided-missile destroyers would virtually level the city. How many would die? Why? The collateral damage list could run into the billions.

"Captain, Communications." The voice burst over the speaker on the bulkhead.

Tom pushed the button. "Go ahead, Sparky."

"Sir, all communications are down. I can't raise anyone."

"I'm on my way." Tom was out the door before his voice transmitted over the intercom.

His cabin being only a few steps from the bridge, the captain was on deck in moments.

"What do we have, XO?"

His executive officer stepped up. "All communications have gone down. We can't even talk to ships we can see."

"Do we have semaphore contact?"

"Yes, Sir."

This could be the excuse Tom needed. He hesitated a moment. "Pass the word to the rest of the squadron. The attack will proceed as scheduled." He turned to the small man at the next console. "Combat Command, prepare to launch missiles."

"Aye, aye. Prepare to launch missiles."

Tension overtook the bridge. Everyone's senses went to high alert.

"Missile Bay," the Combat Command Officer spoke into his microphone, "you are cleared for launch."

Fire exploded from the missile tubes and the long, white rockets charged forth into the night sky. In seconds, their little wings extended, and the missiles hugged the terrain as they flew.

"All tubes launched successfully, Sir." CCO said.

"May God help us all."

And maybe God was listening.

"Sir," the CCO checked his console. "None of the missiles have established contact with the ship."

"What? Double your signal strength."

"Not working. We have no control over those birds, Sir."

Thirty seconds is the blink of an eye, but also a lifetime. The captain and the bridge crew watched the white trails of the missiles as they carried their load of death toward Tehran. But they were out of control; could they be certain that they were headed for Tehran?

"Get Fleet on the line ..." Then the captain realized he had no contact with his superiors.

A yellow fireball lit the night sky. Then another and another. Tom stopped counting when all of the missiles from his ship were accounted for. The explosions continued until every missile launched blew itself up.

The Tomahawk Cruise Missile was programmed to contact launch control as soon as it cleared the launcher. If contact was not established within thirty seconds, the missile self-destructed.

CHAPTER TWENTY-ONE

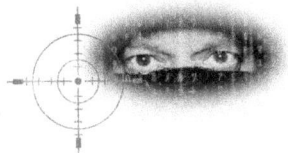

Bear wasn't sure why he was obsessed with whoever released the CryBaby virus. He and Ted had discovered the Denial of Service (DoS) against the Defense Department quite by accident. Something in his gut told him they were related, but he really didn't know how. It really wasn't his business. No one paid him to hunt down the culprit, but he had to know.

Once they figured out how the CryBaby virus spread, it was child's play to determine the method used to launch the DoS attack. It used the same mechanisms as CryBaby. But, it was a time bomb sitting in the Windows source code. Bear needed to learn how it was activated.

So far, he liked working for Ted. Ted didn't question his intentions or tell him what he could and couldn't work on. Bear felt Ted realized he was smart enough to plot his own path. Who knew what he would turn up? It wouldn't be the first time some unintentional discovery made someone buckets of money.

He sat at his workstation and tried trick after trick to find out how the dangerous code got slipped into the operating system. His stomach alarm went off. The clock said eight o'clock. He hadn't been home for dinner in a week. Nancy was always good about this kind of situation, but when the mystery was solved, he would have to take her on a fancy vacation somewhere.

Maybe an Alaska cruise ...

He read through the reports line by line. He could be incredibly anal when necessary. Emails, text messages, phone calls—he looked at any way someone, or something, could access their network. The emails were the most likely. They could contain hidden code or a come-on to go to some website. Once the recipients clicked the button, they were toast.

Bear grudgingly admitted that Ted did a good job training his staff and setting up security. Everything was done the way he would have done it. Maybe the kid did learn something from him.

Something activated the DoS attack. Bear believed that it was sent out in a universal email that the DoD servers would hear. If it went out to all Windows computers, it had to have come into their system too.

Jackknife software allowed him to see all the code in the header and footer packets on each email that arrived at Flaherty & Associates. It was mind-numbing work looking at line after line. A lesser man (or woman) might lose his (or her) concentration, but not Bear. He focused his considerable mental abilities on looking for the one black sheep, the one piece of information that didn't belong.

It was past midnight before he found it.

"Eureka!" He leapt from his chair and did a little happy dance. "I've found you. I've got you dead to rights, you clever bastard."

It was an email that came from a server in Germany. He worked backward to see where the email originated. Before it got to Flaherty & Associates, it bounced off a server in Ireland, then Nigeria, then, what was this? It originated in the States. The IP address—it couldn't be. He had hundreds, maybe thousands of IP addresses stored in his brain. He knew this one. He entered it in the Finder software Ted wrote to trace IP addresses back to street addresses and phone numbers.

The phone rang five times before he heard Ted's sleepy voice. "Hello?"

"Ted, Bear. I've got 'em. I've found where the virus started. You're not going to believe this."

"Huh, what virus?" Ted was obviously fighting to wake up. "What are you talking about?"

"I started out tracking the CryBaby virus. You know that. It was spread by a Windows patch, but something bothered me. I recognized some of the code. We determined it was originally written by the NSA."

"Why are you calling me in the middle of the night with old news?"

"Listen. It didn't feel right. I'd seen that code somewhere before. When I was in high school a bunch of my buddies and I thought it would be fun to see if we could hack the most secure network in the world."

"Huh ..."

"The Department of Defense. We found some cyberwarfare applications they'd written."

"Okay."

"Ted, you know the denial of service attack that hit DoD the other day? The one no one's supposed to know about?"

"Yeah." Ted seemed suddenly interested.

"We found that code years ago when we hacked in. This attack was perpetrated using their own code. And I just found out where it came from."

"Okay, I'll bite."

"It came from a Seattle network owned by Flaherty & Associates. It was sent out under Ted Higuera's account."

———

TED ARRIVED at the office in record time. He inhaled coffee and followed Bear's logic. It was true—he launched the denial of service attack on the DoD.

He walked back to his office and plopped down in his chair. The office still held Catrina's first partner, Jonathon Jackson's dark cherrywood furniture, but it was "Tedized." On the wall opposite his desk was a giant print of a Spiderman picture signed by Stan Lee and Johnny Romita. On his brag wall, instead of degrees and photos of Ted with celebrities, there were pictures of Mexican Revolutionaries, ghetto kids, and American football players.

How did they do it? Why did they use my account? I'm a nobody.

There was zero possibility that some terrorist singled him out for a scape-goat.

And that was the problem. The NSA wouldn't sit on their asses on this one. They had to find out how they were hacked and who did it. *But why me? They could have used any one of billions of accounts to launch their attack, why me?*

"Ted, got a minute?" Mary Beth apparently arrived at work early too.

167

"Uh … I'm trying to work out a problem. Why? What's up?"

Mary Beth didn't wait to be invited in. She sat in the chair across from Ted's desk. "We did an extraction yesterday. By the way, Abiba was marvelous." Mary Beth pried the lid off her paper coffee cup. "There's something about the husband that bothers me that I think you should know."

"Okay." Ted focused his mind on her story. "Whatcha got?"

"The husband is named Samir Hussaini."

Ted held up his hand. "Wait a minute. I know that name." His mind pulled up the relevant data. "I just met with him."

"I would say his activities are suspicious. I don't know what he's doing, but it isn't good."

Ted pulled a yellow tablet and pen from his desk. "What's he up to?"

Mary Beth took a gulp of her rapidly cooling coffee. "Well, he's gone from home for long periods of time. He won't tell his wife where he's been. His presence is unaccounted for. He's not at work; I checked."

"Uhuh … "

"He won't let Jennifer listen in on his phone calls."

"Jennifer?"

"His wife, our client. Her real name is Jennifer Hussaini. She says he has two cell phones. When he gets a call on the one she doesn't recognize, he always clears the room. He won't give her that phone number."

Ted scribbled like crazy on his note pad.

"He can be perfectly fine," Mary Beth went on. "He can be the ideal husband. Then he gets a call on the secret phone and goes crazy."

Ted looked up from his notes. "Any idea who he's talking to?"

"No. It's a burner phone. He's a chameleon. He blends in with American society, he has an important job at …"

"Microsoft."

"Ah … yeah. But he still holds the old country values. He's very strict with his family. He wants America to come under Sharia law."

Ted leaned back in his chair and tented his fingers. "That makes him and about a million other people in this country."

Mary Beth sat her cup on Ted's desk and stared into his eyes. "Ted, we extracted the family because I was afraid he would do an honor killing. This guy's half a bubble off level. I think he's capable of violence. I thought you should know about it because he's a big IT guy. He works for Microsoft. That comes under your domain, doesn't it?"

"Uh ... yeah." Ted closed his eyes and nodded

"I don't like to be prejudiced, but this worries me." Ted looked up at the picture of Spiderman on his wall. "Sam's the head of the Windows security team at Microsoft. He has old fashioned values. I gave him the patch to fix the Wall Street virus. He wants Sharia law. He's a danger to his family." The wheels whirled in Ted's head. "Oh my God."

Ted picked up the phone and pushed the buttons. "Bear, Ted. Listen, do we know if Microsoft has deployed our fix for the Wall Street virus yet?"

Ted listened a moment. "Well find out. Now."

He turned back to Mary Beth. "There was just a major hack against the Department of Defense. Bear traced the source of the hack back to us, me. Someone set me up to take the fall."

His face tightened. "At Microsoft, someone injected the Wall Street virus into their Windows source code. When I gave the fix to Sam, he said he would put it in the next release. If he hasn't done that, I have to ask why?"

Mary Beth nodded.

"He doesn't fix the virus, then somehow, I attack the Department of Defense. It all smells fishy to me."

CHAPTER TWENTY-TWO

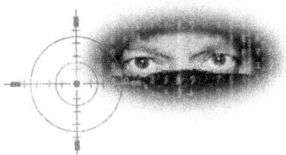

The savanna grasslands stretch on forever, occasionally sprinkled with flat-topped umbrella thorn trees. The grass tears at Abiba's knees as she runs. Something is out there, something stalking her.

It's only steps behind her. She looks over her shoulder, nothing. She hears the heavy breathing. She must find a place to hide, but the rolling grasslands offer no sanctuary.

The tree! The umbrella tree is her only hope. If she could reach the tree, she would be safe.

She runs faster, faster than she'd ever run before.

Then she heard it. The unmistakable roar of a lion. It's right behind her. She looks over her shoulder, nothing there. Then the roar again.

She makes it to the tree. She claws her way up into the branches. She is safe.

At the base of the tree, a massive lion, in all his grandeur, roars up at her. It paws the tree. Abiba shrieks in fear.

The huge lion sinks his front claws into the tree and pulls himself up. Then he anchors his rear claws and reaches higher up the tree. Inch by inch he comes closer.

The lion reaches the lower branches. He pauses and stares at her. Then he roars again.

Abiba moves out further onto the branch. It bends under her weight. How far out could she go? If the lion comes out on the branch after her, would it break?

The lion stares at her. Not making a sound, the big cat slowly inches his way out on the branch. Abiba holds her breath.

Does he dare come all the way out?

The branch creaks and sags. The lion must be twice her weight.

The lion stops and looks at her. There is fire in his eyes.

"I am the Lion of God," the cat says and transforms into a man.

Abiba screams. She knows this man.

She sits up in bed, covered in sweat and tangled in her sheets. Tears flow down her face. Now she knows. She must tell Ted, to save him.

THE SAFEHOUSE WAS DARK, empty but for the Lion of God. Assad might as well have been a statue. He sat staring at his computer screen, not moving. The only sound was the constant tick, tick, tick of the old wall clock.

The infidel is close. He knows who I am.

How could Assad stop Higuera? He'd already tried to kill him three times, but each time the slippery Mexican escaped. What next? He told his superiors he would handle it.

His computer beeped, and a red light flashed on his screen.

They've taken the bait.

Maybe the NSA would do the job for him. Assad had set a flag in the Flaherty & Associates' system to let him know when law enforcement found his little surprise. They were hacking into the system at that moment.

He punched a few keys on his keyboard and a window opened. He could see every keystroke the Feds made.

They've got him. They know he hacked the Department of Defense. A smile spread across Assad's face.

Now is the time.

He'd been waiting for this moment for weeks. When the clumsy government agents finally found his trail of bread crumbs, he was ready to act.

With a few key strokes he initialized a program that gave him access to the FBI's databases. Grinning from ear to ear, he began to insert records.

First, the miserable infidel had been charged with rape in high school. The record was expunged because he was a football star.

Next, he inserted records detailing Higuera's illegal hacking when he worked at YTS security. He hadn't been charged because the law hadn't caught up with the technology and what he did was not illegal.

Next, he made the Mexican responsible for the hidden cameras his crew installed in the women's locker and shower rooms at the Olympic Club. He put the videos on the Flaherty & Associates network when he hacked their system.

Mr. Higuera, you pervert. When they find these records, they will know you are a menace to society.

Finally, he slipped the source code to the CryBaby virus into Higuera's source code control system. It would appear as if the infidel had worked long and hard to perfect the virus.

Days earlier, Assad had opened an account at the Grand Cayman National Bank in Higuera's name. It was time to fill it.

He hacked into Wells Fargo and Bank of America, then moved large sums of money to Higuera's account. He hid the transaction well enough that the average auditor would miss it, but the super-sleuths at the NSA were sure to pick up the trail.

Goodbye, Mr. Higuera. You were a worthy adversary.

***.

Ted awoke to the sound of pounding on his door. He looked at the clock. Two a.m. *What the hell?* Throwing a robe over his boxers and T-shirt, he pulled the nine-millimeter Glock from the drawer in his bedside table and lurched towards the door.

He looked through the peep hole.

Abiba!

He threw open the door. "What the hell are you doin' here at this time of night?"

"Mr. Ted, I have to talk to you," she said. Her normal cultured British accent was slurred with fear.

Ted stepped back to let her in. She wore an unbuttoned coat over a sheer night-gown; it left little to the imagination. *She's not dressed for making social calls.*

She breathed heavily after running from the parking lot and up the stairs to Ted's apartment. "Mr. Ted, I know who is launching these attacks."

"Sit down, Abiba." Ted motioned towards the black leather couch. "Can I get you somethin'?"

"Water, please."

Ted took a few steps to his kitchen and pulled a Britta pitcher out of the fridge.

Ted handed her a glass of water, then sat on the matching recliner at right angles to the couch. "Now, what's this all about? What gets you out of bed at two in the mornin'?"

Abiba gulped a drink of water between gasps for breath. "It came to me in a dream. I know who is causing all the trouble. He calls himself the Lion of God."

"Uh ... Okay, who is he? Where do I find him?"

"You already know him, Mr. Ted." Abiba's breathing slowed down. "He is the husband of the woman we rescued the other day. His name is Samir Hussaini."

Ted scratched his chin. "Okay, I suppose it might make sense. When I met him, he seemed like a decent American citizen, but Mary Beth tells me he's mad at America. He certainly has the technical skills to pull something like this off. No one could do this by themselves, though. He must have helpers."

Abiba reached over and took both of Ted's hands. "I don't know about that, but it is he. He came to me in a dream. He talked to me and said that this was just the beginning. The West Coast was a test. Soon he will launch an attack on the whole country. He said when he was thorough, America would be back in the Stone Age and the Great Caliphate would rise."

"Abiba, you know we can't take a dream to the FBI. We need to have proof."

"I don't know about proof. I just know that it is Samir Hussaini."

ASSAD SAT at his desk in the safe house and stared into space. *Hiquera. He's the key. He knows too much. He must be stopped.*

"Daaim, I need you."

The tall, thin man came to Assad's desk.

"Yes?"

"Can you burn a specific house or apartment?" Assad's left little finger twitched.

Daaim considered for a moment. "If he has a newer microwave. I need to get the IP address. I suppose if I had the target's name and ID information, I could hack the manufacturer and see if he registered his microwave. If he did, I can get it.

"Make it so. We're looking for an infidel named Ted Higuera."

In fifteen minutes Daaim was back at Assad's desk. "It is too easy. The manufacturer never thought anyone would want to get at that information. There is practically no security on their system."

"You have what you need?"

"Yes. I can start the fire immediately."

Assad's eyes sparkled. "Do so tonight, after Higuera has gone to sleep."

"HE'S COMING after me because he knows we're onto the Wall Street virus." Ted sat in a swivel chair in the computer room, talking to Bear. "If we work hard enough, we can probably trace it back to him."

Bear grinned. "If he comes after you, he's going to have to go through me first."

Ted reflected at how easily Bear had accepted Abiba's dream unmasking the villain. Maybe he was coming around. "Okay, here's what we have to do. We need to scour the Internet, find out every scrap of information we can about Samir Husseini."

Bear pushed back from his workstation to look Ted in the eye. "Let's get together after lunch to see what we've learned."

Ted returned to his office and went to work. First, he used NetPI to do a thorough background search on their target. Then he did a general Google search. Next, he targeted specific networks. Schools, government records, honor societies.

The hours went by quickly.

"Mr. Ted." Abiba's voice came over the intercom. "It's after noon. Do you want me to order something in for you, or are you going out?"

"Ah … Thanks, Abiba. No, I don't have time to go out. Order me a California burrito and a Coke."

"Yes, sir."

It took Ted a moment to get back into dogged PI mode. Where else could he search? How about church records. Husseini was a member of a mosque in Redmond.

The mosque records didn't reveal much. He was married there. He had two children. He was a model citizen. *Crap!*

Abiba returned with his lunch. It sat there, uneaten.

His phone rang. "Hi, Bear, whatcha got?"

"I've gone about as far as I can go. Do you want to get together and compare notes?"

"Sure."

A moment later, Bear entered the office, laptop in hand.

"Let's sit at the work table." Ted stood and walked over to the table carrying his unopened burrito.

Bear sat and opened his laptop. "I've gone through the guy's school records. He's impressive. IQ must be off the charts. He got straight A's at Harvard in computer science, then aced his master's at MIT."

"There's no question he's smart, and good, to pull off the stuff he's been doing."

"I've got his immigration documents right here. He came over on a student visa at eighteen. He met Jennifer Griswold in college and got his green card." Bear turned his laptop so Ted could see the screen. "He moved to Seattle after he graduated from MIT. Got a job at Microsoft and quickly moved up the ladder."

"Yeah, I got his wedding at the Redmond mosque." Ted scratched at his head with his ink pen. "I can't find a trace of anti-American sentiment."

Ted looked at his friend. Bear had deep dark circles under his eyes. He looked wan and tired. "When's the last time you got any sleep?"

"I haven't been home in three days."

"Shit, man. At least you could take a shower. You're beginning to get GAPO."

"GAPO?"

"Gorilla Arm Pit Odor."

"Back to the subject at hand." Bear tugged at his fiery red beard. "He's Mr. Clean. I couldn't find a complaint that could be traced back to him."

"It's almost as if he's too perfect. Too clean. No one is that good."

Bear leaned back in his chair. "Unless..."

"Unless?"

"Yeah, unless he was purposely trying to stay off the radar. As if he wanted to get lost in the great melting pot."

"Are you saying that he's some kind of sleeper agent? That he came over here all those years ago just to put this kind of attack in motion?"

Bear laced his fingers behind his head and looked up at the ceiling. "Think about it. Twenty years ago, we didn't have the technology to cause this kind of damage to our economy. Sure, we had computers, but we weren't anywhere as connected as today."

"Okay."

"So, what if someone sent him over here to get educated? To worm his way into our infrastructure. To find ways to hurt us. Over the years, as technology advanced, he saw his chance. He learned all he could and found a way to strike against us."

Ted reached back to his desk to get his Coke. "So, he's Superman. He still couldn't have done all of this by himself. No one's that good. How long would it take you to hack the NSA and modify their virus? How long to hack the sewer systems, the air traffic control, the cities' traffic systems?"

"Okay, so he has a whole crew. They have to be located somewhere. They have to have an office, a place to work."

"Right. That's our first line of attack." Ted wrote on his yellow pad. "We need to trace his utility records, his bank accounts. Find any way we can to locate his office." He unwrapped his lunch and took a bite of the cold burrito.

"Next thing up," Bear said, "is to find out how he hacked into our system. I thought our security was iron clad. How did he get around it? How did he use your IP to launch the DoD attack?"

"Third item." Ted held up three fingers. "We need to get into his files, to see if we can find anything incriminating."

"He works at Microsoft, Hero. They probably have better security than we have. They're virtually unhackable. We'd need a court order to get to his files."

Ted grinned. "Where there's a will, there's a way."

TED'S APARTMENT on Capitol Hill was dark and quiet. Ted lived alone and hadn't had time to ask anyone to look after his apartment for him.

As the clock on the microwave flipped over to 1:00 am, the machine turned itself on. It ran for several minutes.

The microwave was an over-the-stove model with a vent fan included. It sat and hummed. Smoke began to appear from the wooden cabinets around the appliance. Then the box exploded, and flames broke out in the woodwork.

It didn't take long for the fire to spread throughout the kitchen, then leap to the living room. Oil paintings on the walls and the drapes were the first to ignite. Furniture quickly followed.

ABIBA SAT at the reception desk at Flaherty & Associates and thumbed through an old copy of *People* magazine. *I don't know why people are so consumed with what celebrities had for lunch or who is sleeping with who.* But she didn't put the magazine down,

The buzzer for the front door rang. She was happy with the remodel. It would take a Sherman tank to get through the door.

"Flaherty & Associates, how may I help you?" she asked into the intercom.

"FBI. We need to see Ted Higuera."

She sat up and paid attention. On her five-inch monitor she saw an FBI badge held up to the camera.

"Uh ... come on up ... " She pushed the button to unlock the door.

She buzzed Ted's office on the intercom. "Mr. Ted. You better get out here right away."

Moments later two men in Brooks Brothers suits came through the office door.

"FBI," the first man said in his command voice. "We have a warrant."

"What's this all about?" Ted asked as he approached Abiba's desk.

"Ted Higuera, you're under arrest for treason."

"Treason?"

Before Ted had a chance to react, the FBI man spun him around and slapped on hand cuffs.

"You have the right to remain silent. Anything you say ... "

"Abiba, call Hope. Call Chris." And then he was shoved out the door.

Abiba sat, mouth open, too stunned to react.

Mary Beth came running from her office. "Abiba, what just happened?"

"Ah ... two men. Two men just took Mr. Ted."

"Who were they?" Mary Beth's shriek had the volume of a 747 taking off.

"Um ... um ... FBI. They said they were from the FBI. They showed me a badge."

Mary Beth took a calming breath. "Why? What did they say?"

"I don't ... know. Wait. They said he was under arrest for treason."

"Treason?" Bear came running up. "That's all? They didn't say anything else?"

"No, they just took him. Wait a minute, he said to call Miss Hope."

Mary Beth reached for the phone on Abiba's desk and dialed Hope's number from memory.

CHAPTER TWENTY-THREE

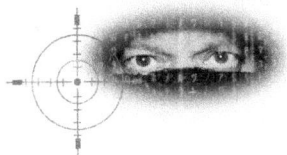

The lunch rush was busy, but Hope's crew handled it with their usual alacrity. Her restaurant was a well-oiled machine. Hope said goodbye to a group of businessmen and headed towards the office. She stopped to pick up a cup of coffee on the way.

She sat at her chair and took a breath. She was still recovering from her injuries and hadn't yet built up the stamina to work a full shift.

Her cell phone rang. The dial tone played "She Works Hard for the Money."

Catrina? No one had heard from Catrina since she took off on her around-the-world trip.

"Hello, Cat!" The excitement showed in her voice. "Where are you?"

"Hope, this is Mary Beth. Something's happened."

Her skin felt prickly, and her body temperature went up. "Mary Beth? What are you talking about?"

"It's Ted. The FBI just arrested Ted. He said to call you."

All of the air went out of her lungs. "The FBI? ... Why? What happened?"

"We don't know. They just came and took him away."

Hope was up, pacing her office floor. Her breath was fast and shallow. Her heart felt like it would burst from her chest. "FBI. Chris. I've got to call Chris."

ASSAD SAT at the desk in his safe house. His hair matted and reeking of sweat. He hadn't been home in days.

As soon as the operation is over, I'll go after my wife and kids. Nothing will stop me from getting them back. Then there'll be hell to pay.

The ringing burner phone broke him out of his reverie. "Yes?"

"You were right. The FBI picked up Higuera today."

Assad slapped his phone shut and shouted. "Yes! It is all coming together. With Higuera out of the way, the operation can proceed."

"LADIES AND GENTLEMEN," the voice on the TV said. "We interrupt your regularly scheduled programming to bring you this special edition of *News Front* with Janet Peterson."

The scene on the TV went from *The Young and Restless* to the studio where *News Front* originated. Janet Peterson sat behind her ebony news desk.

Janet looked directly into the camera. "We're getting breaking news in from around the country. It appears as if the United States is the victim of a full-scale cyber-attack. Our first report was of cell phones going down all over the country."

She held up a smart phone. "There is simply no signal available. We've checked out the phones and they are operating properly, but every cell tower in the country is down."

Over her shoulder, the screen showed a woman turning on a water faucet.

"Water systems are failing across the nation. It appears that the software that controls the water systems in every major city has failed. Workers are trying to restore service through manual intervention, but the systems are so automated that it may take some time."

She held her hand to her right ear. "We have a new story coming in right now." She was silent for a moment. "We are taking you to rural Pennsylvania for a special report."

The picture on the screen changed to a countryside view with two trains, going in opposite directions, derailed over the quiet landscape.

"Thank you, Janet." The camera focused on a silver-haired man. "This is Tom Westmoreland coming to you live from just outside Monongahela in Washington County. At approximately one-twelve pm Eastern time a freight train collided with an Amtrak passenger train coming the other way on the same track. We don't have a casualty count yet, but it's massive. I've already seen the coroner taking away at least three body bags."

The TV screen split with Janet on one side and Tom on the other. "Tom, do we know yet what caused the accident?"

Tom ran his hand through his luxurious silver mane. "Janet, officials are not willing to talk to the media at this point. They've scheduled a press conference for five pm Eastern time. In the meantime, my sources tell me that this is the result of a total collapse of the routing system. I'm getting reports from other parts of the country of incidents like this one."

"Tom," Janet asked, "could this be part of a nation-wide cyber-attack?"

"There's no way to say for sure at this point, Janet, but if I had to bet, I'd put my money on a terrorist attack of some kind."

The screen went back to one picture of Janet. "I'm getting new reports of more problems in the transportation industry. Trucks all over the country are going out of control or refusing to start. If this keeps up, the entire transportation system will shut down."

She put her hand to her ear again.

"Now a new report from Suzanne Sullivan in Cincinnati."

Suzanne stood in front of a huge grocery warehouse.

"Janet, we have new problems here, and from what I can understand, all over the country. Commercial refrigeration is failing. Here at the AFP distribution center, the manager tells me that all refrigeration and freezers have shut down."

The scene shifted to stock footage of the inside of a grocery distribution warehouse with seemingly endless aisles of freezers.

"All of these commercial installations are controlled by remote companies who monitor the equipment and send out repair crews when necessary. According to the manager here, the control centers seem to have crashed."

"What does this mean to the consumer, Suzanne," Janet asked off screen.

"Chaos. With trucks and the railroads down, they can't deliver food to the local stores. With the refrigeration failing, the food supply will run out in two or three days. These attacks, if they are attacks, have effectively put our entire food chain supply in danger."

"What's your recommendation?"

"There are going to be massive runs on the stores. I recommend that our listeners get to their nearest supermarket and stock up right now. I would go so far as to say that if this situation continues for more than a few days, we may see food riots in the streets."

The pictures switched back to Janet Peterson. "Thank you, Suzanne. I'm sorry to cut your report short, but we're getting a live feed from the Oval Office. Ladies and gentlemen, President Jackson Ford.

The screen showed a gaunt, tired-looking President Ford sitting behind his desk in the Oval Office.

"My fellow Americans," the President began. "Today, the United States of American has come under attack as surely as it did at Pearl Harbor or Nine-eleven."

This is his Roosevelt moment. Janet thought.

"I want you to rest assured that this attack will not go unpunished. When we determine who the perpetrators of this cowardly attack are, and you can rest assured that we will, we will punish them to the full extent of the law.

"I made an announcement a couple of months ago that any cyber-attack on the United States of America will be responded to with nuclear weapons. This is our first challenge. You can be sure that we will respond and that this will never, never happen again."

Janet Peterson appeared again on TV screens all across America. "There you have heard it. President Jackson Ford stated that the United States will invoke the Ford Doctrine and retaliate with nuclear weapons. Wait a minute, we're getting in another report."

She looked off beyond the cameras.

"Okay, this is just in. An American citizen has been arrested for launching this attack. We don't have a name yet, but sources close to the investigation say he is a cyber-security expert from Seattle, Washington."

HOPE PACED the floor in her office, constantly wiping the tears from her eyes and wiping her nose with a tissue.

Chris burst through the door. "Hope, I'm sorry it took so long. I was in court when I got your message ..."

"Chris!" She threw herself into his arms. They felt so strong and comforting. She nestled her head against this chest. "They've taken Ted ..."

"Wait a minute. Slow down. Who's taken Ted. Where did they take him?"

Hope sank down on her office chair. "The FBI. No one knows where they took him or why."

"They can't just whisk a citizen off the street. They must have a reason, a warrant." Chris pulled out his cell phone.

"Can you do something?"

"Let me think." Chris began pacing. "I need to call my investigator. But Ted's my investigator. Who do I call? Cat's gone."

"How about Mary Beth? She's taking over for Cat." Hope blew her nose again.

"I don't know her very well. I've seen her around Ted's office. I don't know how good she is."

"Well, do SOMETHING!"

Chris selected the number on his phone. "Goddammit." He slammed down his phone. No signal.

He was silent for a moment. "Wait a minute, maybe this might work."

He brought up his text messaging screen and typed.

<Mary Beth. This is Chris Hardwick>

< the office is in chaos. ted's been arrested.>

<I know. I need to know what happened. Why did they arrest him? Where did they take him? What are the charges?>

Chris waited impatiently while his screen said "Mary Beth is typing."

<We don't know anything. The FBI just barged in and took him away. We're working on what happened now. I have some contacts at the court house that may be able to help. I expect we'll have some answers in a couple of hours.>

< Good. See what you can find out.> He put his phone back in his pocket.

"What?" Hope asked.

Chris let out a long breath. "I read somewhere that even when the phone system is down, you can send texts. They run on different networks."

Hope grabbed Chris and hugged him tight.

"She says they're already on it. She's working with her contacts to see what's going on. So far, nobody knows anything. She'll keep digging until something turns."

Hope buried her face in his chest and sobbed.

"Listen, I know someone at the FBI. We went to law school together. Maybe she can help."

Hope's head popped up. "She?"

"Yeah. I dated her at the U. I'm pretty sure she'll help me."

Chris opened a new chat window.

"You still have her number on your contacts list?" Hope asked.

"I save everyone's number. You never know when you might need them." Chris began typing.

< Barb, this is Chris. ... Chris Hardwick.>

<Chris Hardwick, as I live and breathe. A voice from the past.>

< It's been a while. I need a favor. This is really important.>

Chris winced as Barb answered.

<You need a favor. And you come to me? I still haven't forgotten the last time you asked me for a favor. I ended up going to Planned Parenthood for that.>

Chris gulped a breath down.

< I've said I'm sorry. But that's water under the bridge. I need help and I figure that if anyone can help me, it's you.>

He was relieved to see her answer.

<What kind of trouble are you in, Mr. Hardwick?>

<A friend of mine, Ted Higuera, was arrested today.>

Before he could finish, he saw that she was typing.

<HIGUERA!!!!!!>

<He wasn't taken to county jail. No one at the FBI will talk to me. Could you find out why he was arrested and where they took him.>

<You don't ask for much. That's only the number one topic on every-one's mind today.>

<Why?>

<He's the terrorist, Chris. He's the one who launched the cyber-attacks.>

"No! No, no, no." <That's not true. It can't be true. I know him. He's as loyal an American as you can find.>

<The evidence says otherwise. Okay, listen, I'll look into it as best I can. I don't have much hope for him though. I'll do what I can.>

<Thank you. I owe you one. I'll buy you the biggest steak in town the next time you're in Seattle.>

<Okay—make it a lobster.>

<Anything you want. Bye.>

Chris turned to his fiancée. "She says she'll look into it. It might take a little while. She doesn't want to appear too anxious."

Hope rose and pulled Chris back into a hug.

He tenderly wiped the tears from her eyes. "Don't worry. We'll find him. We'll find out what's going on."

At that moment, his cell phone chimed.

It was from a David Jones.

"You know David Jones?" he asked Hope.

"Yeah, I think he's the guy Ted just hired."

Chris opened the text.

<I know you're working on getting ted released. got some information 4 u.>

Chris pulled out his pen and a small notebook from his suit coat pocket. <What do you have?>

<Ted is on private flight to St. Elizabeth's Hospital campus in Anacos-tia, in southeastern D. C.>

Chris let out a deep breath <Whoa. They haven't even charged him yet.>

<they arrested him under Patriot Act. didn't have to get a warrant. The Attorney General signed the order.>

"The Patriot Act. Holy shit. Ted loses all of his rights under the Patriot Act." Chris thought for a moment. <How did you get this information?>

<You don't want to know.>

CHAPTER TWENTY-FOUR

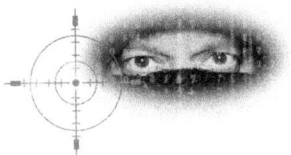

The Alaska Airlines Boeing 737 settled onto final approach for D.C.'s Reagan National Airport. Chris always flew Alaska and Boeing. He was a Seattle boy and wanted to keep his travel dollars in the local economy.

In the morning he would appear in federal court to plea a writ of *habeas corpus* to get Ted's release. He knew it was a lost cause. Under the Patriot Act, anyone could be picked up

without a warrant and held indefinitely if the government deemed them a potential threat. In the

name of security, the country gave up constitutionally guaranteed rights.

An Uber driver delivered him to the Embassy Suites near the convention center. Not a luxurious place, but good accommodations for the money. After checking in, he went to his suite and logged into the Wi-Fi. Scanning his emails, he found nothing to help his case.

Next, he made another Google search on the Patriot Act, looking for something to use.

THE FOLLOWING morning Chris stood in front of the Federal Courthouse in Washington, D.C. It was an unremarkable building, compared to all the flagrant classical architecture in the city. Built of white marble, it was a rectangular building with no ornamentation, totally modern.

A half-dozen news vans jammed the curb. Reporters shoved microphones in his face as he made his way to the building.

"Mr. Hardwick, is your client …?"

"No comment."

He always pictured himself walking up the fanned-out steps of the portico to the Supreme Court when he thought of practicing in D.C. Instead, he walked into this plain building and checked in through security.

Chris found his way to the courtroom and took a seat behind the defense table. Thomas Whitlock, Esq. and a nicely dressed young woman entered and took the other table. Chris saw the anger in Whitlock's eyes.

He's pissed that I'm wasting his time.

A crowd of people fought for seats in the spectators' section. Reporters jostled with sketch artist for the best views.

The clerk and bailiff entered through a side door.

"All rise," the bailiff said.

As the occupants of the courtroom came to their feet, a short, squat man with a bad comb-over in judge's robes entered the room.

"Federal court in and for the District of Washington, D.C. is now in session," the bailiff said. "The Honorable William Tate presiding."

Judge Tate took the bench. "You may be seated." He turned to the clerk. "What do we have on the docket for today?"

Chris looked up and to the right. The computer screen in his head brought up numerous articles about Judge Tate. *Crap. He's a real hard-liner. We don't stand a chance.*

The clerk rose and handed the judge a folder. "*Higuera v. the United States.*"

Chris rose. "Christopher Hardwick for the defense."

"Thomas Whitlock for the people, Your Honor." Whitlock sank back into his chair with a sneer on his face.

"Mr. Hardwick, I see that you are challenging the Patriot Act."

Chris rose again. "Your Honor, we are challenging the right of the United States to hold an American citizen prisoner without charges and without access to his attorney. This is simply a writ of *habeas corpus.*"

"Mr. Whitlock?" The judge turned towards the prosecutor's table.

"Your Honor, this is a total waste of the court's time. It is spelled out explicitly in the Patriot Act that the government may hold any person, citizen or not, for an unspecified time if the government deems that person a threat to national security."

"Mr. Hardwick?"

Chris took a breath. *This is it.* "Your Honor, there is no evidence my client is any threat to national security. He is an upstanding citizen, a business owner, and a valued member of his community. There is no rational reason or evidence for his arrest in the first place."

"What the defense doesn't acknowledge," Whitlock opened his hands to the court, "is that this is classified information. The government is under no obligation to present the evidence to anyone. If the attorney general deems a person a threat to public safety, then he has the authority to detain them." Whitlock turned to the prosecution table and accepted a paper from his second chair. "We are wasting the court's time here. It was found in *Duncan v Kahanamoku* that *habeas corpus* may be suspended under extraordinary circumstances."

"What are the extraordinary circumstances?" Judge Tate asked.

Whitlock looked at Chris, holding his lips together. "It's classified."

Chris stood. "Your Honor, in both *Hamdi v Rumsfeld* and *Hamdan v Rumsfeld*, the Supreme Court ruled that even when being tried for terrorist/insurgent activities, American citizens have the right to file a *habeas corpus* petition."

The judge shook his head. "I'm sorry, Mr. Hardwick, but this is an easy ruling. Under the Patriot Act, the government has the right to detain and hold any person they deem a threat to national security. This arrest has been certified by the attorney general of the United States."

Chris looked at the court reporter. "Your Honor, I understand there is a bit of a split in precedent. I'd like to make an adequate record to send this up on appeal."

"Okay."

"The Fifth Amendment states, 'No person shall be held to answer for a...'"

"The court is well aware of the Fifth Amendment, Mr. Hardwick."

Whitlock chuckled under his breath. "Counsel, the people are also aware of the Constitution."

"Really? Then where's my client's due process? He's being deprived of his liberty without a hearing?"

"Under the Patriot Act, the attorney general performs the investigation," Whitlock responded.

Chris accessed the Second Amendment in his head and quoted word for word. "In all criminal prosecutions, the accused shall enjoy the right to a speedy and public trial…"

The judge tapped his gavel on his desk. "Speed it up, Mr. Hardwick."

Chris looked at the judge. "Your Honor, my client has an absolute right to confront his accuser. How can he do that if we don't know under what grounds he's being held?"

Judge Tate shrugged. "It's an excellent question. One the Supreme Court has hinted at but never resolved. Your failure to present me such a case supports the government's claim that they can, in times of terrorism, hold individuals. Much like Article I, Section 8 provides Congress the power to promote general welfare. It includes the ability to quarantine. In emergencies the government has extraordinary powers."

"But there is no evidence of exigent circumstances," Chris implored. "My client has a right to be informed of the nature and cause of the accusation! How can the court determine if there's an emergency if the prosecution won't provide any information?"

"Satisfied with your record?" Judge Tate asked. "Got enough for an appeal?"

Seething with disappointment, Chris relented. "Yes, Your Honor."

"The court denies defendant's writ without prejudice. It finds the United States has met its burden under the Patriot Act, stating there are exigent circumstances to hold defendant without disclosing confidential information in the interest of national security."

"Without prejudice?" Whitlock asked in disbelief.

The judge left the door open.

"Yes. I may very well change my mind in a few weeks. You can't just go holding people indefinitely. Mr. Hardwick feel free to refile your case in the future."

Chris sank into his chair. Couple of weeks to try again. Couple of months to appeal. *Goddammit. Where do we go from here?*

THE PRISON GUARD opened the door and stood aside. Ted entered the small room. It was a typical interrogation room, blank white walls, two-way mirror, two steel chairs, but no table. The chairs faced each other.

Without a word, the guard slammed the door. Ted was alone. He guessed that someone watched him from behind the mirror.

Time passed slowly. With nothing to occupy his mind, Ted slumped in one of the chairs and closed his eyes. He wished he had Chris's mind. Chris could call up movies on the screen in his head and entertain himself for hours. Ted was just a normal Joe.

Without a clock in the room, and without his smart phone, Ted had no idea how long he'd been in the room.

Finally, the door opened and a middle-aged woman with short brown hair and a pair of reading glasses dangling around her neck entered the room. Ted rose.

"Please, sit, Ted." The woman was wearing a gray pants suit. "Make yourself comfortable. I'm Dr. Moore."

Ted sat and faced her. "Is someone going to tell me what this is all about? Why am I here?"

"That will become plain enough in the course of this interview, Ted."

Growing up in the barrios of East L.A., Ted's contacts with The Law had not been positive. Then there was the time he was arrested for hacking during the Millennium Systems case. He saw no reason to cut this neat, polite woman any slack. "I want to see my lawyer."

"Ted, I'm afraid that won't be possible."

"What do you mean, 'not possible?' I have a constitutional right to see an attorney."

"No, Ted, you don't. You have been arrested under the Patriot Act. Your civil rights have been suspended."

If I can't talk to Chris, how am I going to get out of here?

"Ted," the doctor said, "I'm going to show you a series of sketches. I want

193

you to tell me what happened leading up to the sketch, what's happening in the sketch, and what happens after the sketch."

Ted sat up straight. "What kind of bullshit is this? I'm not talking to anyone without my lawyer."

Dr. Moore seemed the soul of patience as she repeated, "Ted, I'm going to show you a series of sketches. I want you to tell me what happened leading up to the sketch, what's happening in the sketch, and what happens after the sketch."

Ted shook his head and looked at the floor.

The woman put on her glasses, opened the folder, and handed Ted a pencil sketch on cardboard backing. "Ted, look at this first sketch and tell me your story."

Ted reluctantly took the picture. It was of a young girl with an unhappy look on her face. She stared menacingly at a violin on the table in front of her.

He just shook his head. "This is bullshit."

Once again, the interrogator repeated, "Ted, I want you to tell me what happened leading up to the sketch, what's happening in the sketch, and what happens after the sketch."

Rolling his eyes to the ceiling, he held the sketch up in front of him. "Let's see … There's a girl looking at a violin. Okay, before the picture, she got a call from her friend who wanted her to come over and play."

Dr. Moore jotted something down in her notebook.

"Her mom told her she had to practice the violin first, and she's not happy."

When he paused, the interrogator just stared silently at him.

"Uh, let's see … after the picture, the girl practices her violin, then goes to play with her friend."

"Thank you, Ted."

One by one, Dr. Moore gave Ted five more sketches and asked for a story. Ted hesitated each time.

What's this all about? What's she trying to find out?

When he finished the last story, the doctor made a few more notes then got up. "I'm going to leave you for a while. Sit tight, Ted. I'll be back soon." Then she knocked on the door and the guard opened it.

"WHAT DID YOU LEARN, HANNA?" Elaine Jefferson, the head of the NSA's Tailored Access Operations, asked.

Dr. Moore shook her head. "He's very consistent. He values family, maybe above all else. That's certainly something we can use. He's one of the most confident prisoners I've ever interrogated. He's supremely self-assured and totally poised. I don't think we're going to get him to break down in tears." *How do I get to this young man?*

"So ..." Elaine let the word hang in the air. "How are you going to approach the confrontation phase of the interview?"

Hanna Moore looked at her notes. "I'm going to play up the family angle. That's the theme here. Does he want his mother to worry about him, not knowing where he is or what's going on? I'll tell him that he'll feel much better if he clears his conscience, that his family will be able to forgive him if they can understand."

"Okay, go get him, girl."

"Let me make a few notes first. Let's let him stew for a while."

Dr. Moore stared at her notebook. *Is he guilty? I didn't get an iota of remorse from him. I don't have the feeling he's being deceptive. He's going to be a tough nut to crack.*

CHAPTER TWENTY-FIVE

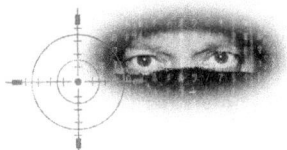

Ted stared at the ceiling. He got up and paced. He sat back down and closed his eyes. The waiting was interminable.

He was familiar with this tactic. He had to wait them out, not get rattled, no matter what they did.

How far will these bastards go? Will they use waterboarding, some other torture? What the hell do they want from me anyway?

He'd been tortured before and wasn't looking forward to it again.

The door opened, and Dr. Moore re-entered the room. "I'm sorry to keep you so long, Ted. Shall we continue?"

She sat in the other chair. "Ted, I want you to listen to me. Don't interrupt, just hear what I have to say.

"Ted, I have a very good friend who has been in your shoes. She was a hacker. She hacked into a big bank and transferred money into her account. She was very smart. She only did it a little at a time. She set up an account for Rose Zeus. Whenever the bank rounded a dollar amount, she transferred the dropped amount into her account. This went on for years and she built quite a little nest egg.

"One day, the bank got a call from a little old lady named Judith Zwicky. She didn't understand where all the money in her bank account was coming from."

"You know what happened, Ted. Rose's hack put the money into the last account on the bank's records. When Mrs. Zwicky opened her account, it was alphabetically after Zeus, so she got the money. If not for that, Rose would probably never have been caught."

Ted sat unmoved. *I heard this urban myth in college.*

"Ted, the story has a happy ending. With someone as talented as Rose, the government couldn't waste all that capability. She now works for the FBI's cyber division."

"What does that have to do with me?"

"Don't interrupt, Ted. Just listen to what I have to say." She hefted a thick file folder in her hands. "I know you, Ted. I probably know you better than you know yourself."

She's a profiler. That's it, that's why she asked me to tell her those lame-ass stories, but build a profile on me? Why? "What's this all about?"

"Don't interrupt, Ted. Just listen to what I have to say." Dr. Moore pulled a sheet of paper out of the file. "I know about your family. How your mom and dad came here from Mexico, how your dad struggled to put food on the table, how he won the lottery and bought the restaurant where he worked. I know about your sister, how she graduated from UC Davis. How she owns one of the most successful restaurants in Seattle. I have to eat there the next time I'm in Seattle. I love Mexican food."

Ted stared down at his folded hands.

"I know you, too, Ted. I know that you went to the University of Washington on a football scholarship." Dr. Moore leaned closer to Ted. "I know that you graduated in computer science and went to work for Catrina Flaherty as a hacker for hire. We've been watching you since you got mixed up with that Al-Qaeda cell in Canada. You've been on our radar for some time."

Ted's mouth dropped open.

"We've wondered how you were involved with the drug cartels in Mexico. How you managed to kill off the leaders so that your girlfriend could take over the drug market in Baja California."

"No!" Ted stood from his chair. *Maria! This is all about Maria.*

"Don't interrupt, Ted. Sit down. Listen to what I have to say." Dr. Moore continued. "We know you have extraordinary hacking skills. We watched you unravel the Millennium Systems scandal. We also know you have exceptional private investigator skills. You worked on the missing bikini barista stand-owner case. You see, Ted, I know all about you. I know who you are and what makes you tick."

"I call bullshit. You don't know anything about me."

"Don't interrupt, Ted. Just listen to what I have to say." Her voice was nice and steady. She pulled a sketch from her file without showing it to Ted. "You met someone in Canada, didn't you, Ted? He was disaffected, felt marginalized by his country. He wanted a way to strike back. That's why they attacked that cruise ship. You understood him. You could sympathize with him because you have been marginalized yourself.

"You grew up in the barrio where it was every man for himself. You didn't fit in the white world. You didn't even start speaking English until you went to elementary school. All of your life, white society put you down. Ted, I understand. What do you think it's like being a woman in a man's world? We have more in common than you think."

Where's she going with this?

"Ted, your resentment grew and grew. Even when you became a successful business man, you couldn't get over the hatred. They scarred you, and they mistreated your people every day. You had to find a way to strike back at them."

Ted shook his head and let out a long breath.

"So, you began the campaign to launch a series of cyber-attacks against your country. You wanted to make them pay. I understand that. I might have done the same thing if I had the abilities you have."

"That's cra ... "

"Don't interrupt, Ted. Just listen to what I have to say." She pulled on both edges of the sketch she held in her hands. "You planned your attacks well; you planned for your escape and made sure you had enough money stashed away to live for the rest of your life."

"Huh?"

"We know about the off-shore accounts, Ted. Over one hundred million dollars pilfered from Wells Fargo and Bank of America. Did you think we wouldn't be able to trace it?"

Ted shook his head in disbelief. *What's she talking about?*

"Ted, it's time to think about your family, your mother, your brothers and sisters. Do you want them to suffer because of you? Do you want them to lay awake at night wondering what happened to you? Where you went? Why you haven't contacted them? Ted, think of the shame they'll have to live with.

"You can help them. I know you love them. Tell me about it. When you shut off the electricity, you never thought they could get hurt did you?" She paused.

Ted didn't respond.

"When you backed up the sewers, it wouldn't affect them, would it? But you went too far. When you started taking control of cars and crashing them, things got out of hand. You never meant to kill anyone."

Ted's eyes widened.

"You must feel an overwhelming amount of guilt, Ted. I'll bet you're relieved that Hope wasn't killed, but you caused her a lot of pain. Why Ted? Why did you attack your sister's car?"

Ted shook his head. "NO! I didn't do it!"

Dr. Moore tried to hide a look of surprise.

"I want to show you this sketch again." She handed it to Ted. "Take a good look at it. Remember it? Remember the story you told me?"

Where's she going with this? Ted looked at the sketch. It was of a young man with his back to the viewer, working on a computer. He looked over his shoulder with a furtive look, as if he was checking to make sure he was alone.

"Your story, Ted, was that he was a hacker. He hacked for the pure joy of it. He hacked into the phone company system and set his and all his friends bills to zero. Do you remember that? And afterwards, his friends thought he was a hero. Remember, Ted?

"Ted, it's time to come clean. Think how much better you'll feel if you get this off your chest."

"Fuck you! I didn't do any of those things."

"Don't interrupt, Ted. Just listen to what I have to say."

"No! It's time you listened to me. I was set up and I know who did it. I know where he's going to strike next. I know he will cripple the country with his next attack. You're wasting your time with me. The real threat is still out there. He's going to attack again; he's going to kill again. I can help you. I can put this guy out of business, but you're so fast to blame this on someone, you grabbed the first easy target."

CHAPTER TWENTY-SIX

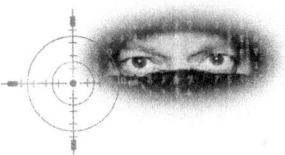

P resident Ford sat in the War Room, tapping his fingers on the table, sweating profusely. He was about to launch the second nuclear attack in history.

How many people will I kill? How many innocent people that had nothing to do with the attack?

"George," the President turned to the secretary of defense, "have we repaired our systems?"

"Yes, sir," the heavy, balding man replied. "All systems up and running."

"And have we hardened them against another attack?"

The SecDef took a deep breath. "As much as we can. We try to anticipate all possible threats, but the bad guys are always coming up with something new. We can patch our defenses against the last attack, but we can't provide defenses against the next attack if we don't know what it is yet."

The President harrumphed. "How about our cruise missiles? That was a sixty-million-dollar disaster. How can we make sure it won't happen again?"

SecDef looked down at this notebook and sighed. "We tracked the problem to a software glitch. Someone messed around with the software on the missiles. They prevented them from establishing contact with the ships, so the missiles self-destructed. We've checked our inventory to make sure none of our remaining missiles have that glitch."

"How did it get in the missiles in the first place," the Veep asked. "And why only those missiles? It's almost as if someone knew that we were going to launch that attack and took counter-measures."

"That we don't know yet, Madam Vice President." The SecDef shook his head. "These people are one step ahead of us. We have airtight security around our arsenal now; we've cut off all contact outside of our buildings. We'll only open those channels when the missiles are launched. I believe that there is no way anyone can mess with the software again."

The President scanned the room. All of his most trusted advisors were there. "Okay, where do we go from here? Do we know enough yet to launch a counter-strike?"

"Sir," General Joseph McNamara, the head of Cyber Command spoke. "I do not believe that we know for certain who launched the attack. I caution restraint in striking back until we know without a shadow of a doubt."

Silence hung in the air.

"Mr. President," Hiram Johnson, the Director of National Intelligence, spoke up. "We have a person of interest in custody. He isn't a foreign terrorist. He's home-grown."

"What?" the President almost came out of his chair. "Why haven't I heard about this yet?"

"We're still interrogating the suspect. We don't have definite proof. We have a pile of circumstantial evidence, but no confession yet."

"What are you doing to get that confession?"

"We have our best man on it, Dr. Hanna Moore. With her advanced inter-rogation techniques, she can get to anyone."

"Well, make it happen, and damned fast. I don't care if you have to use waterboarding. Hell, I can give you one of the CIA's interrogators. They never fail to get what they're after."

"Sir!" the DNI interrupted. "We can't use torture against an American citizen."

The President pulled himself up to his full height. "This is war, Mr. John-son. We'll do whatever we have to, to defend ourselves."

"We need to consider all possibilities. It has come to light that another attack is planned. Maybe this Ted Higuera can help us stop it. We don't want to alienate a potential source of information."

"Mr. President," the Director of the FBI broke in. "We arrested Higuera. He has a long history of criminal behavior. We firmly believe that he is the unsub. I see no reason not to lock him away for life. If he's locked up, he can't launch another attack."

"Gerry," the DNI said. "Think about it a minute. No single human being could've caused the devastation we've seen. He must have helpers. A whole team of disaffected hackers. If we take him out of the picture, the others will continue on with his master plan."

"We've pinned the source of the attack down to Seattle." The FBI man said. "If it came from Seattle, then Higuera is involved. He's hacked some of the most secure systems in the country."

"Shit!" The President banged his hand on the table. "Don't we know anything yet? What are we, the Keystone Kops? This is the most powerful brain trust of the most powerful nation in history. You find out who this Higuera is and what he's up to or heads will roll." He stopped to let that sink in. "Do I make myself clear?"

THE GUARD LED Ted into a different interrogation room. This one had a table and three chairs. The single chair on one side of the table was bolted to the floor.

The guard herded Ted towards the chair and pointed with his baton. Ted sat. The guard unlocked one of Ted's handcuffs and locked it to a steel ring jutting out of the table top.

After the guard left, Ted looked around. With the exception of the table and an extra chair, it was identical to the last room.

Two chairs ... that means that there will be two of them this time. Playing good cop/bad cop I'd think.

He didn't have to wait long to find out. Dr. Elaine Jefferson, head of the NSA's Tailored Access Operations (TAO) entered the room with Dr. Hanna Moore in tow.

"Mr. Higuera," Elaine said.

Ted sat silent.

"Ted," Dr. Moore started, "we need more information. I'm inclined to believe that you had nothing to do with the cyber-attacks."

"Then let me the fuck out of here."

"Others in the NSA hold a different opinion."

Ted rattled his handcuffs. "At least get me out of these things while we talk."

"Mr. Higuera," Elaine put a folder on the table and leaned towards Ted. "If what you say is true, then you can help us determine the identity of the cyber mastermind."

"I'm not saying another word until you unlock these." Ted lifted his left hand to show the cuffs. *I have to exert some sense of power. I have to show them that they aren't in charge.*

Elaine pulled a key from her pocket and unlocked the cuff. "Okay. Tell us what you know."

"I already told you, I know who he is, where he lives."

"Then share that information with us."

"No way. I'm not telling you anything until I'm released."

"Ted, that can't happen," Dr. Moore interjected.

"She's right. I can't let you go until we have this madman in chains," Elaine said. "So start talking."

"I'm not saying anything without my lawyer. You want my information, you're going to have to negotiate a deal with him."

He was delighted to see the look of frustration in their faces. "You can hold me 'til the cows come home. I'm not saying a word. When the whole economy comes crashing down around your ears, it will be your fault. You had the chance to stop it and you didn't."

"Ted, think of your country, your family," Dr. Moore said. "Can you really stand by and let this terrible thing happen that will do irreparable harm to them?"

"I want to talk to my lawyer."

"WHAT DO YOU THINK?" Elaine asked Hanna Moore as they walked down the hallway.

"I'm inclined to believe that he knows something. Maybe something important. I also think that he won't say a word unless we meet his terms."

Elaine pushed her hair back out of her eyes. "He has no legal right to demand such a thing. If we give in to him, we're setting a dangerous precedent. I'd need to run this by the attorney general."

Dr. Moore stopped. "Elaine, what happens if the AG won't let him see an attorney?"

Elaine sighed and lowered her head. "They have other methods of extracting information."

"No. You can't." Dr. Moore's eyes widened. "He's an American citizen. I'm not even sure he's involved in this crime."

Elaine started walking again at a brisk pace. "It doesn't matter. He holds information vital to our national security. If he's not willing to divulge this himself, then we will have to find a way to force him."

"Is it true, the rumors I heard?" Dr. Moore struggled to keep up with the taller woman. "Did the President really authorize you to use CIA interrogators?"

MARY BETH ENTERED the break room and went directly to the coffee machine.

Bear sat at the table, with a can of Diet Coke in his hand and a bag of potato chips in front of him. *Go to jail, directly to jail, do not pass Go, do not collect two hundred dollars.*

He didn't understand why Mary Beth didn't like him. He couldn't think of anything he'd said or done to make her feel this way. He'd never said a word to her that wasn't the truth.

"Hi, Mary Beth."

"Hi." She didn't even turn to see him.

Bear took a swallow of Coke. "May I speak with you a moment?"

He could almost feel the wrinkling of her nose.

"What do you want?"

"I have a problem. It's about Ted."

That got her attention. She sat down opposite him.

"What? Have you heard anything?"

"No." He grabbed a chip from his bag. "That's the problem. I can't find a trace of him. It's like he was abducted by aliens."

A tear formed in Mary Beth's eye. "We've got squat. My contacts have looked everywhere. He just disappeared."

"Okay, so here's my dilemma." He turned the bag towards Mary Beth.

She shook her head.

"We know he was arrested by the FBI. The asshole that took him said something about the Patriot Act."

"Un-huh."

I've done a lot of research on the Patriot Act. I've talked to his lawyer, Chris Hardwick, about it."

"I know Chris."

He felt an air of superiority from her. "As far as Chris can tell, no one has ever been released from the Patriot Act by their lawyer's actions. He says it's all but impossible."

"Okay, I get that." Mary Beth sniffed.

"I ... uh ... I shouldn't be telling you this. It could land me in prison if it ever got out." He munched another chip. "Mary Beth, I know we got off to a rocky start, but I really need your help. We're trying to accomplish the same goal."

She stared silently at him.

"I need to tell you something, ask your opinion. But you can't tell anyone. Can you keep this a secret?"

She thought for a long moment. "I'm a woman of integrity. Cat taught me that. If you lose your honor, you can never get it back. I can't promise you I'll be silent until I know what it is. I won't participate in anything illegal or immoral."

He ran his hands through his bushy red hair and interlocked them behind his head. He stared at the ceiling.

"That's just it. It isn't exactly legal. We do this kind of stuff here all the time. We hack into people's lives to help our clients. Can't we do it to help our boss?"

Mary Beth sat her coffee cup down with a thud. Coffee spilled over the rim. "Bear, what are you getting at? You want to break the law to help Ted?"

"It's a bad law. The Supreme Court should toss it out. It takes away our constitutionally guaranteed rights."

"The Patriot Act?"

"Yeah. I know how to hack into the NSA's system. I can get in and out without them ever knowing it. But the question is, should I?"

He crumpled his Coke can and tossed it towards the trash can.

"You know that goes in the recycling?"

He ignored her. "I'm thinking, if I can find Ted's records there, maybe I can do something. You know ... like changing the records or ordering his release. I know it's wrong, but we're talking about Ted. Should I do it?"

"Jesus, Bear. You sure don't bring me the easy ones." She got up from the table and began pacing. "Let's see. Ted was arrested for something he didn't do. We think. We don't even know why they arrested him."

She turned to face Bear. "The law he was arrested under is questionable but has never been tested in court. You say you can get into their system and change his records ...'

"I didn't say I could. I said I might be able to."

"... The question is, should you try?" She shook her head. "My heart tells me to do whatever you can to help him, but my head says it won't help him to do something illegal. If they find out, you'll both end up in prison."

Bear fingered the collar of his SLUT T-shirt.

"I know. If it was just me, I wouldn't even hesitate, but I have a family. What happens to them if I'm in prison?"

He saw that his comment hit Mary Beth hard.

She sat back down at the table. "You can't do it, Bear. You have responsibility to your family." She thought for a moment. "But ... you could ... Do you know anyone else who's as good as you are, who doesn't have a family to consider, who might do it for the thrill?"

Bear smiled and crushed his now empty bag of potato chips.

CHAPTER TWENTY-SEVEN

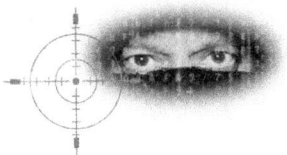

Chris sat in the interrogation room, drumming his fingers on the table. *How long is this going to take?*

Eventually he heard noise in the hallway and a guard's voice.

"Turn around," the guard said as he unlocked the door.

Chris watched Ted turn to face the guard. The guard removed the handcuffs. Ted shook his hands to get the circulation going again, then turned to enter the room.

'Chris!' Ted leapt forward and grabbed his best friend in a big *abrazo.*

"Take it easy, Tiger." Chris pushed him off. "We don't want your fellow inmates to get the wrong idea." *And we don't want the Feds to know how close we are. We're just client and attorney.*

The guard closed the door and Chris heard a loud click. It wasn't the first time he'd been in a prison cell, but the click had the sound of doom to it.

"Man, I'm so damned glad to see you." Ted wiped a tear from his eye. "How'd ya get in here? They told me I couldn't talk to an attorney."

Chris seated himself on one side of the table and gestured to Ted to sit. "Something happened. The NSA contacted me and said they wanted me to talk to you. You know anything about this?"

Ted smiled. "I just told them I wouldn't talk to them without my attorney. I was expectin' them to waterboard me."

"How's it going?" Chris asked. "Are you all right?"

"The food's not bad." Ted grinned at his friend. "I have a clean bed to sleep in and a hell of a lot lower stress level in here than if I was at home workin'."

"Still the wiseass, huh? I hope you're enjoying your vacation."

Ted started to speak, but Chris raised his hand, palm out.

"Before we say anything, you need to know that attorney/client privilege doesn't apply here. Under the Patriot Act, the government can listen in and record conversations between an attorney and his client." Chris lowered his hand and sighed. "You could spend the rest of your life in Guantanamo Bay if the attorney general thinks you're a threat. Let's not give them anything to work with."

"Shit. These guys don't mess around, do they?"

Chris shook his head. "No, they don't. They have a huge problem, and they're looking for a scape-goat to blame."

Ted shook his head and reached out for one of Chris's hands. "Chris," he said in a soft voice. "I know who did this."

"By this you mean ..."

"Everything. It's all comin' together. He released the CryBaby virus; he took control of those cars and crashed them; he started the microwave fires. Everything. He even tried to kill me a couple of times."

Chris just whistled. "Okay, so tell them and maybe they'll let you go."

"What kind of lawyer are you, Bro? What I know is the only leverage I have. If they discover the culprit while I'm in here, they'll just let me rot. If I don't tell them, they'll torture me. One of the guards was joking about it yesterday."

"So, what can you do?"

"No, what can *you* do. I want you to negotiate a settlement for me with the Justice Department. They release me and let me work on this in my office, and I'll tell them everything I know."

Chris leaned forward and turned his head slightly. "What do you know?" He kept his voice soft so that the microphone couldn't record it. "I have to know what my bargaining chips are."

Ted leaned towards him and whispered in his ear. "I know who did this. I suspect that he had many helpers. I suspect that he has a secret hideout some-where, where he can run his operations. I know what he's planning next. It's big. If he's successful, he'll bring our whole economy, maybe the whole world's economy, crashing down. I've already written the code to stop him; we just need to distribute it."

"Whew," Chris whistled. "You don't settle for small change, do you?'

Ted shrugged.

"Okay. I'll talk to them, to see what I can work out. Don't talk to anyone. Don't even tell them your shoe size."

BEAR SAT in his office at his Bellevue home. It was the penultimate man-cave with a big-screen TV, surround sound, a refrigerator and microwave, and sports memorabilia all over the walls. A pennant from BYU, a framed Ken Griffey Jr. jersey, a signed Edgar Martinez bat, and a life-time of other trinkets and toys.

He sat behind a locked door. His family was all asleep. The hands on his Seahawks clock ticked over to four a.m. Time to get started.

He reached in the fridge for another Diet Coke and picked up a burner phone. He wouldn't dare make this call on his own cell phone.

The phone rang six times, then he punched in a code and hung up.

The waiting began. Was she even there? This was how she said he could reach her. *Funny, her. The most feared hacker in the world and it's a her.*

A bell rang in his computer and a message popped up on the screen.

<Activating VPN>

A Virtual Private Network. Using Peer to Peer Tunneling Protocol (PPTP), she drilled a tunnel through the Internet that no one else could break into. This was the most secure mode of communication Bear could think of.

A log-in screen appeared, and he entered his user name and password. He thought he would never use this.

When he met the Joker at DEF Con in Las Vegas, the world's largest hacker convention, he couldn't believe his eyes. Of course, she didn't announce herself to the world as the Joker, but he knew. From things she said and questions she asked, he uncovered her secret identity.

She was a small woman, no more than five-foot-one, and probably didn't weigh a hundred pounds. Her short black hair was cut in a page-boy. She wore no makeup and dressed in sweats.

After the conference, Bear tracked her down. He learned everything he could about her. As much as he liked to say he was the world's best hacker, he knew he wasn't even close. This small woman put him to shame.

She had been in the Army, working for Cyber Command. She discovered leak after leak, hack after hack, and her superiors wouldn't let her do anything about it. Russian, China, North Korea, and Iran all intruded into America's cyber backbone. She wanted to strike back, but the powers that be wouldn't let her. They didn't want the enemy to know they were on to them.

When her hitch was up, she melted into civilian society and began her path towards revenge. She restlessly attacked the states and organizations that invaded American cyber-space. During the election, she changed the Kremlin's home page to tell them that if they didn't stop interfering in American politics, she would destroy their systems.

Bear waited. In a couple of minutes, he got a message inviting him to a video chat. He accepted.

A window opened on his screen with the Joker herself staring back at him.

"Uh, hi," Bear said.

"Hi, Bear." She didn't sound overly friendly. "I never expected to hear from you."

Bear looked at his screen. She was in some sort of computer room. There were servers in the background, and he could hear the constant humming of the air conditioning.

He felt sweat on his brow. "I never thought I'd need to talk to you. I figured I'd just hunker down and let you do your thing."

She took a sip from a cup on her desk on the screen. "Well, now that you're here. What's up?"

"I have no right to ask you this." His palms felt sweaty. "But I don't know what else to do."

"Ask me what?"

"My boss, Ted Higuera ..."

"I've heard of him."

"... was arrested by the FBI. You know all the cyber-attacks that have been happening all over the country? They think he did it."

A slow grin spread across her face. "Then he should rot in hell." She reached for her mouse.

"No! No, wait." Bears eyes got big. "He didn't do it. We know who did. We know what's going to happen next. We went to Microsoft to try to fix the problem, and they just ignored us."

She leaned back in her chair and tented her fingers. "So, what does this have to do with me?"

"Vicki, we can stop the attack. We can save the country, but not if Ted's in a jail cell. We need to get him out. We need to hack into the NSA system and find a way to release him."

She laughed out loud. "Are you serious? The NSA? That's harder than breaking into Fort Knox. Can't happen."

Bear smiled to himself. He did something that even the infamous Joker couldn't do. "I can get in. I know a back door. I've been in their system."

She stared at him for a moment. "You've been in?"

"Yeah."

"Then why do you need me?"

"I … I can't do it. I mean, I have a family. If I got caught, I'd spend the next twenty years in prison. I can't leave my family all alone with no one to take care of them."

"And you think I can?" Her eyes flared. "Why is your family so much more important than mine? Why should I put myself at risk for someone I don't even know?"

Bear's heart pounded in his chest. "I don't mean it that way. This is defending your country. You've already shown that you're on a crusade to punish those hackers who mess with your country. Well, this is the big one. They've already caused billions of dollars in damage; they've killed people. Are you going to stand by and let them do more damage, kill more people when you have the opportunity to stop it?"

She looked down at her clasped hands and was silent.

After several moments, she began to speak. "Okay, Bear. What do you need?"

THE ORIENT AIR'S Gulfstream G-5 lightly touched down on the runway at Suvarnabhumi Airport outside of Bangkok, Thailand. Orient Air was a CIA front.

A flight attendant opened the hatchway and lowered the steps.

"Get up," the tall CIA agent ordered and hauled Ted out of his seat.

It had been a fairly comfortable flight, with the exception of the handcuffs. As Ted stepped out of the air-conditioned plane, he was overwhelmed by the heat and humidity. By the time he reached the ground, his clothes were soaked through with sweat.

Two hardened Humvee's waited on the tarmac. Ted was shoved in the back of the second one and a black bag was pulled over his head. The vehicles leapt forward, made a large circle, and drove off the runway.

He lost all sense of time. The ride could have been an hour or a day. When the vehicles stopped, Ted was pulled out and his bag removed.

He was in the middle of a dense tropical jungle. A large clearing surrounded a white concrete-block building.

Clear field of fire, Ted thought. If anyone attacked the building, there was no cover for a hundred yards.

The CIA men led Ted into the building. The cold air-conditioned air was a gift from Heaven. Armed guards, posted at the door and every fifty feet or so down the hallways, wore black fatigues with no markings, carried AK-74's and wore sidearms.

They led Ted to a plain white room with a table and four chairs. It didn't have the two-way mirrors of his former interrogation rooms, but Ted picked out two tiny video-cameras on the ceiling.

He sat handcuffed in an uncomfortable steel chair. His sweat soaked clothes stuck to his body and were uncomfortable in the cold air.

After a life-time, the door opened, and Dr. Elaine Jefferson entered the room.

"Mr. Higuera, I see you made it. I hope you had a comfortable flight."

He flashed a grin at her. "I hated the in-flight movie, the beer was watered down and the chips were stale."

"We'll see how humorous you are when we get finished here."

"I won't talk to no one without my lawyer."

Elaine smiled. "We'll see about that. Do you know where you are? Do you have any idea what's going to happen to you?"

Ted stared at her with cold eyes. "I'm not an innocent. You've whisked me off to some kind of CIA black site. You're going to torture me and probably kill me. You're even more stupid than I thought."

Elaine rose from her chair and walked around the table. "Mr. Higuera, you are gifted with insight. What you need to know is that you have two options." She ran her fingers over Ted's jaw line. "You can tell us what we want, then spend the rest of your life at Gitmo. Or, you can hold out, in which case you will most surely die here."

A sliver of ice ran down Ted's spine. *Can they really do that?*

Elaine walked behind Ted's chair, grabbed his hair with both hands, and pulled his head back so that he was staring straight up at her.

"You don't exist. You have disappeared off the face of the planet. No one can help you. No one knows where you are." She released his head and walked back to her side of the table. "Like they say in the movies, 'you can make this easy or you can make it hard.' It's up to you."

She pulled the door open. "I won't be seeing you again. That's kind of a shame. They use some really effective nude techniques to extract information here. You have a delicious body. Too bad it will be withered and broken by the time we finish with you."

She stepped through the door and shut it.

Holy shit. I'm so in over my head. I want to say goodbye to Mama, Hope. He sat and stared at the walls. *What can I do? Should I tell them everything? That would get me off the hook, but I'd still spend the rest of my life in prison. If I hold out, they're gonna hurt me bad. And what will it get? Can I still trade information for my freedom?*

His stomach churned, and he could hardly breathe. He took deep, slow gulps of air. He felt his heart beating wildly in his chest. The room faded from focus.

Goddammit. Get control of yourself.

With a supreme effort of will-power, Ted brought his breathing under control. He cleared his mind and thought about Maria.

They were on a beach. A lone sailboat was anchored in the lagoon. The turquoise water was bath temperature, and the sun beat down relentlessly on the white sand.

They were on a blanket under a palm tree, a bucket of Coronas at hand, they lay naked in the sun.

Her body was incredibly beautiful and soft. She had long legs and a perfect round ass. Her tiny breasts bobbled and pointed towards the sky. Fair skin, green eyes and red hair made her flawless.

Somewhere in the distance, Ted heard a baby crying. *Mijo, I'm coming.* It was his son. Soon he'd find a way to meet him, be part of his life...

Two large men in back fatigues, with a pistol on one hip and a police baton on the other, burst into the room. "On your feet."

They grabbed Ted and pulled him up. They took hold of his upper arms and dragged him out of the room.

By the time Ted had his feet underneath him, he was halfway down a drab white hallway. The men led him to a steel door, like all the other doors in the hallway, and unlocked it.

"Inside," one said.

Ted stepped into a room with half a dozen dog-sized cages. *What do they need kennels for? Do they use dogs here?*

"Strip," the guard said.

"Huh?"

"You heard me, strip. Take off your clothes."

Ted hesitated.

The other guard slammed the end of his baton into Ted's gut. Ted let out a surprised gasp and bent double.

"When we say jump, you say how high? Got it?" the second guard growled.

"Uh ... yeah." Ted pulled off his T-shirt and unbuckled his jeans.

When he was naked, the first guard unlocked and opened one of the cages. "Get in."

"Huh?" It wasn't big enough for a man.

The guard smacked his baton against Ted's head. "You're a slow learner, aren't you? I said get in."

Ted got on his hands and knees and crawled in.

"Turn around."

Ted complied. The second guard grabbed his left hand and snapped it into a cuff at the top of the cage. Then he secured Ted's right hand. Ted was partially suspended by the cuffs, half his weight on his knees and the other half pulling his arms from his shoulders.

"See ya in a couple a days," the first guard said. They turned and locked the door behind them.

CHAPTER TWENTY-EIGHT

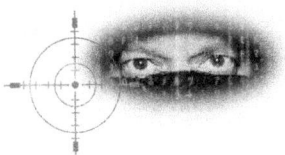

The buzzing and vibration in Bear's desk drawer brought him out of his trance. He stared at the drawer for a moment, then pulled it open and grabbed his burner phone.

"Yeah…"

"I've got some good news and some bad news," a female voice said. "Which do you want first?"

Bear ran his hands through his bushy red hair. "Give me the bad."

"I couldn't find out where they're holding Higuera." There was a note of sadness in the Joker's voice. "He's disappeared off the face of the Earth."

"Shit." If the Joker couldn't find Ted, then nobody could.

"I do have some good news though."

Bear perked up a little. "What?"

"How would you like some information on the head of the TAO?"

Bear pulled at his fuzzy red beard. "TAO?"

"Yeah, the Tailored Access Operations. They're the NSA's cyberwarfare group."

"Never heard of them."

"That's because they're a gray organization. Congress funds them, but no information about them is ever released to the public."

What does this have to do with Ted? Bear sighed and gazed around his cubicle. The Star Wars bobble heads on his desk stared back at him in silence.

"They're the ones who made Ted disappear," she continued.

"Huh?"

"I found a document passing custody from the NSA to TSO. I also found presidential authorization to do 'whatever is necessary to collect pertinent information' from Higuera."

"Oh, God." Bear rubbed the back of his bushy red head.

"Here's the good part, Dr. Elaine Jefferson has been a very bad girl.'

A TALL, slender red-haired woman sat at the head of the table. Dressed in a powder blue power suit, with four-inch heels and finely manicured nails she emanated power. Her blue eyes scanned the four dark-suited men around the table and then fell on the monstrous Harlequin Great Dane who sat on the floor at her side.

"I hear we have a problem," she said in Spanish in an icy voice.

"I'm afraid so, Reina," a man with a scar down the left side of his face and a Pancho Villa mustache replied in Spanish. "But first, more pleasant things. How is the *bebe?*"

The woman smiled. "Eduardo is doing fine. He's strong and handsome, like his papa."

Maria Gonzales, a Mexican-American woman, the head of one of Mexico's most infamous drug cartels, started out her professional life as the curator of the pre-Columbian exhibit at *Museo Nacional de Antropología,* the National Anthropological Museum, in Mexico City.

She met and fell in love with an American boy, and transferred to teaching at the University of Washington in Seattle.

Her father was killed in Mexico's drug wars, and she returned home to take over the family business, bringing her unborn child with her.

"Tell me about this computer problem."

"Señora," a slender light-skinned man on her left said. "We have been attacked by the CryBaby virus. If we don't pay the ransom, all our data will be lost."

Maria reached over to pet her Dane's, head. "So, how bad will that be for us?"

"It will be a disaster," a tall, thin man, known as El Razor, said. "All of our client information, supplier information, all of our business is there."

"How much do they demand?"

El Razor, the *jefe* of accounting, looked down at his notebook and said, very softly, "One hundred million dollars, U.S."

Maria's face was cold as stone. "That is outrageous. What can we do?"

Martin Flores, a young man in his late twenties, spoke up. "Señora, I suggest we pay the ransom. We cannot operate without that data. Then we find out who did this to us and we make them pay."

Maria's eyes rolled skyward and drew a deep breath. She knew what she had to do but couldn't bring herself to do it. "How will we find out who did this?"

Martin gave Maria a sad smile. "You know, Señora."

CHRIS SAT AT HIS DESK, bouncing the eraser on his pencil on a yellow note pad.

What else can I do?

He had exhausted every legal avenue to secure Ted's release. The Federal Government was no longer even interested in talking.

His gaze fell on a framed photograph of a blue sailboat taken from a helicopter. Dressed in red foul-weather gear, the crew hung over the side as his father steered the *Defiant* on a close tack. He was the small red figure hanging off the rail.

God, it's been a long time.

His dad's boat, the *Defiant*, had led Ted and him on their first adventure. Ted saved his life after the al-Qaeda cell filled his body with bullets. What could he do to save Ted now?

The phone on his desk rang.

"Mr. Hardwick, it's a David Jones," the voice said.

"Put him through."

"Hi, Mr. Hardwick, this is Bear."

"Bear?" he scanned his internal memory banks. "Please, call me Chris." He turned his pencil business end down. "You work for Ted."

"That's right, and I've got some information for you that may help."

"Don't say another word. This phone line is not secure. We need to meet in person."

"Okay, where?"

Chris thought a minute. "You know the Shilshole Bay Marina?"

"Yeah…"

"Meet me there in half an hour. Dock D. I'll be waiting at the gate to let you in."

A WIND STIRRED ripples on the bay and seagulls circled overhead, cawing. *It's been too long,* Chris thought as he waited by the gate. *I've got to get back on the water when this is over.*

A short, stocky man with fiery red hair and a bushy beard got out of a blue Volkswagen Tiguan. Chris recognized him from Ted's office. He was some kind of super-nerd.

"Chris Hardwick?" Bear asked.

"Yep, that's me." Chris extended his hand.

Bear shook his hand and looked around. "We're going to meet here?"

"Let's go down to my boat." Chris unlocked the gate and led the way.

In slip D-56, a bright red boat rolled gently to the breeze. The forty-three-foot sloop looked like a sailing Ferrari sitting at the dock.

"Holy crap," the red-head said, "this is your boat?"

"Yeah. The last present my dad gave me." Chris hopped aboard and spun the combination lock on the cabin door. "Come below. We can talk and not be afraid of any listening devices." He climbed down the companionway ladder.

Bear followed and spun his head in awe. "I didn't even know they made boats like this."

The teak walls and bulkheads were highly polished. A table hung on a brass pole that ran floor to ceiling. The galley, to Bear's left, looked like it was ready for a gourmet chef. Wine glasses hung in a rack above the sink.

"Beer?" Chris asked.

"No thanks. You got a Coke?"

"Sure." Chris retrieved the can from the fridge and pulled out a Dos XX for himself. "What do you have for me?" He waved Bear to the starboard settee and sat opposite him.

"I had one of my hackers looking for Ted and he found some interesting information. I don't know if you can use it or not, but I thought you should have it."

"Okay." Chris studied Bear's blue eyes. *He seems earnest. Can I trust him?*

"It's about a Dr. Elaine Jefferson..."

"I've met her. She's the head of the TAO."

"That's right." Bear couldn't suppress his grin. "She's been a very naughty girl."

Chris leaned forward. "What did you find?"

Bear leaned back and crossed his legs. He took a long drink of his Coke set the can on the table and twirled it around. "There's a warning in her file. It seems several people in her employ filed sexual harassment charges."

"What?" Chris started as if he'd been hit by an electric shock.

"That's right." Bear's smile lifted his beard at least an inch. "She used her position to pursue her employees."

Chris ran his hand over his long, blond hair and down his ponytail. "I don't get it. How did she harass male employees?"

"Not just male, some women filed complaints too." A smile crossed Bear's face. "This gets even better. The women say that she showed them pictures of various penises, then told them who they belonged to and how good they were in bed." Bear put his elbows on the back of the settee. "I've got the files. Would you'd like to see them?"

"No, thanks." Chris had to gasp for air. *Could this really be true? It might be the key to get Ted out.* "I'll take your word for it."

"I have photos of her having sex with several different men in her employ."

Chris popped up the computer screen in his head and replayed his meeting with Dr. Jefferson. *There it is.* He focused in on her left hand. *She's wearing a wedding band.* "She's married?"

"Right oh. Two kids, both going to expensive private schools in D.C. I don't think her husband knows anything about her behavior."

"Christ. Is there more?"

"I'm just getting started." Bear uncrossed his legs and leaned toward Chris. "She's had two of her paramours fired and one transferred." His voice lowered. "The fourth man just disappeared. His name is Daniel Wilson. No one knows what happened to him."

"Jesus God," Chris just stared at the super-hacker for a moment, his mind totally blank. He had to keep his head clear. "You have evidence, proof of these claims?"

Bear dug in his computer bag and pulled out a memory stick. "It's all here. And the cover-up. The Department of Homeland Security swept this under the bridge. The secretary himself said she was too valuable to fire."

A smile slowly spread across Chris's face. "Okay, anything else?"

"Would you like to know her favorite food? My hacker found out everything about her."

"Who the hell is your hacker?"

"The Joker."

Chris whistled. "I've heard of him. How did you get him working for you?"

Bear leaned back again, his face split by a smile. "Oh, I pulled a few strings."

"How did he get this information?"

"You don't want to know."

———

CHRIS FLIPPED through his file of business cards in his head until he reached the "J's." He pulled out his phone and dialed her number.

After several rings, a voice came on the line. "Department of Homeland Security, how may I help you?"

"I would like to speak to Dr. Elaine Jefferson." Chris felt the storm of wasps in his stomach."

"Do you have an appointment?"

"No, but she wants to talk to me."

"Who may I tell her is calling?"

"Daniel Wilson."

———————

TED COULDN'T REMEMBER the last time he slept. He was so exhausted, he wanted to die. The pain in his shoulders was excruciating. His knees cried out for relief and his back was on fire. He was too tired to realize how thirsty and hungry he was.

How long had he been in this cage? He was in a white concrete room with no windows. The lights stayed on twenty-four hours a day. Rap music blared from the speakers 24/7. He had no sense of time.

He was naked, on his knees with his hands chained to the top of the cage. There was no way to get comfortable.

He closed his eyes. Maybe this time they'd let him alone.

As he slumped off to sleep, the door opened. One of the black-clad guards entered with a bucket in his hand.

"Wake up, Higuera," the man said as he doused Ted with the ice water.

"Huh?" The water pricked Ted's skin like a thousand ice picks.

The guard unlocked the cage. "We're going for a little walk."

The first guard stepped back as a second guard unlocked Ted's handcuffs.

"Get up." The guards grabbed Ted under the arm pits and hauled him to his feet. One guard pulled Ted's hands behind his back and the other slapped on the cuffs.

"Let's go."

Ted couldn't stand. The two men easily lifted his one hundred and eighty pounds and dragged him out the door.

They hauled him to yet another white-walled interrogation room. This room had a device that looked like a giant wooden X standing vertically in the center. On the backside of the X was a table with gimbles to allow the X to move in any direction. Along one wall was a workbench covered with neatly ordered power and hand tools.

A tall, well-muscled man stood behind the X. "Let me introduce myself. I'm TJ MacLeod, I'll be your interrogator today." He had a sly smirk on his face.

A tiny skinny black man with a shaved head sat behind a computer in the corner of the room.

Ted looked at the interrogator. His blue eyes were like machines with no trace of humanity. He wore a tight white T-shirt from which his muscles bulged.

MacLeod nodded at the guards. They led Ted to the giant X and strapped his hands and feet to it. He couldn't hold himself up and sagged towards the floor, his wrist straps held him upright.

The interrogator laid the X flat. Ted looked up at the torturer. McLeod reached down with large, calloused hands and flipped Ted's balls up and down.

Ted's face reddened. *Madre de Dios.* "Leave the privates alone, dude."

"You need to understand that you're totally helpless." McLeod spun the X around and around until Ted was dizzy.

MacLeod turned back to the table with the tools and picked up a leather apron. He put on the apron, then a pair of latex gloves. Finally, he pulled a pair of goggles over his eyes. His movements were slow and deliberate. He hummed "Margaritaville" to himself.

"Mr. Washington here is going to ask you questions." He nodded his head toward the man sitting behind the computer. "You will answer them."

Washington got up and attached electrodes to Ted's chest, wrists and thighs, then strapped Ted's head down and put more electrodes to his forehead.

McLeod picked up a cordless electric drill and walked back to Ted.

"Make no mistake, you will talk." He pulled the trigger on the drill and let it run long enough to make Ted shiver.

MacLeod put the drill in his left hand and slapped Ted in the abdomen with an open right hand.

"Ooompf." The slap was hard and unexpected.

MacLeod grabbed Ted's face in the free hand. "Are you listening? You need to understand that you are not going to walk out of this room alive. The only question is, how long it will take you to die and how painful it will be? I'm very good at this you know. I can keep you alive for days."

Ted's breath was fast and labored. He felt a chill flow down his back and through his veins. He closed his eyes and tried to think of Maria, Mama, anything.

He received another hard slap to the abdomen.

"You call this little thing a dick?" MacLeod pulled on Ted's penis and twisted.

Ted gritted his teeth, then smiled up at McLeod. "You get off playing with other guy's junk?"

McLeod ignored him and pumped the power drill again. "First, let me show you I'm not kidding." He grabbed Ted's ear and punched the drill through an ear lobe.

"Yaaaaa"

"You like that?" He drilled Ted's other ear.

Ted screamed.

"Now we're getting to understand each other." The torturer ran the drill through Ted's nose.

"Nooooooo"

"I was thinking about drilling your tongue, but tongues bleed a lot. you might die before we have a chance to finish that conversation."

Ted clinched his teeth and breathed hard. "What happened to you? Your mama didn't love you?"

The man ignored Ted's comment and turned back to his table, put down the drill and took a neatly folded towel from the surface. He walked over Ted. "You're going to appreciate this."

This baboso gets off on hurting people.

"I've always admired a man who enjoys his work." Ted smiled up at the torturer.

Ted was blinded by the towel, but heard the water pouring. He felt his face get wet, then he was drowning.

He tried to hold his breath but couldn't keep it for long. Finally, he gasped. He took in a lung full of water. He coughed and spit, but it did no good. Every time he tried to breathe, he got water.

"How you likin' it so far?" MacLeod asked and pulled the towel free.

Ted gratefully took in a lung full of air and was wracked by deep coughs.

McLeod turned to the black man. "Mr. Washington, you may proceed."

"You want to tell us how you managed to shut off the power grid?"

"I didn't do it," Ted sputtered.

"Okay, round two." The torturer covered Ted's face with the wet towel.

He hummed "Georgia on My Mind" as he gingerly poured water over the towel.

Ted stiffened and held his breath. Once again, he gasped and took in a bucket of water.

This continued for several minutes, then MacLeod pulled the towel free. "Feeling better, buttercup?" he asked.

Ted sputtered and gasped for breath.

The man grabbed Ted's balls and twisted.

Ted howled in pain.

"You gonna talk?"

"I ... don't ... know ... anything." Ted gasped for breath. "Believe me ... if I did, I'd tell you."

Washington watched his computer monitor and shook his head.

MacLeod grabbed a pair of pliers from the table. "Let's take another tack." He opened and closed the pliers in front of Ted's face.

Washington said, "Let's talk about your claim to know who's behind the attacks."

McLeod put the pliers on Ted's big toe on his left foot. Ted struggled against the restraints straining his neck to see what McLeod was doing. McLeod jerked.

Ted cried in pain as the toenail came loose. Blood squirted from his foot.

"He works for Microsoft."

"Now we're gettin' somewhere." MacLeod jerked off the next nail.

"AIEEEE ... " Ted strained against his bonds to no avail.

"Who is this mysterious stranger?" Washington asked.

I can't tell him. Then I've lost all leverage. Ted's mind raced. *I can't take this anymore. I have to tell him.*

The door opened, and Dr. Elaine Jefferson entered the room.

"You can take a break. I want to talk to Mr. Higuera alone."

McLeod jerked another toenail free.

CHAPTER TWENTY-NINE

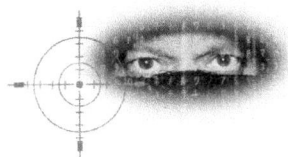

Maria Gonzales sat on a chaise lounge on the deck of her Spanish-Colonial-style ranch house and looked out over the azure waters of the Sea of Cortez. She spent most of her life on the ranch, but the view never failed to inspire her. The deep blue water lapped against the brown land dotted with cactus and mesquite. Blue and white pangas were pulled up on the gravel beach below her. She could just see the three large cement crosses on the point to her left.

She held a small fidgeting bundle to her chest. "Patience, Mijo," she said in English. "Mama's just about ready."

She unbuttoned her blouse with one hand and pulled the Velcro-fastened cup from her bra. "Here you go, baby." She pulled the cover off the baby's head and held him to her breast. He immediately started sucking.

"Oh, Mijo, what are we going to do?"

She heard footsteps behind her.

"Hey, Sunshine, would you like a glass of lemonade?" her mother, Theresa Gonzales, a middle-aged blonde woman said, offering Maria a tray with two frosty glasses on it.

"Thanks, Mom."

"It looks like he's eating well."

Maria smiled. "I've never been so happy in my life as when I'm with him. If only ..."

"Let's not go there, honey." Theresa set the tray on the table and sat in the deck chair next to Maria.

Maria picked up her glass. "Mom, we have to talk."

The words hung in the air.

Finally, Maria spoke again. "Something's happened. We've been hacked. All our computer systems are down."

"Oh." Theresa's eyes widened.

"It's that CryBaby virus we've heard so much about. All of our data was lost."

"My God." Theresa put down her glass and turned full on to her daughter. "What're you going to do?"

"Martin recommended we pay the ransom, so we can keep doing business, then find out who did it and take care of them."

Theresa stared out over the blue water. "Martin's a smart boy." A large white boat with four white sails cruised by in the distance.

"We paid the ransom and got our data back, but Martin and Razor both agree, we need to pay back this hacker. Everyone has to know that you can't mess with the Baja Cartel."

"You know what you have to do, don't you?"

Maria lowered her head, fussed with the baby, then changed him to her other breast. "Mom, I can't. You know that as well as I. If I call him, he would come back into my life, into Eduardo's life. It can't be."

Theresa reached over and took Maria's hand. "How else are you going to solve your problem? Is there anyone on the payroll who could do this for you?"

Maria shook her head, her long red hair tumbling down her shoulders over her baby's head. "We just don't have that kind of talent."

Theresa looked at her daughter. "You've put family first before. You need to think of all the people that depend on you, the interest of your business. Is there another way?"

The baby fussed in Maria's arms. She put him on her shoulder and patted his back.

"Let Grandma take him." Theresa reached for little Eduardo.

Maria pulled her bra cups closed and buttoned her blouse. "Martin talked to some people in Mexico City. They're not even in Ted's class. I don't know anyone as good as he is when it comes to technical stuff."

"I think you need to do a little research. Find out who is good with this kind of stuff, pay them a little visit." Theresa stood and rocked the baby in her arms.

"I'll look some more, but I don't think there's anyone else as good as Ted."

"How will you get him to work for you?"

Since Maria took over control of the Cartel, she had to do many things she didn't like. The hardest thing for her was a face-to-face confrontation. She hated making a threat so powerful that the other person had to comply.

"I'll solve that problem when we get there."

***

"Mr. Higuera, we need to talk." Dr. Elaine Jefferson stood over Ted and stared down at his naked body.

"Then get me outta here."

Elaine ran a fingernail up the inside of Ted's thigh.

He felt embarrassed that his cock started to stir.

"I've been talking to your attorney." She ran her fingers over Ted's hard abdominal muscles. "I think we may have room to work out an agreement."

She touched Ted's bloody toes, then raised her fingers to her lips. "Mmmm. Nothing tastes as good as fresh blood in the morning."

She stepped back and stood the giant X up so that Ted was vertical. "I wish we had toys like this at home," she said in an aside.

"I'm taking you back to D.C. When we get there, you're going to help us find this hacker you say you know. You will be in our custody until he is neutralized."

***

The Gulfstream G-5 touched down lightly at Joint Base Anacotia-Bolling outside of Washington, D.C.

231

Ted looked out the window at the lush Virginia country side. *I thought I'd never see that again.*

He was grateful that Elaine rescued him from the torture chamber but was mad as hell that he'd been put through it in the first place. *I'd kill her in a heartbeat if I had the chance.*

The old saying kept going through his head. *I love my country but fear my government.*

A pair of black Chevy Suburbans with darkened windows waited for them on the ground.

Dressed in sneakers, jeans, and a black sweat shirt, Ted hadn't spoken since he was taken down from the X. He stared at Elaine and felt his temperature rise and tingling in his limbs. He clenched his fists to stop his hands from shaking.

"Okay, Mr. Higuera, it looks like our ride is here." Elaine removed her seat belt and rose.

Two men in black suits with bulges under their left shoulders, motioned Ted to get up. His stomach muscles screamed when he tried to get up. He sucked it in and didn't let them see his pain, then followed them down the ramp. He limped behind them, putting his weight on the heel of his left foot, as best he could.

He was loaded into one of the Suburbans and the mini-motorcade drove off the airstrip. An hour later, they entered the compound that served as NSA headquarters at Fort Meade, Maryland. The main building looked like a giant shoe box, with black mirrored windows covering the entire surface.

The guards whisked Ted to the sixth floor and deposited him in a well-appointed meeting room. A mahogany table that accommodated eight people filled the center of the room. Cabinets and a counter ran along the inside wall. At one end of the rectangular room, a flat-screen television filled the wall.

One guard motioned towards a stuffed rolling chair and said, "Take a seat." Then the two guards turned to leave the room.

Ted waved to them "You boys have a great day," It hurt to talk with his sore tongue. "It's been a pleasure doin' business with ya."

One guard wrinkled his nose and left.

Ted walked to the windows and looked out. Tree-covered hills surrounded the complex and, in the distance, he could just barely see the Potomac River. He wasn't free, yet, but this was a hell of a lot better than the jungle site in Thailand. He nervously fingered the bandages on his ears.

Ted turned when the door opened, and Elaine entered followed by a tall, thin, bald man and Chris.

"*Hermano*," Ted squealed in delight. He saw the hardness in Chris's eyes and didn't embrace him.

Elaine introduced the other man. "Mr. Higuera, this is Thomas Whitlow, a staff attorney. He and Mr. Hardwick have worked out an agreement that you are going to sign." Elaine sat at the head of the table and the others seated themselves to her left and right.

Ted looked to Chris. "Well, *hermano*," he mumbled, "what is this? Do I sign it?"

"It's a contract laying down the terms for your release. You'll help the NSA capture the person or persons responsible for the cyber-attack; you'll sign a release that absolves the U.S. Government of all responsibility for your incarceration and any hardships you may have endured during said incarceration."

Ted and Chris had always been close. Often, Ted thought that he could hear what Chris thought. His dry recital told Ted the message underneath. *I did the best I could for you, bro. I'm sorry."*

Ted reached for the leatherette document. "I think I need to read this before I sign anything." He trusted Chris implicitly, but he needed to know what he was agreeing to.

"Go ahead, Mr. Higuera," Whitlow said. "I'll find us coffee service." He got up and left the room.

Ted read through the document, blanking out all external stimuli. *Bullshit! The bastards want me to sign a release saying I won't sue 'em for torturing me.* His hand went subconsciously to the bandage on his nose. *Want me to work for 'em until they're satisfied the crisis is over. That could be forever.*

"I got a couple of issues here," Ted said. "First of all, I ain't gonna stay here in Washington under house arrest. You want my help, you let me go home to Seattle and work in my own lab."

Elaine raised her eyebrows but remained silent.

Whitlow re-entered the room, followed by a young woman in a black skirt and white blouse pushing a service cart with a silver coffee service.

"Coffee anyone?" he asked. "Did I miss anything?"

"Mr. Higuera wants to renegotiate the contract."

Whitlow poured himself a cup of coffee and turned to Ted. "You know, don't you, that this is our last best offer? We worked very hard with Mr. Hardwick to get you the best deal we could. There's no room for negotiation here."

Ted stared at him, poker faced. "And I want an end date for my indentured servitude. I ain't gonna work for you for the rest of my life."

"That's totally unacceptable." Whitlock's eyes widened, and his eyebrows raised.

"I'll sign the NDA, and I won't sue you for my kidnapping and physical abuse, but I reserve the right to bring any or all of my staff in on this project."

"You don't seem to understand," The veins in Whitlow's neck bulged and he breathed deep, heavy breaths. "This is it. Take it or leave it."

"Ted," Chris reached out for Ted's wrist. "This is it. The best I could get out of them."

Ted smiled. Smiling hurt his face. "Then take me back to Thailand. I ain't gonna tell you nuthin'." He folded his arms across his chest and leaned back in his chair.

The room fell silent.

After several moments, Whitlow said, "Elaine, take him back."

A slow smile spread across Elaine's face. "You must be one hell of a poker player, Mr. Higuera." She shook her head. "Agreed. I'll have Mr. Whitlock rewrite those clauses."

Whitlock whipped his head in her direction, his mouth hanging open. After a moment, he mumbled "Yes, ma'am."

Elaine turned towards Ted. "While we're waiting for the new document may I ask you a few questions, on good faith?"

Ted looked at Chris. Chris nodded.

"Shoot."

"You say that the terrorist spoofed your IP address to send out his viruses. How did he do that?"

Ted looked at Chris again, who nodded again. "He bounced his requests off servers all over the world. He covered his tracks well. That's why you couldn't get beyond my IP address to see where the attack originated."

Ted closed his eyes and took a deep breath. His body screamed at him, but he wasn't going to give the bitch the satisfaction of showing it. "My partner, David Jones, wrote an app that let him dig deeper. That's how we found the bastard..."

CHAPTER THIRTY

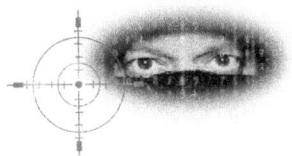

"M r. Ted, you have a call." Abiba's cultured British accent flowed out of the intercom.

"Take a message. I don't want to talk to anyone right now." Since his return from Washington, D.C., Ted had locked himself in his office, with a bottle of Tequila handy, and didn't want to talk to anyone. He stared at the portrait of his father on the wall.

"You're going to want to take this call." Abiba hung up and the light on line one flashed.

"Goddammit. I thought I was supposed to be the boss around here." Ted reached for the phone and pushed the button for line one. "Ted Higuera…"

"Teddy, it's so good to hear your voice."

"Oh my God … Maria." Ted's heart stopped. He felt dizzy and the world swam in front of his eyes.

"You sound funny. Are you eating ice cubes?"

"No, it's a good idea though. I had a slight run in with our government."

"Ted, I don't have much time. I have an emergency here. I need your help."

"I'm on my way." Ted started to rise from his chair. His stomach muscles cramped.

"Stop and listen to me. I'll pay you whatever your normal rate is. I've been hacked, and I don't know anyone as good as you on these kinds of things."

"Pay me? Maria, you're family. I'll fix whatever you need. How's the baby? What's his name?"

"He's doing great. He's the joy of my life."

"I need to see him, Maria." His palms sweat.

"No, Ted. You can't come here. I'm offering you a contract, a business deal, nothing more. You offer a service no one else can provide. Do you understand me?"

The world crashed in on Ted. He stared at the wall and closed his eyes to fight off the tears. His head felt like it weighed a ton.

"Can you at least tell me his name?"

He could almost feel her anxiety in the silence on the phone line.

"I named him after his papa."

"Eduardo, Eduardo Higuera!" Ted had never experienced anything like this in his life. A son! He had a son.

"No, Ted. I named him after his father. Not you."

Ted dropped the phone and stared into space.

"Ted? … Teddy? … Are you still there?"

The voice seemed to be coming from somewhere outside of Jupiter. With a great act of will, he shook his head and picked up the phone. "Yeah."

"Will you help me?"

Life was no longer worth living. "Yeah, I'll see what I can do. Are the passwords still the same?" He reached for a pencil.

"Everything's the same."

"There's your problem. You know you should change your passwords every ninety days. I told you that. You're just askin' to be hacked." Ted rubbed his rapidly healing nose.

"We don't have time for recriminations. I just need this fixed."

"Okay. I do need payment though. If I do this for you, you have to let me see my son."

There was a long silence on the phone.

"I'm sorry, Ted. He's not your son. No, you can't see him. You can't come down here. You need to make your own life up there."

What's she up to? Why can't I see him? I know he's my son. He couldn't be anyone else's.

"Ted, you don't know how hard it was for me to make this call. All I want is to be left in peace to live my life. To raise my son. I can't take any more of the turmoil that comes with being in love with you. You have to do this for me, then let me go."

Ted's heart beat so fast that the world faded out of focus. He felt a chill rise up from his toes. The pencil broke in his hands. "Okay, tell me what happened?"

"We got the CryBaby virus. We had to pay one hundred million dollars, U.S., to get it fixed."

"If you got it fixed, why do you need me?" He reached for another pencil.

Another long pause.

"Because ... we need to find out ... who did this. We need to make sure it never ... happens again."

"So, you want me to reinforce your security systems."

"No, I want you to find out who did this."

Ted stared at the Spiderman poster. The web slinger was flying right at him. *Dios mío. Can I do this?*

LEAH SYKES WAS NOT a traditional beauty. At six feet tall, she was skinny, and all arms and legs. Her curly hair reminded Ted of nothing so much as a red Brillo pad. She wandered around like a lost puppy since her best friend, Catrina Flaherty, disappeared.

"Leah, I'm glad you could make it in." Ted knew that Leah did occasional work for Catrina as a forensic accountant. Despite her appearance and her personal flaws, Cat always said she was as good as they come. "What's new?"

Ted really liked Cat's friend, but she wasn't pretty enough for him, and there was the issue of her being twenty years older.

Leah lowered her gangly body into one of Ted's chairs. "I think I've met The One."

Oh Christ.

"Every time I see you, you think you've met The One."

"This time, it's real. He's tall and handsome. He has a good job, owns his house outright, and has a body that would stop traffic. He's got the biggest pe

..." She put her hand over her mouth and said, "Oops. Let's talk about business."

Thank God. I don't feel like being her girlfriend today.

"Here's the problem. The FBI says I have a hundred million dollars in an off-shore account. They say I stole it from Wells Fargo and Bank of American..."

"What's the problem? Let's head for the Caribbean."

"I didn't steal that money. I didn't set up those accounts. I didn't know anything about it until I was arrested."

Leah opened her suitcase-sized purse and pulled out a leather-covered notebook. "Go on."

Ted leaned back in his chair and put his fingers to his forehead and his thumbs to his cheeks. "The NSA is willing to drop the terrorist charges against me if I help them, but the FBI wants to prosecute me for the theft."

Leah scribbled on her pad.

"While I'm busy tryin' ta save the world, you've gotta be lookin' for whoever set me up. You've gotta find out who opened those accounts and moved the money."

The conversation went on for another half hour as Leah interrogated Ted about the most minute details.

"Well, I think I have enough to get started," Leah said.

"Oh, I almost forgot." Ted reached into his desk drawer. "I got another card from Cat."

"Oh, let me see." Leah leaned over the desk.

Ted handed her the card. It showed the Leaning Tower of Pisa. On the back it said "Having a great time. Wish you were here."

Leah held the card as if it was a stink bomb. "You know, there's something wrong here." She fanned herself with the offending card. "Oh, God. I'm having another hot flash." Her normally pale face lit up bright red and sweat ran down her forehead.

"What's wrong?" Ted wrinkled his forehead.

"I've got big news, bro," her and it doesn't look like her handwriting."

"But it has her name in the return address ..."

TED AND CHRIS had met at the Jock and Jill Gym every Wednesday night since college. They worked out, they talked, laughed, and sweat. Then they headed to Ted's place where he had a gourmet meal waiting.

The gym was about as generic as it could get. Large windows, bunches of exercise machines, free weights, a mirrored wall with a cushy mat in front of it. Ted liked it because it wasn't a pick-up joint. No one seemed to be primarily interested in hooking up with someone of the opposite sex. Or the same sex, for that matter. They were all there to exercise.

"I've got big news, bro," Ted said between breaths as he pounded the treadmill. His foot still hurt, and his abs ached, but he worked through the pain.

"Yeah? What?" Chris kept up an easy pace and had more breath.

Ted reached up to the controls and slowed down the treadmill. "I heard from Maria."

"No shit!" Chris stopped and looked at Ted. "What'd she want?"

Ted's breathing started to return to normal. "She's been hacked." Ted stopped his machine. "The CryBaby virus. She had to pay one hundred million dollars to get her data back."

Chris looked over at his friend and raised his eyebrows. "So, why did she contact you? She's stayed away from you ever since we got back from Mexico."

"She says she's looked for help all over the place, and she can't find anyone as good as me."

"Beware of Mexicans bearing flattery."

"No, she really needs help."

"If she paid the ransom, why does she need you?

Ted wiped his brow with the towel around his neck. "She wants to find out who did this. She wants to keep it from happening again."

"You know what that means, don't you? It's a euphemism for she's going to kill the dude."

"We don't know that." Ted's head hung down. "Maybe she has ways of convincing him of the error of his ways."

Chris shook his head in disgust. "You're so in love with this woman, the head of a drug cartel, that you're willing to help her commit murder."

Ted stepped off the treadmill and spread his hands "Look, she's in danger from the Sonora Cartel. They're behind this. They hired the Russian Mafia to do the hack."

"You can't possibly know that." Chris turned and started towards the locker rooms.

Ted reached out and grabbed Chris's arm. "Hold on, amigo. I have proof."

"You what? Ted, you can't be working on this. You signed an agreement with the NSA. They own you."

"Look, I found an exchange of emails between Juan Miguel Mendoza and the Russian Mafia. He hired them to do it. He's coming after Maria. If he takes her out, he'll kill my son, too. I have to protect my family."

Chris turned and put his hands on Ted's shoulders. "You need to hold off, buddy. If the NSA finds out you're working on something else on their dime, it's off to Guantanamo for you."

CHAPTER THIRTY-ONE

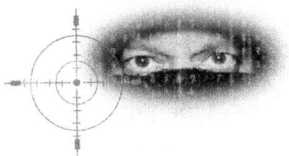

"How did you find him?" Dr. Elaine Jefferson asked Ted as they stood outside the perimeter of Chevy Suburbans surrounding the house.

"You don't really want to know."

"Mr. Higuera, you are under a legal obligation to tell us all you know. Think about how lovely it is in Guantanamo this time of year."

Ted pawed at the ground with his foot. "We got a little help from our friends."

"Your friends?" Elaine's eyes got big. "You know this is a matter of national security?"

"I also know that our agreement let me bring in my staff to solve the problem."

"Who else knows?"

"My people, and ... uh ..." Ted dropped his head and lowered his voice. "The Iceman and the Joker."

"The Joker!" Her head spun so fast that Ted thought it might pop off. "Are you out of your mind?"

"Cool your jets. We got what you needed, didn't we?" Ted fumbled with the Kevlar vest with the bold yellow letters "FBI" on it "We knew his name and Abiba knew his alias. I found several property transactions under the name Assad al Allah. But the key was my forensic accountant. She found the transfers of money from Samir Hussaini's accounts to Assad's. As Leah always says, 'Follow the money.'"

Ted stood behind the cover of a SUV. His Glock nine-millimeter slung on the right side of his utility belt. On the left side were four extra magazines of ammunition and a Maglite. He wore a small Maglite pen light on a tether around his neck.

"I don't give a damn how you found him. I just want to stop him," Brice Holloway, the special agent in charge, said. Tall, broad shouldered, dark hair and brown eyes, he was the prototypical FBI agent. He looked as if he could tear apart the entire ISIS army with his bare hands.

Ted saw men in black combat fatigues with assault rifles moving around the perimeter of the property. Uniformed police officers, with flashing lights on their cars, blocked off all access to the neighborhood. Police officers went door-to-door evacuating nearby families. Men, women, and children in their night wear funneled out of the area, directed by police officers.

"Sir, we've found an escape tunnel two lots down," a man in an FBI jacket said.

"Have you blocked it off?" Holloway asked.

"Yes, sir. We have four agents stationed at the opening."

Holloway put his radio to his lips. "All units, check in."

One by one, the various SWAT teams, agents, and police officers checked in.

"We're a go," Holloway said to Elaine.

"Then let's do this."

"ASSAD, our motion detectors have gone off. I can see soldiers on all our hidden cameras. We're surrounded."

Assad laughed. "The fools. How little they know. EVERYONE, OUT. USE THE TUNNEL," he shouted.

The twelve men in the house ran down the basement stairs. A tall, thin man with a scar on his face pushed the freezer aside and opened a door. "All of you, out."

The men ran down the dimly lit tunnel. Some hundred feet down the tunnel, a ladder led up to a hatch. The tall man waited until all his subordinates were at the ladder.

He climbed the ladder and unlatched the hatch. He slowly pushed it open and began to climb out.

"Freeze." An M4 muzzle stared him in the face.

The tall man dropped down inside the tunnel. He locked the hatch behind him.

"Back, everyone. Now."

Assad sat at his workstation. He clicked on an icon that brought up an application labeled "Death to the Great Satan."

The tall man dashed back into the room. "Assad, they have sealed off the tunnel. We are surrounded."

Assad closed his eyes and shook his head. "Then this is the day we will see paradise." He pushed the button on the screen starting the Death to the Great Satan application.

The other men began to accumulate in the living room.

Assad pulled up another application titled "Darkness to the Satan." He saw a timer on his screen. He set it to fifteen minutes. He had to have time to let the Death to the Great Satan application do its work before shutting down the power grid to the entire United States.

"Samir Hussaini, this is the FBI," a voice said over a megaphone. "We have you completely surrounded. There is no chance of escape..."

"How little the fools understand," Assad said to his followers.

"Throw down your weapons and come out with your hands up."

Assad opened his desk drawer and flipped the clear plastic cover off a small metal box with a red switch on it.

"Allahu Akbar," he screamed and flipped the switch.

TED STOOD behind the Suburban with Elaine Jefferson and the special agent in charge. He watched as the SWAT teams moved into position. He held his breath as they pulled flash-bang grenades from their vests.

They stood frozen at their posts, waiting for the word.

"Samir Hussaini, this is special-agent-in-charge, Brice Holloway. Put down your weapons and come out. This is your last warning."

The world exploded in a ball of fire. Ted felt the concussion and was thrown to the ground. He felt the sharp, stinging pain of hundreds of pieces of shrapnel hit his face.

The air was forced from his lungs. He couldn't breathe. He gasped, but no air would come in. He panicked.

Holding his throat, he climbed back to his knees. He tried breathing. He thought he was going to die. Then he felt the lifegiving breath enter his body. He sucked in hard and blew out, joyous to be able to breathe.

He felt his face with his hands. He picked small pieces of wood and glass from his face. His hands were covered in blood.

As he got his wits about him, he looked around. The house was gone. Small fires burned everywhere. The neighboring house's roof was on fire.

Black-clad bodies lay strewn about the scene. He didn't have the brain power to count them, but he knew that there had been two dozen men and women in the strike force.

He turned to look at Elaine Jefferson lying on the ground beside him.

"Oh God!" She didn't have a head.

Holloway lay bleeding on the ground. Ted dropped to his knees and examined the FBI agent. He had a large splinter stuck in his leg. Without thinking, Ted pulled it free. Blood gushed out of the wound, pulsing with each heartbeat.

From somewhere far back in his mind, Ted recognized arterial bleeding. He pulled the belt off the wounded man and wrapped it around the man's thigh. Then he picked up a nearby stick and put it under the belt. He began to twist the stick to tighten the belt. The bleeding lessened, then stopped.

"Medic!" Ted screamed at the top of his lungs. "I need a medic over here. Man down."

In an instant, a team of paramedics dropped their boxes next to Holloway and took over without a word.

Ted stood and looked at his blood-covered hands. He looked around him at the devastation. He uttered the word, "Why?"

CHAPTER THIRTY-TWO

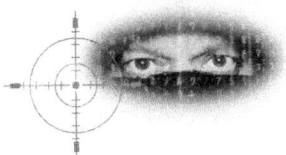

I van Gregorovich.

He'd done it. Ted followed the maze of spoofing, the leaping from server to server, network to network. He sat at his desk, sweating. It was the middle of the night. No one else was around.

Bear was taking a weeklong vacation after the cyber-attack to get back in touch with his family. Abiba left early to watch her daughter's performance. Mary Beth was at Jennifer's house, consoling her new friend.

Ivan Gregorovich.

What should he do with that knowledge? Ted got up and walked to the break room. The only thing to drink in the fridge was a lone diet A&W root beer. He popped the lid.

What to do? If he gave Maria the name, she'd have him killed.

No, she wouldn't. She's not that kind of girl.

Who the hell do I think I'm kidding? She's the queen of a drug cartel.

He wandered back to his office.

Maybe she wouldn't. Maybe she had another way of making sure the hack would never happen again.

He had to think about his son. The boy was in mortal danger. He could save him. Would he kill one man to save his son?

He picked up the empty tequila bottle from his desk and hurled it across the room.

Family is everything.

THE SHORT, dark, powerful man with curly black hair and a unibrow sat in his gold-claw-footed tub, sipping vodka. He'd really done it. A hundred million US dollars.

Ivan Gregorovich couldn't be happier. He had everything he'd ever dreamed about in his life. Money, power, women. He could have any woman he wanted with that kind of money. Why stop at one? Maybe two or three. Maybe a whole harem.

His thoughts turned to later this afternoon. He had hired a girl. When the service asked him what he wanted, he replied, "Wild and kinky. Let her surprise me." He felt a tingle in his loins just anticipating the evening.

There was a tap at his door. "Room service."

Ivan stepped from the tub and wrapped himself in a towel. He reached for the Marakov semi-automatic pistol on his night stand.

"Room service? I didn't order room service."

"It is your complimentary breakfast. Courtesy of the hotel."

He peered through the peep-hole in the door. What he saw was a tall, gorgeous woman with heavy black hair pulled up in a bun. With an incredible body she filled out her waiter's uniform perfectly.

Hmmm ... Could this be my call-girl? She's very early.

Ivan unlocked the door and let the server in.

"What do we have?" he asked.

She smiled at him. His heart melted, but something was bothering him. He sat his pistol on the side-table.

"Eggs sunny side up, sausage, coffee, orange juice and toast." She lifted the cover off the plate, replaced it and reached into the pocket of her apron. "And this." She produced a small semi-automatic pistol.

"What?" *Oh, I get it. This is the wild and kinky.*

"Back slowly into the bedroom. And drop the towel."

Ivan laughed. "That is a toy. You don't really expect me to cower, do you?"

The server produced a silencer from her pocket, screwed it into the pistol, and waved the gun at him. "I said now."

"Very good. You are very convincing."

The woman pulled the trigger. There was a soft "thwatt" and Ivan felt the bullet pass close to his ear. The mirror on the wall behind him shattered.

"Holy God," he shouted and jumped aside.

"Now do you think I'm serious?"

Ivan slowly backed into his room, heart beating wildly.

"Lay down on the bed."

She is very good. He sat on the bed and swung his legs up.

"Spread your arms and legs."

The gloves. She was wearing latex gloves. Why did she need those?

She pulled a pair of handcuffs from her apron and latched them on Ivan's hand, then fastened them to the bed post. She did the same with his other hand.

"Now," she said, "we can have a little conversation."

"You are very good, da? What do you have planned for me?"

She set the pistol on the side-table. "This will be beyond your wildest imagination."

He smiled. This was worth whatever he had to pay for her.

She took two pieces of velvet rope from her apron and tied his legs to the bed.

He lay there spread eagled, grinning up at her.

"Now, that's better." The woman pulled off her black wig and shook lose her short blonde hair. "That wig was driving me crazy."

Da, she is much better as a blonde.

"I suppose you're wondering what's going on here?" She laughed. "I bring you greetings from La Reina."

La Reina? That's the Baja Cartel. Oh, God. How did they find me?

"She wants you to know that she didn't appreciate your little stunt." The woman pulled a switch-blade knife from her pocket. "Just to set your mind at rest, she wants you to know that she's already transferred the hundred million dollars back to her accounts."

Ivan tried to yell, but she stuffed a napkin in his mouth. He struggled against his bonds.

"It's of no use. You will die in this bed."

He stared up into her cold blue eyes. She was easily the most beautiful woman he had ever seen, but to die like this. He tugged at the ropes.

The woman pushed the button on the knife. The blade sprang into place.

"I want you to know that this is very sharp." She picked up a cloth napkin and dropped it on the knife. The blade cut through the napkin. "I don't want you to worry that I might be using dull tools on you."

She's mad. What does she want?

She gently touched the blade of her knife. "There is no sense fighting this, Ivan Gregorovich. You fate is already settled."

She put her left hand to her chin.

"Hmmm ... What else can I tell you before you die? Oh, yes. Your employers, the Sonora Cartel, will receive the message. Three of their top deputies have been killed. When they learn of your death, they will understand that no one messes with the Baja Cartel."

Ivan twisted, turned and made gurgling sounds. He tried to spit the napkin out of his mouth.

If I could talk to her. I could offer her twice what they're paying her. I'm sure she would listen to reason.

"My name is Heidi," the woman said. "I just thought you would like to know who is sending you to hell." She flipped his penis to one side with her knife. She grabbed his balls.

Aieee ... He screamed in terror.

She took her knife and cut his balls off. Blood flowed from the wound. Next, she took hold of his penis and sliced it off his body.

"This is La Reina's trademark. From now on, when she kills a man, he will have his privates cut off and stuffed in his mouth."

She pulled the napkin from his mouth and shoved the parts in.

Blood poured from the cuts in his crotch.

Ivan yelled and squirmed, but Heidi just stood and stared at him, a smile spreading across her face. "This is so much more satisfying than taking you out with a sniper rifle. It is so much more personal."

Two hours later, the Syrian maid entered Ivan's room. She noted that the room service breakfast had not been touched.

"Hello? Is anyone here?" she called.

No one answered.

She lifted the cover off the plate, dropped it, put her hands to her face and screamed.

A testicle was stuck in the center of each egg and a penis lay between the two sausages.

CHAPTER THIRTY-THREE

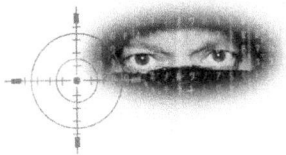

Ted sat at his desk, staring at the empty bottle of tequila, holding a half-empty glass in his hand. The door opened.

"What the fuck? Doesn't anybody knock anym ..." He froze.

Standing in the doorway was a tall red-headed woman with pale freckled skin.

"Maria ..."

She stepped into the room.

Ted leapt to his feet.

He rushed to embrace her. She stood stiff and held out her hand, palm out.

"Stop, Ted. I'm here for business."

"Business?"

She reached into her purse and produced an envelope.

"I'm here for two reasons. First, I need to pay you for your services." She handed him the envelope. "I want to thank you for the help you gave, that only you could have given me."

"Gregorovich? What happened to him?"

"You don't need to know that."

Ted tossed the envelope on his desk without looking at its contents.

"Maria, my son. I need to see him."

0

She glared at him. "That's the other reason. You need to get this idea that he's your son out of your head. He's not your son."

Ted slumped onto his desk. "Then who is his father?" His voice rose. "Tell me that."

Maria closed her eyes for an instant. Her lips curled in a grimace. "His father is, was, El Pozolero."

"El Pozolero?" The room spun around Ted. He grasped the edges of his desk to keep from falling over.

"El Pozolero. While he held me prisoner, he raped me every day. He got me pregnant. It's not your baby."

TED STOOD and looked up at the Henry M. Jackson Federal Building. The tall, buff-colored building soared into the late summer sky.

He had been summoned, not invited, to attend a meeting by FBI special-agent-in-charge Brice Holloway.

The security screening at the entrance was at least as rigorous as the boarding lines at the airport. Ted always felt violated as he passed through the portal. He rode the elevator to Holloway's office on the seventh-floor. Once again, security stopped him before allowing him to proceed.

"Mr. Higuera," a pretty receptionist said. "They're already waiting for you. May I bring you coffee? Water?"

"A cup of coffee would be nice. One packet of sweetener."

Ted opened the heavy wooden door and stepped in.

The office felt like a movie set. Pictures of Holloway with various presidents, FBI directors and celebrities hung on the walls. The oak desk was spotless, and no clutter existed anywhere.

"Higuera, good to see you." Holloway eased himself gently from his chair. He had a bulge under this left trouser leg.

"Mr. Holloway," Ted said as he accepted Holloway's hand.

Holloway turned to the third man in the room. "I want to introduce you to John Archer, assistant director of TAO. He's temporarily stepping into the number one seat while Homeland Security decides on a replacement for Elaine.

He didn't even blink when he said it. Ted didn't know the woman that well but was crushed to see her lifeless body in the grass.

"Mr. Archer." Ted shook his hand.

"I think we've just about wrapped up this case," Holloway said. "Hussaini's attacks failed, thanks to you. Microsoft got your patch out in time, and our cyberwarfare team put an impenetrable firewall around the nation's electrical systems."

Ted nodded his head.

"The President wants you to have this." Holloway picked up a framed letter from his desk. "He wishes to express his gratitude for a job well done."

Ted took the letter. He stared down at it. Even if they went way outside the bounds of U.S. law when they tortured him, even though he didn't agree with anything the President did, he was impressed.

The letter had the presidential seal and a well-written expression of gratitude.

"The President, and the whole nation, wish to thank you for your service …" The letter began.

Archer stepped forward. "There's more. We at the TAO have reviewed your file. We've seen you work. I must say, I'm impressed." He reached his hand out to Ted again.

Ted shook his hand. *What's this baboso up to?*

"On behalf of the Secretary of the Department of Homeland Security, I would like to offer you a job. We want you to come to work for us."

TED'S HEAD was still spinning when he returned to his office. Should he accept the offer? But then what? Leave Catrina's business to flounder?

And how about his son? He knew that Maria was lying to him. He knew in his soul that he was the father.

A yellow manila envelope lay in the center of his desk. It was from a friend at Seattle PD's CSI unit.

Ted opened it and pulled out a stack of postcards and a one-page report. He quickly read the report.

Someone had been faking the postcards from Catrina. They didn't have a single one of Cat's fingerprints on them.

Holy crap. What does this mean? Why would someone send postcards from all over the world with her name on them? She's in trouble.

The End

POSTSCRIPT

I hope you enjoyed reading Ted's latest adventure. This book took me a lot longer than planned to complete and the world changed rapidly while I wrote. I had to go back and re-write or add several scenes as new hacks popped up in Internet Land. The latest hack, brought to you by your friends in Iran and North Korea, of the CIA's systems led to the deaths of over thirty CIA operatives. I just didn't have time to add this to the book. This stuff is really happening every day, folks.

Reviews are the life-blood of independent writers. The more reviews we get, the more Amazon and others promote the book. If you want to see more Ted Higuera adventures, a review would go a long way towards allowing me to write more books. If you liked the book, I ask you to write a review of *Cyberwarfare* on Amazon.com, Goodreads or wherever you go for your book information. Thank you so much, it means the world to me. If you didn't like the book, then please disregard this paragraph.

I'd love to hear your comments and criticisms. Who knows, maybe some of your ideas will appear in a future Ted Higuera novel (As a matter of fact, this book was suggested by a reader). To contact me click here or use the Contact Penn form on my web site at www.pennwallace.com.

Ted will be back next year. He'll head to the steamy jungles of Vietnam in search of a long-lost uncle. Keep track of the progress of his next adventure on my website at www.pennwallace.com. Better yet, sign up for my readers' list and you'll get my monthly newsletter with all my latest progress, book recommendations, give aways, and more. Sign up at http://pennwallace.com/sign-up-page.html.

For now, if you liked this story, you can browse my other books and short stories at http://www.pennwallace.com/index.html.

Thank you very much for reading my book. I hope you enjoy my other works and don't forget to write.

Pendelton C. Wallace
November 13, 2018
San Diego, California

ACKNOWLEDGMENTS

First of all, I need to thank the members of my authors' critique group: David Larson, Mike Gibbs, Christina Buffington, Marla Anderson, and Brian Hogan. They've suffered through the whole manuscript with me and made many suggestions that I've incorporated throughout the book. Thank you.

Brandi McCann designed the cover for this book. She did her customary outstanding job in taking an idea and bringing it to life.

I would like to thank my editor Larry Edwards. He did an above and beyond the call of duty job.

Donna Rich was my proofreader. If there are any errors left in this book, they are wholly my fault.

Mike Gibbs, a retired San Diego police officer, was my mentor and helper in shaping the police scenes. He corrected my errors and helped me write the fights and cop-speak dialog.

I want to give a special thanks to Adam Van Sustern, my attorney consultant, who helped me shape Chris's appeal to the Federal Court. He made several suggestions that made the court case work.

I must thank my beta readers who saw the first draft of the manuscript and helped me smooth out the rough edges. You know who you are.

I also want to give a big shout out to my Advanced Readers. They put the finishing touches on the book and provided reviews on launch day.

I have to thank Mama. She's been in my corner from the beginning. She encouraged me when the night seemed the darkest. I would not be publishing my tenth book without her. *Muchas gracias.*

And finally, I have to thank you, dear reader, especially those of you who have taken the time to write to me with your thoughts and comments. Without patrons, artists don't last very long. The fact that you read and enjoy what I write drives me onward. Like Thomas Jefferson, I believe that a free society must read to maintain its freedom. You are all freedom fighters.

Pendelton C. Wallace
November 13, 2018
San Diego, California

AUTHOR'S NOTE

I hate to tell you that *Cyberwarfare* is based on real events. No, there was no massive cyber-attack against the United States, but there could be. All of the hacks and attacks in this book have either already happened or are technically possible. I spent twenty-five years as a software engineer and cyber security analyst, so I know what I'm talking about.

To paraphrase the old *Dragnet* TV show, the story you have just read is true, the names have been changed to protect the stupid.

I hope you enjoy the Ted Higuera Series. If you like Ted's stories, you need to read the Catrina Flaherty Mysteries too. You may have noticed that Catrina was absent from *Cyberwarfare.* That's because she's up to her neck looking for a serial killer in Panama. I can't wait to share this story with you.

I'd love to hear from you. I've already gotten a couple of ideas for future books from readers like you. I've also had several people point out proof-reading errors that I correct and publish in future editions of my books. Most of all, I get praise from people who have been to the locations I write about. I also get a lot of questions. Why did Ted do this? Was Chris really thinking about that? I'd love to hear your thoughts and I promise to answer each one of your emails.

You can contact me from my web site, www.pennwallace.com, using the Contact Penn tab or email me at penn@pennwallace.com

As Dean Martin used to say (am I giving away my age here?), "Keep those cards and letters coming in."

Pendelton C. Wallace
May 27th, 2017
San Diego, California

CATRINA FLAHERTY MYSTERIES

Mirror Image

Based on a real-life tragedy, *Mirror Image* is a heart-stopping tale of horrific abuse.

Female PI Catrina Flaherty tackles one of her most difficult cases. Cat specializes in women's issues: infidelity, messy divorces, spousal abuse, sexual harassment, etc. But her newest client, Mandy Alcott, has an unusual problem; her abusive husband is the chief of police.

Who you gonna call when your abuser is The Law?

Cat Flaherty.

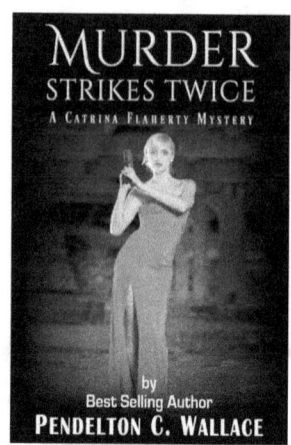

Murder Strikes Twice (Catrina Flaherty Mystery 2)

When her daughter dies in a tragic accident and the daughter's husband's second wife does the same, what is Eleanor Johnson to think? The police have ruled both cases accidents and closed them, but something doesn't feel right. Is it possible to believe that two tragic deaths are mere coincidence, or was something more sinister at play? Who's Eleanor gonna call?

Cat Flaherty.

Murder Strikes Twice, the second book in the Catrina Flaherty Mysteries, is based on an actual case.

When Cat starts looking into the Barrett Case, something smells rotten. She and her team scour Seattle for clues as the pieces start falling into place, but can she make a case that the D.A. will take to court? Did Murder Strike Twice or will Brody Barrett get away with killing both of his wives?

Catrina is known for administering vigilante justice. Will Brody finally have to pay for his sins?

The Chinatown Murders (Catrina Flaherty Mystery 3)

WARNING: This book contains graphic sexual violence. Not intended for younger readers. Based on a true story. Someone is raping women working at massage parlors in Seattle's China Town. He selects his victims because they are undocumented aliens. They can't go to the police or they risk deportation. Now he has escalated to murder. Who you gonna call? Cat Flaherty. The Man leads Catrina on a danger-fraught chase through the ancient streets of Chinatown in a race against time. Neither Catrina, nor her ex-lover, Detective Sergeant Tom Brennen, can stop the monster as the body count piles up. With a shock ending that you'll never predict, the latest Cartrina Flaherty Mystery is a page burner.

The Inside Passage (Ted Higuera Series Book 1)

Somewhere on Canada's Inside Passage, terrorist plot to blow up a cruise ship filled with celebrities and VIP's. Ripped from today's headlines, a group of Canadian-born terrorist plan to bring their war to the Western Hemisphere. Ted Higuera and his friends stumble upon the al-Qaeda plot to blow up the cruise ship and the clock starts ticking.

Can Ted and his friends act in time to save the thousands of people aboard the *Star of the Northwest or will the terrorists take them out of the picture?*

Hacker for Hire (Ted Higuera Series Book 2)

If Clive Cussler had written *Ugly Betty*, it would be *Hacker for Hire*. *Hacker for Hire*, a suspense novel about corporate greed and industrial espionage, is the second book in a series about computer security analyst Ted Higuera and his best friend, para-legal Chris Hardwick.

When you're already in the top 1% of the country's money makers, how much is enough?

Ted and lovely PI, Catrina Flaherty, are led deep into Seattle's Hi-Tech jungle as they stalk a killer. But the killer is also hunting them. Can they find the killer before the killer finds them?

This is the introduction to Cat Flaherty. If you're a fan of hers, you have to read this book.

The Mexican Connection (Ted Higuera Series Book 3)

IN *THE MEXICAN CONNECTION*, the third book in the Ted Higuera series, Ted and Chris are lured to Mexico by an old nemesis. They are dragged into Mexico's drug wars and have to confront the corruption of Mexico's law enforcement. They meet a colorful cast of characters as they search from border towns to the cosmopolitan Mexico City to ancient Aztec ruins.

In the meantime, Cat is in Mexico on a mission of her own. Her client, a Seattle housewife, is thrown into jail when her drug-dealing husband disappears, leaving her holding the bag.

You will meet old friends, make new ones and encounter new villains as our heroes cut a wide swath through our neighbor to the south. Throw in a magical Jaguar and an Aztec god and you have a rollicking adventure tale.

Bikini Baristas (Ted Higuera Series Book 4)

BIKINI BARISTAS IS a tale of Dick Randall, the owner of a chain of bikini barista stands in the Seattle area and Clayton Johnson-White, a teenage kid who thinks he's smarter than the rest of the world.

The story begins when Dick's pickup truck is discovered burned-out in the California desert. What happened to him? Did he fake his death to escape his sleazy past or did the past catch up with him?

Catrina Flahery and Ted Higuera are hired by his wife to find out what happened.

To get away from his trailer-trash life, Clayton drops out of school and runs away into the woods of Camano Island. He breaks into vacation homes and steals what he needs.

The case is handed to Ted's best friend, Chris Hardwick, his first grown-up lawyer case.

What do these two cases have in common? In the end, they come together with the force of two colliding freight trains.

The Cartel Strikes Back (Ted Higuera Series Book 5)

Ripped from today's headlines, the world's most wanted criminal, Mexican drug lord, El Posolero, escapes from prison and vows revenge on the man who sent him there: Ted Higuera.

Ted finally gets up the nerve to propose to Maria. What happens next will take your breath away. As Maria runs away to Mexico and El Posolero moves in, the body count soars.

The Cartel Strikes Back ends with a shock you won't see coming.

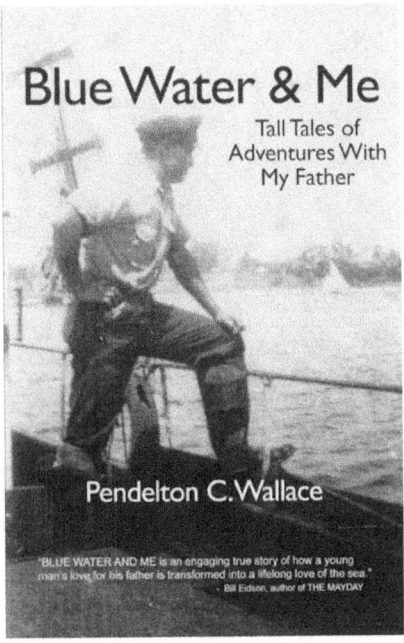

Blue Water & Me, Tall Tales of Adventures With My Father

Blue Water & Me is a high-adventure true story of author Penn Wallace's magical first summer fishing with his father, Blue Water Charlie, off the coast of Mexico at age eleven.

Christmas Inc.

AMAZON.COM'S #1 bestselling political satire.

What would happen if Santa decided to go public and sell shares of Christmas on the NASDAQ? What would happen to the elves if he outsourced toy making to China?

WARNING: **This is not a children's book. Exposure to children under 12-years old may cause the child to stop believing in Santa Claus or take a cynical view of Christmas.**

ABOUT PENDELTON C. WALLACE

Pendelton Wallace is the author of
*Blue Water & Me, Tall Tales of
Adventures With My Father,
Christmas Inc,* the Ted Higuera
Series, and the Catrina Flaherty
Mysteries.

If Chevy Chase had played Indiana
Jones, he would be Penn Wallace.
Penn has a thirst for adventure, but nothing ever seems to go exactly as
planned.

Penn graduated from the University of Oregon (Go Ducks!) and has had
three careers. He owned and operated two restaurants and worked for several
major chains. In 1990, he went back to school, got his MBA in Information
Systems and embarked on a new life.

After his wife died in 2010, Penn lost all interest in work. He left his career
as a software engineer and bought a big old sail boat. He spent the next two
and a half years restoring the vessel.

In the fall of 2012 he set sail for the warm blue waters of Baja California in
his 56-foot sailboat, the *Victory,* picking up a gorgeous blonde and a couple of
Great Danes along the way. You may read an account of this adventure on his
blog at pennwallace.com. This is when Penn started his third career, as a
writer.

Penn currently resides in San Diego, but expect him to pull up anchor and
set sail back to exciting new ports soon.

You may contact Penn at:

pennwallace.com/contact-penn.html

and visit his web site at

pennwallace.com.

Follow Penn on Twitter at **@pcwallace1**

pennwallace.com

penn@pennwallace.com